Count It All Joy

Count It All Joy

Ashea S. Goldson

www.urbanchristianonline.com

Urban Books, LLC
78 East Industry Court
Deer Park, NY 11729

Count It All Joy Copyright © 2011 Ashea S. Goldson

ISBN 13: 978-1-60162-803-9
ISBN 10: 1-60162-803-X

First Printing October 2011
Printed in the United States of America

10 9 8 7 6 5 4 3 2 1

Distributed by Kensington Corp.
Submit Wholesale Orders to:
Kensington Publishing Corp.
C/O Penguin Group (USA) Inc.
Attention: Order Processing
405 Murray Hill Parkway
East Rutherford, NJ 07073-2316
Phone: 1-800-526-0275
Fax: 1-800-227-9604

Count It All Joy

By

Ashea Goldson

Dedication

To my daughters, Anais and Safiya. I love you both with an undying love. As you face the storms of life, my prayer is that you will keep the faith, stay the course, and count it all joy.

Acknowledgments

To my Lord and Savior Jesus Christ: Thank you for giving me the gift of creative writing, for filling my head with ideas, stories, and words, for filling my spirit with wisdom and compassion, and for filling my body with strength to go forward on this literary journey. Without your love and guidance, I would be nothing.

To my husband, Donovan: Thank you for chauffeuring me around to all of my many writing events without complaint, for enduring countless hours of silence while I type away on my laptop, for listening to me go on and on about my dreams as well as my disappointments, and for praying for and with me in the midnight hours. I thank you.

To my children, Anais, Safiya, Jamal (my son-in-law), and Syriah and Jamian (my grandchildren): Thank you for being uniquely yourselves. I wouldn't have it any other way. Thanks for your artistic and technological help, your support, and your love.

To Mommy: You never cease to amaze me in your doings. You just keep getting better and better as the years go by. Thank you for always having a positive word for my soul. Thank you for continually praying for me and thank you for being an example of faithfulness I can aspire to.

To Grandma: Thank you for reading my last book in record time. I appreciate your encouragement and your love.

Acknowledgments

To Dad and my many siblings from your side of the family: Although we may not be as close as I would've liked, I love and appreciate you all.

To the McCloud family: Tamicka, Darryl, Emmanuel, Hannah, Faith, LaShydra, and Cameron: Thank you for being more than friends, more than godchildren. Thank you for being my family.

To my long-time friends: Bernadette Page (in particular), Joy Jones-Garrett, Hope Raymond, Sherri Holmes-Knight, and Alfonso Jackson: Thanks for being consistent in your support of me, from our childhood "glory days" until now.

To Leandra Goldson: Thank you for being more than family and a devoted friend. God bless you, Brandon and Breanna.

To the Franklins, Thomas, Erma, Grandma Patton, and Linda: Thank you for taking good care of my baby so I could focus on writing.

To LaToya Forrest-Heard: Thank you for being my number-one fan and adopted goddaughter. May all your literary dreams come true.

To my editor, Joylynn Jossel: Thank you for editing with both precision and the Holy Spirit. You have undoubtedly been instrumental in my writing success.

To my Urban Christian family, especially Kendra Norman-Bellamy: Thank you for being supportive at every turn.

To my literary agent, Sha Shana Crichton of Crichton & Associates: Thank you again for keeping my literary business in order.

To the Faith-Based Fiction Writers of Atlanta: Thank you for the literary sisterhood you represent.

To Tyora Moody: Thank you for doing what you do, bringing together literature and technology through blog tours. God bless you.

Acknowledgments

To Light of Joy Word of Faith Church, World Changers Church International, and Joyce Meyers Ministries: Thank you for keeping me filled with the Word of God while I do this Kingdom writing.

To my Anointed Minds students: Thank you for filling my workdays with love and laughter.

To all the Christian fiction authors, my fellow writers, bloggers, social media organizers, book clubs, reviewers, and radio hosts: Thank you for either paving the way, promoting, or encouraging me in some way.

To all family, friends, or writer-sisters who have not specifically been named, to those in Atlanta, New York, North Carolina, or around the world: Thank you for being a positive influence in my life in one way or another. If you have ever gone the extra mile for me, know that I remember and I appreciate you.

To my readers and fans: Thank you for continuing to buy my books. Thank you for your feedback, and thank you, most of all, for believing in me. God bless you all!

Chapter One

Alex

How could a good-looking, fairly confident, church-going woman like myself fall into the abyss of depression and self-loathing while she was still a newlywed and married to one of the most impressive catches of the season? I'll tell you how—with one bad thought at a time.

One thing I've heard my whole thirty-one blessed years on this earth is that no matter what trials I may face, and I've seen a few, count it all joy. Now, I try to embrace this scripture, James 1:2–3, and truly count it all joy when I fall into divers temptations; knowing that the trying of my faith worketh patience. To tell you the truth, when I was walking through the fire, neither joy nor patience were on my mind.

Besides, Joshua and I were still on our honeymoon in Nairobi, Kenya, when a series of complications began to surface. I mean, we were right in the middle of a serious round of newlywed kissing when all of a sudden, a familiar gentleman by the name of Seger Abasi interrupted us. Now ordinarily, that wouldn't mean much to honeymooners, but Seger just happened to be the missionary who had more than just a friendly interest in me. Seger was a hottie too; tall and Mandingo warrior-style, if you know what I mean. Running into him at the beach was awkward because even though

Joshua had only met Seger once during Joshua's brief stay in Nairobi a few months ago, I could tell my husband sensed the attraction. Not that I had a thing for Seger, because I was a happily committed woman, but the brother made it more than obvious he had a thing for me.

So our first few days of matrimony had its challenges, with my fine, caramel-honey husband looking into Seger's smooth, Belgium-chocolate face, sizing him up like brothers do. I don't know how I survived the shock and the evil glaring. Now you know a sister had to put on the ever so humble wifey role, reassuring my husband again and again that he was overreacting, that Seger was nothing more than a friend, and that my husband was the only man for me, ever. In my world, this was the truth because I was paying Seger no attention. I'd worked too hard and been through too much in the last year to mess up this relationship. Eventually, Joshua realized I was right and was able to put Seger out of his mind. Then remembering that I was his sexy new bride, he kissed my face and neck, massaged my back, and gave me every reason to thank Jesus over and over again. Yes, I was in heaven.

Kenya was one of the most beautiful places I had ever seen, which is one of the reasons we decided to honeymoon there. We enjoyed stunning landscapes, beautiful wildlife, age-old architecture, enchanting beaches, sleepy coastal towns rich in culture and history, and impeccable hospitality. Everywhere we went the natives were so friendly and eager to help. They were also excited to show us many of their traditional customs, like their tribal dances. There wasn't enough time to explore all I remembered from my missions trip so many months ago, but I was content just hanging out with my handsome new husband.

Besides our frequent romantic lounging, we had time to hit a few of Kenya's hot spots, like the Kenya National Museum, The Kenyatta Conference Center, and The Nairobi National Park, which was only fifteen minutes from the center of Nairobi. My favorite was one of the five restaurants at the Safari Park Hotel where we were staying, The Nyama Choma Restaurant.

There, we enjoyed a five-course meal where the main course was nyama choma, which is grilled meat. We were surrounded by waiters who carried skewers of sausages, beef, lamb, pork, crocodile, alligator, and chicken. This reminded me of a Brazilian steakhouse. While we were eating, we were entertained by a musical theatrical show called the Safari Cats. Then the band played and took requests while some people actually danced around the restaurant in a chain fashion. Joshua and I, although we were in a festive mood, decided not to participate. Instead, we spent the rest of the evening holding hands and staring into each other's eyes.

Later that evening we were rolling around on our bed in the hotel room, laughing, talking, and playing the way lovers do.

Suddenly Joshua became serious. He sat up and took my hand. "I'm glad we're married."

"So am I, especially since we almost weren't," I said, sitting up also.

Joshua looked into my eyes. "What do you mean?"

"We came so close to breaking up after all I put you through—"

"Shhh. Nonsense." Joshua put his finger over my lips and shook his head. "You're worth anything I ever had to go through."

"No, really. I should've never kept such a big secret from you."

"I didn't make it easy for you to tell me with my bad attitude. I was so judgmental about the abortion issue back then."

"You had a right to be. Delilah was your wife. She had no right to do what she did to your child, and to think she had no intention of telling you." I shook my head, imagining the pain he had experienced.

"It's amazing that I was never supposed to find out, but I guess she never planned on dying in the process." Joshua took a deep breath. "But the wages of sin is death."

"And I should've learned from her mistake that keeping secrets doesn't work. I should've never accepted your proposal in the first place without telling you what I had done. I was just so afraid of losing you, and hiding it was tearing our relationship apart."

Joshua held me against his chest. "Yes, but all of that's over now. You're my wife. You're never going to lose me, and the best is yet to come."

I laughed, happy that the mood had lightened again. I certainly didn't want our future to be tainted by the past. "Go ahead, Deacon."

"I'm the happiest man alive." Joshua wrapped his arms around me.

"No, I'm the happiest woman alive."

"All I want now is to make beautiful babies with you," Joshua said, stroking my hair.

Now that is when the conversation really went wrong. I cringed at the idea, a little uncertain about all that would mean for me and for our relationship. Something about this just didn't seem right. A new baby, along with my stepdaughter, four-year-old Lilah, the child we planned to adopt from Kenya, Kiano, plans for graduate school in the spring, and working in the ministry were a

tall order for any new bride. Then there was that lingering question of whether I could even become pregnant.

Yes, I had issues with that too, thanks to an abortion
I was talked into almost eleven years ago. It had stolen
every ounce of dignity away from me until I was delivered from the spirit of condemnation. Jesus cleansed
me of all my sins, that I knew. But would my uterus be
as forgiving?

The infection had been terrible. Blood everywhere.
Unimaginable pain. It sure felt like my uterus was
damaged. If my body had sustained at least half the
damage that my soul had, I knew it was over for me.
My poor lost twins. Gone forever because of youthful
ignorance.

Maybe I'd be able to have twins again one day. My
thoughts threatened to overwhelm me but the sound of
Joshua's voice brought me back to the present.

Joshua shook me a little. "Babe, are you okay?"

"I'm fine, but don't you want to wait awhile?" I sighed.

"Nope. I want to get started on making a son, an heir
to the Benning estate."

"Benning estate? Now you sound like your parents.
Don't you think that's a little premature?"

"Premature?" He kissed my cheek. "No."

"But we've only been married three days. Can we
give it a little time at least? Besides, we're already starting the process for an international adoption. I mean,
we don't want to take on too much at once."

Suddenly Joshua squinted his eyes and stared directly into mine. "Are you saying you don't want to
have my baby?"

"Of course not. I want nothing more, but can we just
please get back to the U.S. first?" I playfully pushed
him to lighten things up. I didn't want him to think for

one second that I was anything like his deceased wife, the one who never really wanted kids in the first place, the one who broke his heart.

"Sure, I'll let you get back on American soil, but after that, it's on." He wrapped his strong arms around my waist. "And still, there are no guarantees on what might slip through the cracks, even here in Kenya."

I giggled, but I popped my birth control pill into my mouth happily, knowing I didn't want any slips until the time was right. That had been my whole reason for getting the new prescription from the clinic in the first place. This was the first time in years I had to use a contraceptive. I was a married woman now, and those last four years of abstinence, hallelujah, were over.

Early the next morning, I woke up to the sound of running water. As soon as Joshua stepped out of the shower, I went in and showered quickly. When I came out wrapped only in a hotel towel, Joshua wrestled me to the bed and smothered me in sweet-smelling kisses.

Finally, I was able to glance up at the wall clock.

"Oh, look at the time. We're not going to make it if we don't hurry," I exclaimed.

Joshua looked at the wall clock. "You're right. Let's get going."

After quickly dressing, we went down to the U.S. Embassy to start the process on our international adoption, a vision God had given me when I visited Kenya the first time. Back then, during a time of temporary estrangement from Joshua, I was able to clear my head and subsequently hear God's voice. After several weeks of simultaneously working on a public relations assignment and in missions, I renewed my vow to work with children. Joshua, who wanted me back, was happy to agree to the idea. He would've agreed to anything at that time, including sipping my bathwater.

Down at the embassy, Joshua and I scoped a list of various attorneys and chose one from the list. We were blessed that he was able to meet with us immediately. Mr. Nyuoso was a short, wide man with a wide face and big features. His office was neat and functional, but quite plain compared to the American lawyers' offices that I was accustomed to.

"I tell you that Kenya is very strict now about you Americans adopting our children and taking them out of our country. There are new laws," Mr. Nyuoso had said with a very heavy Kenyan accent.

Although he spoke English, it was a little challenging to understand what he was saying.

"Okay. What do we need to do?" I listened intently.

Mr. Nyuoso spoke slowly. "Well, the process is a very complex one, but you can overcome it if you are serious."

"We're very serious." I punched Joshua in the ribs.

"Yes, we're dedicated," Joshua said.

"Good. Good. It's not that our government is totally against the international adoptions, but there have been so many bad things that happen to our children. They are very cautious now." Mr. Nyuoso began to take papers out of his desk.

"I understand." I turned to look at my husband.

"Yes, we understand," Joshua said, on cue.

"The government will want proof that the two of you are authorized and recommended as morally fit and financially capable to adopt a foreign child. Subsequently, you'll be required to prepare a dossier. I will tell you everything that is required for it." Mr. Nyuoso handed me an envelope full of papers.

"Anything to ensure the welfare of the children." I nodded my head in agreement.

Protecting the children, was, after all, my main interest.

We spent an hour with him as he explained the requirements for getting Kiano back to the United States. He told us how we'd be required to live with Kiano in Kenya for at least three months before the adoption would become final to ensure bonding and security for the child. He explained many other procedures as well, how we were no longer able to apply for an immigrant visa for the child to enter the United States, that the entire adoption process had to be completed in Kenya. He told us that we had to be sponsored by a local child welfare agency, that the agency had to complete a home study, take our fingerprints, and do a criminal background check. He also told us that bank references and an income-tax assessment would also be necessary. Then he started detailing the fees involved, starting with the application and filing fees. All that information made my head hurt, especially the expense part. With Joshua's school loans and other debts from his glamorous deceased wife, we could barely afford it. That was why Brother and Sister Benning stepped in and volunteered to help out with Kiano's adoption. But they hadn't written the check yet. So Joshua and I handed over a very small deposit with the promise that the remainder of the funds would be forthcoming. We shook his hand and left Mr. Nyuoso's office hopeful.

The next step was to go visit Kiano, whose name meant full of joy. His full name was Kiano Adoyo. He was the child I'd developed the most special bond with during my original visit here a few months back. He was the one Joshua and I had talked about, prayed about, and had decided that we would welcome into our new family. Yet Joshua had never met him.

Kiano lived in an orphanage in the slums of Nairobi. His parents and grandparents were both killed in a brush fire when he was very young. Now that he was six, an impressionable age, his curiosity often outweighed his sense of good judgment. He was a strong, happy-looking boy, despite the hardships I knew he faced daily. Although I loved all the children in the orphanage, he was the boy with a special place in my heart.

When I saw him I ran over and wrapped my arms around him. He squeezed me so tight around my waist I almost lost my balance. Then he jumped into my arms and I held him.

"You're back." Kiano's dark eyes danced in the sunlight.

"I told you I would be," I said.

"You really came back. I'm so happy now."

"I'm happy too. And look, I not only came back, but I brought my husband with me this time."

Kiano's smile disappeared. "Husband?"

"Yes, I'm married now." I showed him my wedding ring. "This is my husband, Joshua."

Joshua stepped forward and kneeled down to Kiano's eye level. "I've heard a lot about you, big guy."

"Hello." Kiano cast his eyes downward.

"No need to be shy. Come on over and give me a hug too." Joshua held out his arms.

"I've heard so much about you I feel like I know you already."

Hesitantly, Kiano climbed out of my arms and went over to hug Joshua.

We spent the rest of the afternoon together, explaining to Kiano that we wanted to adopt him, but that the process would take awhile. Needless to say, we made his day and his lifetime all at once. Before we left, we were arm in arm discussing the adoption, and the plans we had for our family.

"But I don't want you two to leave me here." Kiano started to cry.

"We'll be back, I promise." It was so hard to say good-bye. Tears were welling up in my eyes also.

"We will be back for you soon, we promise," Joshua said.

I looked at my husband and with the strength of his words, both Kiano and I wiped our tears away. It was funny how a simple promise made it all better.

By the time we actually started walking toward the exit, Joshua started rubbing my shoulders and talking about all that baby stuff again. I was hearing him, but my mind was far away.

"It'll be so nice to have Kiano, Lilah, and the new baby—"

"Come on now. Give me a chance to settle in with Lilah and Kiano before you start saddling me down with more babies," I said, cutting him off.

Joshua smiled and gave my shoulder a little squeeze. "At least one more."

"But can I catch my breath first? I mean, I'm gonna be the mother of three kids." I gasped. "Wow."

"Yep. I can't wait."

I rolled my eyes and smiled. "I see."

"I can't wait to have another baby." He touched my stomach.

Since I had recently worked so hard to get rid of the excess flab, I slapped his hand away.

He growled. "Ouch. That hurt."

"Well, there's more where that came from. I just got my abs down to the size they are now." I twirled around showing off my newly toned figure. "Please don't mess a sister up."

"Don't worry about that, you're beautiful."

"That's easy for you to say. You're not the one that has to carry around an eight-pound baby."

Joshua laughed and shook his head. "Got that right."

I playfully punched him in the arm, and we let the conversation wean itself off like stars in the dusk.

I remembered how I used to be in such bondage, worrying about my mistakes as if Jesus didn't die on the cross for my future, present, and my past. Today I was a different woman than I was then. Even though I wanted babies, my past was trying to manifest a new fear in me, the fear of conceiving and carrying Joshua's child.

As we were walking out the front door of the orphanage, we ran into Seger again.

As if once wasn't already enough, I sighed at the thought of having to stroke my husband's delicate ego one more time. Humph, men.

Seger smiled with milky white teeth. "Well, Sister Alex and Deacon . . . uh . . ."

"Joshua." Joshua's chest rose and fell.

"Yes, Joshua. It's good to see you again." Seger extended his hand and Joshua shook it in an obligatory way.

"Nice to see you too, Seger," I said.

"I won't be in Kenya much longer. Just a couple more months and it's back to the States for me," Seger chuckled.

I remembered our missions work together. "Oh, your mission assignment will be over?"

"Yes, yes. I'll be heading back home to the U.S." Seger didn't take his eyes off of me.

"Mmm." Joshua glared at Seger. "I thought that Kenya was your home."

"Yes, I was born here, but I was raised in the States." Seger turned to face Joshua.

Suddenly Seger turned back to me. "Have you seen Kiano?"

"Yes." I could feel myself glowing with the thought of being Kiano's mother. "We're going to adopt him."

"Really? That's wonderful." Seger looked back and forth at our faces. "He always wanted to be adopted so badly."

Joshua squinted his chestnut-brown eyes. "Oh, so you know Kiano too?"

Seger turned to look Joshua straight in the eyes. "Yes, yes. Alex and I spent a lot of time with him, and the other kids too, of course."

"Right," Joshua said.

Eventually, Seger turned away from Joshua's stare. "I'm sure he couldn't ask for better parents."

"Thank you," I said.

"Yeah, thanks," Joshua yawned.

"Well, take care of yourselves. I've got missionary duties." Seger, probably sensing the tension, gave a quick wave and disappeared through the orphanage doors.

I smiled politely, and let out a semi deep breath now that he was gone.

Joshua took me by the hand and spun me around.

"Why didn't you tell me you and Seger were involved with Kiano?" Joshua squinted his brown eyes.

"We weren't involved with him. But we did serve the orphans together, all of the orphans. Sometimes Kiano just got a little more attention than the others. It wasn't intentional."

"I'll bet."

"Now, what's that supposed to mean? Would you have preferred we ignore Kiano and all the orphans?"

Joshua took a step back. "Of course not. But you could've given me a heads-up that you and Seger had a special relationship with him."

"We had special relationships with a lot of kids. We worked together with them for many weeks. I told you about that."

Joshua gritted his teeth. "But you and he apparently had a special one with this particular kid."

"Okay, so does that change anything?"

"No, but I wish you had told me," Joshua sighed.

"Well, I didn't think it was important at the time." I threw my hands into the air in mock surrender. "I'm sorry."

Joshua grabbed one of my hands as it was coming down. "I'm sorry too. Is there anything else you're hiding about you and Seger?"

Chapter Two

Alex

Two days later as I lay in my bed, I still had a bad taste in my mouth from Joshua's question and the mean look on his face when he asked it. Despite his quick apology, my own personal time in prayer, and a seventeen-hour plane ride from the Jomo Kenyatta International Airport to the JFK Airport, the sting of his words still rang in my ears. I was confident that with being back in New York now, away from Seger, the added tension from his presence would be alleviated from my marriage.

With the window open, the fall breeze brushed against my skin. Fall was undoubtedly my favorite time of year. I looked over at Joshua and saw that he was still asleep. The alarm clock hadn't gone off yet, so I decided to let him have his last fifteen minutes of sleep while I showered. Under the refreshing spray, I thought about my twin sister, Taylor. Now that I was back in the States and back to my trendy downtown Brooklyn neighborhood, I could hardly wait to see her. Ever since the car accident impaired her ability to walk, she had become a different person, a better person, and I missed her. I smiled at the thought of her finally using a walker and at the thought that she had finally found someone to love. By the time I came out smelling of tangerine body splash, Joshua was waiting for me, wearing only his little satin robe.

"Good morning, sweetheart," Joshua greeted.

"Morning." I took his hand and led him to the kitchen while he groped me at every chance. After fixing a hot breakfast of grits and eggs with cheese, and serving orange juice, I sat down to join him at the table.

The sun flowed through the pastel blue curtains and onto the white lacquer table. I made a note to myself that I had to change the decor ASAP. Now that I was the woman of the house, definite changes were going to have to be made, starting with this dull kitchen.

"What's on the agenda for today?"

"I'll be at the bank 'til five. Then I have my class at Missionary."

"Yep, your last one. Aren't you excited? Can you believe it's almost over?"

"I can't wait." Joshua filled his mouth with grits. "Can't wait to minister."

It was already October, and Joshua only had two months more of Bible school. He had worked extremely hard over the past few years, both at the bank and in school, and I was very proud of his accomplishments.

"I can't wait to be a minister's wife." I leaned against him, smiling.

"Just a couple of months, and then I'll be able to preach anywhere."

"Yep, Missionary Church, your parents' church, and one day soon you'll be preaching at our own church."

"Hold on, Mrs. Benning. I haven't gotten that far yet." Joshua tapped me playfully on the head. "I'm taking one day at a time."

"Well, don't tell your mama that."

Joshua smiled. "That woman is impossible."

"You didn't hear it from me." I laughed as I stuffed my last forkful of eggs into my mouth.

"By the way, when is Lilah coming home? I mean, your mother has had her ever since before we left for our honeymoon."

"I'm sure she'll bring her home soon."

"No, but seriously though, I think that your mother is poisoning her against me."

Joshua laughed. "What? You're paranoid?"

"No, I'm not. I can feel it."

"Lilah will be home soon, and you and her will be as close as mother and daughter can be."

I put my hands on my size twelve hips. "Really? Are you sure she's not afraid of sending her home to the wicked stepmother?"

"No, it's not that at all. Mom is not so bad, you'll see."

Given our history, I wasn't too sure about that.

There I was down at Missionary Bible Institute, walking down the long stretch to Dr. Harding's office. I felt much better about working here now since I had come to grips with my past and my purpose. Thankfully, Dr. Harding agreed to let someone else handle public relations while I worked at my same office job. I needed a job with less responsibility until I finished the classes necessary for me to receive my teacher certification. It was a good deal, but sometimes when I was really bored, I wondered why I turned down the more glamorous position. It didn't matter though. Before I knew it, I would be teaching and that was all that mattered.

Besides, if I was going to be a mother to Lilah, I needed a less demanding schedule anyway. My new part-time hours were the perfect arrangement for my new family duties, even though I hadn't fully tried the mother role yet. Joshua and I had only been married for two weeks. Then Joshua was tripping, always all over me, talking about having a baby. Was this brother crazy? Didn't he realize that we were newlyweds and that there was plenty of time for that?

I slapped my girl Marisol a high five. "What's going on, girl?"

"Hey, lady. How are you?"

"I'm good." I leaned across Marisol's oak desk.

She winked at me. "I'll bet you are."

"Don't start."

"Well, how is married life?"

I gave her a big cheesy grin.

"That's what I thought. Too bad Joshua doesn't have a brother."

My girl, Marisol, I laughed to myself. "It's good to be back."

"Yeah, I thought you were gone for good when you turned down that PR gig."

"Well, that public relations position would've really been something, but all I want to do is eventually get certified to teach, so this is fine for now. Dr. Harding agreed to let me come back part-time." I stood up straight and tucked my blouse back into my skirt.

Marisol put both her elbows on her desk. "Oh, part-time?"

"Yes, and that schedule works well with me going back to school in the spring, and with my new motherhood role."

"Of course. How is Lilah anyway?"

"She's doing good, thanks." I pulled her close and whispered in her ear. "But that husband of mine wants me to get pregnant right away."

"Wow, he doesn't waste any time, does he?"

"No." I laughed. "I mean, Joshua has lost his natural mind."

"Girl, I could live with that if I were you."

I gave Marisol a fake punch in the arm. "Traitor."

"I'm just saying," Marisol giggled as I walked away. "I'm just glad you're back, *chica*. I missed you."

"I missed you too, girl," I said.

The rest of the day went fairly well, considering it was my first day back at the office.

As soon as I had a break I called my sister to check up on her. Although, we engaged in frivolous conversation, I detected pain in her voice.

"What's wrong, Tay?" I leaned back in the swivel chair.

"Nothing." Taylor paused. "I'm okay."

I wondered what was bothering her. "Are you and Keith going anywhere special tonight?"

"Nope, I'll be solo tonight," Taylor said.

"Oh. Well, do you need me to come over?"

Taylor's voice wavered. "Naw, girl. You better stay there with yo' new hubby and make him happy. I'm fine."

"No really, I can . . ." I started.

Taylor snorted. "I'm okay. Just go home and do your thing."

"Okay, but if you need anything, you let me know," I said.

"I'm still me, so you know I will."

"You're right about that," I laughed. "Talk to you later."

"Bye." Taylor hung up the phone.

I clicked off my cell and put it into my purse. Knowing my sister, I knew something was wrong. I made up my mind that I'd have to pry it out of her later.

It wasn't until evening that things began to get complicated. After Joshua returned home from work, we sat in the living room, wrapped in my favorite flannel blanket, cuddling. We discussed his plans for starting an urban-contemporary church after he graduated, my plans for graduate school in the summer, plans for expanding the Young Women's Giving Life Ministry, and, of course, our plans for expanding our family. That's where it got really tricky. I closed my eyes every time he brought up the subject of having a baby with me.

I really wanted to give Joshua what he wanted, and what he deserved, although I whole heartedly believed he was moving too fast. My own immediate goals were to adopt Kiano and work on developing our ministries before I committed to carrying a child. Adoption was one thing, but the physical demands of having a baby were more than I was willing to deal with. Sure, I knew that motherhood was full-time responsibility no matter what my schedule was, and whether I actually delivered a biological child. It was that serious for me.

Mama always said a woman didn't have no business having babies if she wasn't ready to take care of them. So that was it for me. I wanted to make my mark in the Kingdom of God first.

As Joshua came up behind me and touched my shoulder, I shivered, and not with passion but with fear. Maybe it was fear telling me I wasn't ready. In any case, he had insisted that I stop taking my newly prescribed birth control pills so the heat was on.

When the doorbell rang, expecting it to be my mother-in-law, I pried myself away from Joshua, straightened my blue cotton skirt suit, and hoped I looked good enough. Then I opened the door to Mother Benning and Lilah.

"Hello, dear." Mother Benning kissed me on the cheek.

I looked down and there was Lilah. I reached out my arms to hug her. "Hi, sweetie, how are you?"

"Fine." Lilah ran across the room and jumped into Joshua's arms. "Dad, I had so much fun at Big Mommy's house."

There was that word again. Maybe if Mother Benning wasn't so much of a "Big Mommy," I'd have half of a chance to be "Mommy." I dropped my arms and sighed deeply, not that anyone probably noticed.

Mother Benning unbuttoned her navy blue, fitted suit jacket and held it out for me to take. I took it and motioned for her to come into the living room.

"Can I get you something to eat or drink?" I made sure to make eye contact and smile.

"Maybe just some coffee, dear." Mother Benning sat down on the leather couch.

I walked to the kitchen to put a pot of coffee on. I hoped it would be good enough for her. Somehow I pictured her more of an herbal tea or latte drinker. Joshua loved raspberry tea himself, and I did the occasional mocha latte. Diet Coke was actually my drink of choice.

By the time I came back into the living room, Joshua and his mother were already huddled together on the couch. Lilah sat on the floor playing with her doll. I walked over to Mother Benning and served her coffee.

"Excuse me." I held the serving tray in front of my dear mother-in-law. "Sugar or cream?"

"No, thank you, dear. I'll take it straight black." Joshua's mom took her cup and put it down on the center table. "I don't know how to tell you this."

"What are you trying to say, Mom?" Joshua repositioned himself on the couch.

I gave Lilah a cup of apple juice. Next I walked around to Joshua and served him a cup of his favorite tea. He smiled and mouthed a quick "Thanks." I could tell something serious was going on because the atmosphere had changed. So I lured Lilah to her room and quickly returned, perching myself on the arm of the couch next to Joshua.

Mother Benning looked into Joshua's eyes. "Joshua, your father is very ill."

Joshua looked directly at his mother without blinking. "What's wrong with him?"

Mother Benning looked away for a moment as if she were holding back tears. "It's prostate cancer."

Joshua dropped his head in his hands and dropped his voice to a whisper. "How long have you known?"

"We've known for a while now; but I've been waiting for the right time to tell you."

Mother Benning took a sip of her coffee.

Joshua raised his eyebrows. "The right time?"

"Yes. We knew you'd be graduating soon so we were trying to wait until then," she said. "Unfortunately, his condition has deteriorated even in the past few weeks."

"I wish you had told me sooner." Joshua took his mother's hand. "Don't worry about me. I can handle this."

"We didn't want it to be a strain on you with all you're already dealing with." Mother Benning peeked around at me and smiled.

She'd only been here about twenty minutes and already she was pushing it. Yet, I forced my lips to remain closed. No drama tonight I promised myself.

"What about you?" Joshua looked into his mother's eyes. "How are *you* holding up?"

Mother Benning spoke slowly, methodically. "I'm doing as well as can be expected. It's a lot, but I'm coping. We're coping."

I looked into Joshua's mother's eyes, and I saw an unusual vulnerability, not the same manipulative, conniving woman who had single-handedly tried to undermine and destroy my relationship with her son not that long ago. In fact, I attempted to forget the way she tried to set Joshua up with single women from her church while we were officially courting. One after the other, she encouraged a string of Christian debutants to make their move on Joshua. Thankfully, Joshua remained a man of integrity. I didn't want to remember the way she constantly badgered Joshua about whether he was sure I was really "Benning material" or whether I would be a good mother to Lilah. The ultimate disgrace though, was when she had a private investigator dig up my college sweetheart, Ahmad, in the hopes that she would prove me unfaithful. Yes, Mother Benning certainly had her volatile moments, but this was not one of them. Instead of her normal flawless self, she looked drained.

"I'll be taking a leave of absence from public office so I can spend more time taking care of your father. And, of course, he'll need a private nurse as well." She ran her fingers through her long, jet-black hair. Not a single gray strand in sight.

Mother Benning had been a council woman for years, was currently the president of the City Council, presiding at City Council meetings, appointing members and chairpersons of council committees, signing all ordinances, resolutions, subpoenas, and other documents issued by the council. She had actually considered running for Congress a few years ago. Ultimately, it was her love for the ministry that thwarted any greater political ambitions she had.

"Right," Joshua said, leaning over to hug his mother.

Mother Benning pursed her lips. "Of course, you know we're going to handle this aggressively."

"So what's the next step, Mom?"

"Exercise, change in diet, more rest, etcetera," she said.

"Good call." Joshua stirred his tea with his spoon.

Mother Benning shook her head. "It's not my call. I've been preaching to him about his health for years. It's doctor's orders."

Joshua looked up from his teacup. "Well, maybe now Dad will listen."

"He has no choice. In any case, I'll need to know where you stand." Mother Benning put her hand on her son's knee.

Joshua searched his mother's face. "Stand?"

Mother Benning folded her hands in front of her. "Yes, Joshua. I need to know what you intend to do."

"I don't know what you mean." Joshua stood up. "You know I'll help in any way I can."

Mother Benning stood also. "Oh, Josh. I'm so glad to hear you say that."

"What?" he squinted his eyes.

"We need to know that you'll be there to pastor the church when your father steps down." Mother Benning grabbed Joshua by both arms.

I looked at her and shook my head, having no idea what Josh would say to that. I didn't envy his position at all. How could he turn down a plea by his desperate mother to help his ailing father in his time of need? Yet, at the same time, how could he ignore his longing to fulfill the specific dream God had placed in his heart, which was to build a dynamic church in the inner city, not take over an established one in suburbia? We'd had many intense conversations about him starting his own little church wherever God called him, and about how glad he was that he didn't have to pastor his father's church and deal with the constraints of his father's leadership.

I just stood back and watched Joshua tug at his mustache. Clearly, he was nervous because that was the only time he fiddled with his face like that.

Mother Benning let go of him. "Joshua, are you okay?"

"Yes, Mom." Joshua walked away from her.

"Are you sure?" Mother Benning followed him. "You seem a little withdrawn."

Now *that* was an understatement. My guess was that my very articulate husband didn't want to say the words that would undoubtedly break his mother's heart.

"I'm sorry, Mom. It's just that this has all been such a shock to me," Joshua said with his back still turned to us both.

"I know. Josh, when your father was first diagnosed three weeks ago, this took us by surprise too. But I need to know you'll stand as you father's successor." Mother Benning walked in front of him.

"Dad's not going to die now." Joshua hung his head down.

Mother Benning sighed, and then sat down. "I didn't say he was going to die, but he has been warned about slowing down, and pastoring a church of our size can be very strenuous."

"I know that." Joshua shook his head and sat down next to his mother again. "I'll have to talk to dad about cutting back on his responsibilities."

Suddenly Mother Benning frowned up her face. "Why don't you talk to me about your responsibilities?"

Joshua's voice was filled with frustration. "What are you talking about, Mom?"

"I'm no fool. You still haven't answered my question." She put her hands on her modest hips.

"It's a big question." Joshua drummed his fingertips on the side table.

Mother Benning looked directly at Joshua. "With only one right answer."

"Maybe you two—" I started.

Mother Benning put up her hand to cut me off. "Please, dear. Stay out of this one."

My first reaction was to disappear from the room, but I decided not to let her bully me in my own house, so I stayed put.

"Joshua Douglas Benning the Third," Mother Benning said.

Oh, it was on now.

Joshua sighed. "Yes, Mother?"

"You're our *only* child, the *only* heir to our estate." Mother Benning's jaws looked like they were tightening as the words sneaked from her lips.

"I know, Mother." Joshua clasped his hands.

Mother Benning patted her foot. "Then *why* can't you give me a straight answer? Are you or are you not going to pastor our church?"

He dropped his hands and looked his mother straight in the eyes. "No, Mom. I'm sorry, but I can't."

Chapter Three

Alex

Two weeks went by with Joshua's dad's condition gradually worsening as well as his relationship with his mother. According to him, his mother never directly mentioned the incident again, but she alluded to it all the time. She even mailed a personal postcard invitation to a church event to our home and addressed it to her *only* son. Still, I couldn't believe that fourteen days had passed and she had not even called. Not once. Not even to speak to Lilah. Apparently no one ever said *no* to a woman like Mother Benning. She was, after all, very powerful, both in political and religious circles. Not to mention that she was a powerhouse in the family circle as well. Joshua walked around, moping most of the time, yet he refused to talk about it or to admit that he was hurting.

In the meantime, he found solace in fulfilling his vision of having a child with me, trying every chance he got to get me pregnant. Not that trying wasn't fun most of the time, but the stress was unbelievable. All I wanted to do was have an intimate connection with my husband, but all he was concerned with was fertilizing eggs. Not exactly something to get a girl in the mood. Finally, when the romantic flames had fizzled out, along with my patience, we sat down to have a serious conversation. Now that's what I was really afraid of—

talking. Talking always led to *doing* in our household. We talked mostly about my feelings following the abortion. Our talk revealed the fact that although I spent years in and out of illicit relationships trying to become pregnant again, I never could. Joshua handled the information well because he knew that old things were passed away and that I was a new creation.

Against my better judgment, I finally agreed to visit a fertility specialist, one who came highly recommended by a couple from our church. Joshua and I agreed that even though we were both nervous, we would surrender our anxieties to the Lord in prayer.

One week later, a strawberry-scented nurse led us to Dr. Henley's office, which was decorated in mahogany. His degrees and licenses covered the mint-green-colored walls. Joshua and I sat in matching green leather chairs, staring through the window at the panoramic view of Manhattan. Finally, the doctor entered the room. He was tall, with blue eyes and dark hair with gray around the edges.

"Good afternoon, I'm Doctor Jason Henley." He extended his hand.

Joshua shook his hand and pointed to me. "Hello, I'm Joshua Benning, and this is my wife, Alex."

Dr. Henley turned toward me with a smile. "Nice to meet you both. Is Alex short for Alexandria?"

"No, sir," I stuttered as I shook his hand. "Just Alex, sir."

"No need to be so formal. I want you to feel comfortable here," Dr. Henley said.

He first asked us about our specific concerns, and believe me, there were many.

Then he explained that since we had only been trying for three months that there might be absolutely nothing wrong with either of us. However, he did agree that with me being over thirty, and since women's fertility normally decreases after age thirty-two, that it was wise to be tested for problems sooner than later.

Then he proceeded to check our general health, and thank goodness, we were both fine.

He asked us questions about our lifestyle, like smoking, alcohol, and caffeine consumption.

He also asked about possible environmental exposure to eliminate other factors that might cause infertility. Finally, he tested Joshua's sperm count.

"So no other births? Live births, miscarriages, or abortions?" the doctor questioned.

It took everything in me to answer. "I aborted twins about eleven years ago, when I was in college."

"Were there any complications?" Dr. Henley looked over his glasses.

"It was sloppy, and I contracted an infection where I almost bled to death a week later," I said.

Joshua held my hand. "That's the main reason she's afraid she can't conceive."

"I see." Dr. Henley steadily wrote notes in his pad.

"We'll have to test for PID, pelvic inflammatory disease." Dr. Henley looked up from his notes and his eyes met mine. "It's a very serious pelvic inflammation resulting from untreated vaginal or cervical infections. It does damage to the reproductive tract, often scarring and blocking the fallopian tubes. Scarring like this prevents fertilization from ever occurring."

I couldn't believe what I was hearing. "That sounds so harsh."

"Unfortunately, it is. PID is one of the main causes for infertility in women. But the good news is that I believe in the supernatural healing power of God above all else."

"Amen," Joshua said.

"I've seen many babies born since I've been in this field. About two-thirds of all infertile couples are able to have a child. There are the natural remedies like medicine, surgery, artificial insemination, or assisted reproductive technology. And then there is the mighty hand of God. My colleagues don't necessarily agree with all my methods, but prayer changes things." Dr. Henley set his clipboard down.

"We agree with you, Doctor," Joshua said.

Dr. Henley smiled. "Good."

I was too shaken up to say anything.

One month later I trembled at the thought of even seeing Dr. Jason Henley again.

One more test. One more doggone needle or urine sample and I was going to scream. We were monitoring my body temperature, positioning, diet, and anything else that was recommended. I was tired, stressed out, and ready to give up trying at what seemed to be so impossible. Obviously, I just wasn't up to the task.

"Why don't you try those breathing techniques right before you leave home so you'll be more relaxed by the time you get here," Dr. Henley said.

I couldn't hold it in any longer, so I broke down right on the table. Tears began to run down my cheeks. I wasn't sure why I was even crying, but Dr. Henley consoled me with his gentle spirit.

"Why don't you go on home and talk to your husband," he suggested.

I nodded in agreement, but I knew that Joshua would never truly understand. Everything I was going through was for him. Everything I was feeling was because of him. And even though he was kind and alluring, I had absolutely no desire left in me.

When I came home, I threw down my purse and sat in the dark hunched over for two hours, waiting for Joshua to return from work.

I heard his keys in the lock, but I didn't move.

"Hey, baby. What's wrong?" Joshua walked over to where I was sitting on the couch.

"I'm tired, Josh."

"Why don't you let me help you to bed then?"

"No, I'm tired of trying, tired of everything." Tears dripped freely from my eyes.

"Oh, come on, baby, we can't give up now," Joshua said.

"That's easy for you to say, but you just don't know the humiliation I endure week after week." I blinked away the tears. "I'm just tired now."

Joshua sat down and placed my head on his strong shoulders. He stroked my hair with his loving hands, and all my cares seemed to slip away instantly.

"Let's pray," he said.

"Okay," although, honestly, I was too numb to have any real expectation.

"Dear Lord, we come before you humbly thanking you in advance for what you're about to bring into fruition. We've planted the seed. We've been faithful and diligent throughout the process. We're expecting a manifested harvest in Jesus' name. We have touched and agreed that everything would be okay. We thank you that everything in this family is better than okay. In Jesus' name. Amen."

"You're right. Everything will work out." That was what I loved about him. He was so secure in the things of God. I remembered when I used to be like that. What in the world was happening to me? Was I losing my faith?

Joshua wrapped his strong arms around me, and I felt so secure in them. He touched my hair and my cheek with his fingers, and for once, I was almost able to relax.

When the phone rang, I clung to Joshua, not willing to let go of the moment. I hesitated to answer it until I saw that it was Dr. Henley on the caller ID. Joshua and I looked at each other in silent anticipation. *Could it be?*

Chapter Four

Alex

Too bad Dr. Henley's phone call was nothing short of catastrophic. For such an educated man, he had bad timing and an awful way of communicating disappointing news. He stuttered and mumbled, something that was totally out of character for him. Since our last attempts of conceiving had failed, he thought it was time for us to consider other options.

Needless to say, this upset me beyond reason. Joshua tried to smooth it away as he usually did; hugged me tight, massaged my back, and even kissed me deeply, but secretly, I wasn't convinced.

So I did what I always did, hid my sorrows in service. I went on with my life, serving in ministry, working, and praying, but what nobody knew was that underneath my sanctified exterior, I was a cowering shell of a woman.

Nevertheless, I went on with the façade even while working at the church. Joshua and and I went down to Missionary to help Aunt Dorothy and Sister Trudy set up for the annual children's health fair. Two hours after we arrived, Taylor showed up in her wheelchair, which came as a shock to me because ever since she started using the braces a few months ago, she had put it aside.

Still, she was my beautiful sister, an almost perfect replica of me, or at least a better looking me. How my sister kept everything together from her wheelchair was a complete mystery. So she'd totally earned my respect. I could hardly maintain my figure, and I was standing on two good legs. She spoke to everyone in the room, and then rolled over to me.

Seeing me sitting on the floor gluing letters on a paper sign, Taylor scooted out of her chair, onto the floor next to me, and immediately joined in.

When Joshua walked into the room, Taylor asked him if he was excited about his impending graduation.

"Do I look excited?" Joshua gave her a fake smile and walked away.

"Uh-oh." Taylor pushed her neck back. "What's wrong with Rev?"

I leaned over and whispered in her ear. "Leave him alone. He's just a little stressed out, that's all."

"Excuse me. I didn't know I was bothering him in the first place," Taylor said.

"No, I didn't mean it like that." I looked around to make sure everyone else was occupied. "It's just that his mom kind of has him backed up against the wall, threatening him with guilt."

Taylor reached into her pocket and pulled out a piece of gum. "Why is she tripping anyway?"

"She wants him to take over his father's church." I leaned in close to Taylor's face.

"So what? I mean, his father is a middle-aged man, so he shouldn't be retiring anytime soon."

"Well, actually, he's having some health challenges so . . ."

"Oh, I see. So ol' girl wants Josh to step in for the ol' man, and Josh turned her down 'cause he's planning to have his own gig, right?"

"Something like that," I said.

"She still doesn't have to be so stink about it," Taylor said, pushing a strand of her weaved hair from her face.

I stood up with the sign. "No, she doesn't have to be, but she is."

Taylor laughed "Well, it's your mother-in-law."

"Don't remind me," I said.

"You'd better be glad you weren't forced to attend his parents' church."

"Girl, you know when I met him he was running from their church. No offense to his parents, but Joshua has always been more comfortable at Missionary."

"With all his parents' stuffiness, I don't blame him."

"Well, I think it was more than that. I think he knew if he stayed at their church, he'd never be able to break away. They'd always control him, what he did, where he went . . ."

"Who he married," Taylor completed my sentence.

"Girl, you know they tried that," I laughed.

"I'm glad you can laugh about it."

"I can now, but I wasn't laughing when Mother Benning was steadily setting up Joshua with the members of her social circle." I shook my head. "That wasn't funny."

Suddenly I began to feel dizzy. I sat down, hoping that the feeling would go away.

Shortly after drinking a glass of water that Joshua brought me, I felt better. So I continued helping with the decorations. At one point, I stood on a medium-sized ladder taping balloons to the usually dull-looking beige walls. Then the dizziness started again so I climbed down and sat on the floor.

"What's wrong?" Joshua entered the room abruptly.

"I'm dizzy again. Just not feeling too good."

He sat down by me and placed my head on his shoulder. Then he cleared his throat and came out with it. His words were soft. "Do you think that you could maybe be . . .?"

"I don't know . . . maybe." My heart raced at the thought.

He smiled at me, and I smiled back. There was no way he'd know the fear I held in my heart.

Now fear had a way of tangling my nerves and tearing me apart as the inner workings of my mind proceeded to wreak havoc on my spirit. God said that fear was never intended for us Christians. Mama used to say fear gets the best of folks, specially ones afraid of every little thing, even their own shadow. Mama didn't believe in being afraid, but heck, she did believe in instilling fear. Taylor and I knew better than to underestimate Mama. She never did play.

I, on the other hand, wasn't sure what I believed about fear. Sure, I knew God didn't give us a spirit of fear but of power and a sound mind. But what did that mean for me? Did that make that churning in my belly every time Joshua talked about babies any less real? Every time he pushed up on me, I'd wondered if it was genuine love and passion, or if it was just a calculated attempt to get me pregnant. Was my frantic, chaotic mind really just a figment of my imagination, or had my fear become a familiar, yet unwelcome part of me?

In any case, I ended up in the Brooklyn Hospital emergency room, and although Joshua and I both hoped I was pregnant, it turned out to be a disappointing false alarm. Apparently, my blood sugar was low. Imagine that. Low, with all the ice cream I'd been consuming.

Sometimes it seemed like the thing I wanted the most was the thing that kept eluding me.

Sure, I was depressed, and yes, I buried my sorrows in Baskin Robbins double chocolate fudge, but that wasn't enough to make me forget the commitment I'd made to Joshua and to myself.

It was that same commitment I was praying about when guess who walked through the church doors on Sunday morning? Sister "too much to take" Yvonne twisted her way up to me, with her naturally red ringlets bouncing against her shoulders.

"Good morning, Sister Alex." Yvonne had her lips pinched so tightly together that her fakeness exuded from her pores.

"Good morning, Sister Yvonne." I gave her a fake smile in return. *Lord, forgive me.*

She gave me a pitiful version of the church hug, picked a piece of lint off the shoulder of my linen suit, and then sauntered up the aisle with her too tight skirt about to split, like she didn't know better.

It was hard on me, smiling at this sister, knowing that just a few months ago she had tried to seduce Joshua. She had come boldly into the church, pretended to be helpful, volunteered to help Josh, who was then my fiancé, with the homeless project, and then, *bam.*

When she had finally earned Joshua's trust and happily watched ours dwindle, she went for the kill. Thank God a brother came to his senses just in time. 'Cause I knew she was wicked from the very beginning, and she had evil plans for my man. A good man like Joshua, heck, I couldn't blame a sister. Guys like him were scarce.

She had disappeared from the church for a while, ever since Joshua and I got married, in fact. The word on the street was that she was modeling uptown. Now I wasn't believing that at all. Dancing around on a pole, maybe. But legitimate fashion modeling, never. There she sat on the front pew next to her troublemaking aunt, Sister Winifred, with her legs crossed and half of her thigh exposed. I wondered why she came back to Missionary. *Lord,aren't I going through enough?* Something inside told me she wasn't back to save her soul.

Chapter Five

Joshua

It was the day of my commencement ceremony at Brooklyn Missionary Bible Institute. It was two weeks before Christmas, and it was colder than usual. The crowd rustled around in thick leather coats and fur-lined boots. The wind whistled in the background as the familiar school noises took center stage. First, there was the familiar beat of pomp and circumstance as all one hundred of us marched down the center aisle in our caps and gowns. It was also an ordination ceremony for twenty-five of us, and I hadn't felt this proud of myself in a long time.

I remembered when God first called me to preach. I had been hurting pitifully after my first wife, Delilah's, death. I was not only devastated that my wife and unborn child were gone, but I was also devastated because my wife died trying to get rid of my unborn child, the one I never knew I had. Yet, I was left with a baby girl and I didn't know what to do. I didn't know where to go. No one even knew what to say to me except that they were sorry. The few spiritual ones, like my father, told me to give it time, that God would use my pain for His glory, but I didn't want to hear that. I didn't see it either. In fact, I thought my father had lost his mind. Didn't he know how this thing was tearing me apart, that I'd probably want nothing more to do with God?

Didn't he understand that God had betrayed me by allowing the woman I loved to become a Jezebel, to love her career more than she loved me or our children?

"It will all be revealed in the fullness of time," he said.

And every day I went to work to keep busy, to stay alive and to stay sane until my parents begged me to move away from Rochester. I decided to move for two reasons: to get away from the memories of Delilah around me, and to be closer to my parents so I'd have some help with raising Lilah. I didn't expect to marry again any time soon, so I knew I needed help.

Mother was ecstatic because she never liked me living in Rochester while they lived in Long Island. She also never liked me being married to Delilah. I'm not saying that my mother was glad Delilah was gone, but I honestly don't think she lost any sleep over her death either. So I moved to Brooklyn, and I became heavily involved in the church, throwing myself in and never looking back. It was either Jesus all the way or death. That's how I felt. So I kept myself busy; too busy to hurt, too busy to even feel. I didn't want to feel anything. I just wanted to work hard, day and night, and maybe even work myself to death.

As time went on, my busy work became more content driven. I began reading, and studying, and hearing God's inaudible voice. So I signed up at Missionary Bible Institute to help me understand what I was experiencing. The next thing I knew I was ordained as a deacon and feeling the nudge to preach the gospel. The more I went to God about it, the more I was pulled in, sucked in, like I had to do it to save lives—and to save my own.

After I received my master of divinity degree, all of my family and friends gathered around to celebrate with me, including Alex's Aunt Dorothy who gave me one of her usual warm hugs. Her arms were snug and soft, and she always smelled like vanilla. Alex's dad came over and shook my hand firmly. Then he looked me up and down kind of suspicious-like, but I knew he just wanted to protect his daughter so I tried to over-look it. I mean, brother to brother, I respected the man. He had given me Alex and despite his shortcomings, that was all that mattered. My sister-in law, Taylor, was there too, but I noticed that Keith, her fiancé, stayed a safe distance away from her. I figured Taylor had prob-ably been nagging him about something.

Women could get on a brother's nerves fast.

"Congratulations, Deacon Joshua, uh, I mean, Rev-erend Joshua," Minister Harris said.

"Oh, that's okay. Don't worry about titles. I'm still me," I said. "Thanks."

The Missionary church choir sang. Pastor Martin led the ordination ceremony. My dad and mom spoke briefly. Dr. Harding did his usual speech on vision and fulfilling the will of God for our lives. And I received my degree right on time. I felt really good, like everything was coming together. Everything except one important thing.

Now that I was officially a minister, all I had to do to have my life on track was to just get this baby thing right. Thanks to Alex, that was becoming a real mess. She kept fighting it, making excuses. Then there was that terrible thing she did to her body all those years ago. I mean, she was forgiven, but man, why did I have to deal with that same issue again? After Delilah died, I thought I was done with the whole abortion issue. I mean, how many men have their wives die while mur-dering their child? And I knew those were harsh words, but that was how I felt about it.

I had gotten past it, but sometimes I didn't know how much more I could take. I needed to fix everything, to have a son with Alex and finish my family once and for all.

I looked at her across the room and wanted to hold her right there on the spot, to tell her everything was going to be okay, that I was going to make sure of it.

"I'm proud of you, son." Dad pulled me into a bear hug, but he felt thinner than usual. My heart jumped as I thought about the possibility of losing him.

I looked across the crowd at my mother. She turned in her very snug two-piece suit and winked at me. I remembered when I'd earned my MBA, how I looked out at my parents and my mother winked at me from the audience. Eventually she made her way over to me and gave me her longest motherly hug, with just a bit of warmth and a hint of discipline. It was good to know she still cared, even though I recently disappointed her. Mother was always tough.

"Congratulations, Brother Benning." Sister Trudy walked toward me with open arms and hugged me as if I were her own son.

"Thank you." The vision was all coming to pass.

Then Sister Winifred waltzed over with her lips pursed tightly. "Deacon Joshua. So glad you made it through, dear. I was a little doubtful about you being called at first."

"Hello, Sister Winifred. Thanks for coming." I was determined not to let her get to me.

"Many are called, son, but few are chosen." Sister Winifred looked around. "Where is your wife, dear?"

I pointed over to Alex. "My wife is right over there."

"I see her now. Looks like she gained a little weight." Sister Winifred adjusted her glasses on her nose. "You two aren't expecting, are you?"

I took a deep breath before answering. "No, ma'am, we are not expecting."

"Well, I guess I should go over to say hello." Sister Winifred left me and walked in the opposite direction. Her smell of Bengay ointment made my nose tingle, reminding me of my great-aunt Mildred in Chicago, the one who carried hot sauce around in her purse.

The crowd remained lively up until the time we dispersed for the graduation luncheon back at the church. Everything was decorated nicely with black and green balloons, compliments of Sister Dorothy and Sister Trudy, the official hospitality team from Missionary. If there was ever an occasion to make guests feel welcome, these two ladies were on it.

Alex came up and put her arms around me. "I'm so proud of you, Minister Benning."

"And I'm so glad I have you to share all of this with." I looked into her dark eyes. "I couldn't have done this without you."

I knew that at this moment the only thing that mattered was getting this family thing right, no matter what I had to do.

The next day I was still high from yesterday's events. At the job I did my usual prayer before I got started, and then settled down in front of my computer screen. As the assistant vice president of loan accounting for the retail loan department, it was my job to approve new loans and also to check on those accounts. When I did my checks and balances, I noticed a few figures were out of line, but not necessarily enough to become alarmed. I double-checked the columns just to make sure I was seeing right. I was used to handling multiple financial transactions and everything coming up straight. So I made a mental note to go back to the beginning of each transaction and check everything more thoroughly. Since my boss, Simon, the president of loan accounting, was a cool guy, and it was only he and I who had access to this information, I knew that it was probably just a computer glitch. Yet, when I took one final look at the spreadsheet, something in my spirit told me trouble was coming.

Chapter Six

Alex

On Christmas morning Joshua and I were awakened by Lilah jumping into our bed. She was wearing Winnie the Pooh-footed pajamas, and her hair was standing wildly on top of her head in several puffs.

"Wake up! Wake up! It's Christmas, Daddy." Lilah landed on top of her father.

"Merry Christmas, sweetie," Joshua said.

I touched the top of her fuzzy little head. "Merry Christmas, Lilah."

"Merry Christmas. Now, come on. Let's go." Lilah grabbed her dad's hand and pulled.

"Okay, okay. We're coming." Joshua smiled as he slid his feet into his slippers.

Lilah looked at me and smiled. "Come on, Sister Alex."

My heart fell.

"Sweetie, didn't we have a talk already about you not calling Alex that anymore?" Joshua sighed. "We're married now, so Alex is your new mommy, remember?"

"It's okay, Josh." I shook my head to indicate my disapproval of him reprimanding her. I could tell by the look on Lilah's face, the title would have to be earned.

"But Grandma said that Alex is not really my mommy," Lilah said.

Joshua and I looked at each other in horror, and then I squeezed his hand.

"Don't worry about what Grandma said," Joshua replied.

I hopped out of bed and leaped past both of them. "Let's see what Jesus blessed us with this year."

I marveled to myself at the way I had decorated the apartment, with fresh holly, a live tree with lights, porcelain ornaments, and stringed popcorn around the tree. Each of the windows had silver lighted angels in them, complete with silver tinsel as well. Yes, I was very pleased with myself.

After I got dressed in a simple green and black pantsuit and we opened the gifts, we played one of Lilah's new video games with her, then gathered one of her new dolls and we went down to the church to serve meals to the homeless.

First, we set up the chairs and folding tables with red and white tablecloths and little fake holly centerpieces. We hung up a huge banner that read "The King is Born" before the men, women, and children started filing in. Some of the people looked like they had been down on their luck for a long time, but others looked like average people who maybe had a bad month or a bad year. Maybe they were recently widowed or unemployed. Maybe their spouses were laid off, or they had an unexpected family emergency that set them back. Maybe they had become ill and had fallen behind in medical bills. Whether they were low on cash or low in spirit, we had to rescue them. Whatever their reasons for being there, they were human beings, and they deserved to be served with as much dignity as possible.

We took so many privileges for granted on a daily basis, living the good life whether we saw it that way or not. We were unequivocally blessed, and therefore, we had a responsibility to pass that blessing on, not just with natural food but with spiritual food as well. Pastor Martin blessed the food, and everyone proceeded to eat a mixture of turkey, stuffing, collard greens, rice with gravy, fried chicken, cranberry sauce, candied yams, baked macaroni and cheese, cabbage, red velvet cake, and peach cobbler. Loose conversations spun off between tables before Pastor Martin came forward with a brief holiday message.

"I'm not going to preach today, but I am going to say what Christmas is not. It's not about jingling bells or snowmen, reindeer or elves," Pastor Martin said. "It's not even about pretty decorations, parties, or receiving gifts. The meaning is deeper than this. You see, Jesus is our gift, and His gift to us is His love. The very miracle of His birth and life is what we celebrate during this season, not the commercial items we are bombarded with in the media every day. No matter how hard they push us to buy, buy, buy, Jesus is still king and He still sits on the throne. So sing a song about Him today and get into the *real* holiday spirit. Come to Jesus."

Then the choir sang "Oh Come All Ye Faithful," followed by an altar call.

The church was so packed with volunteers, members, and nonmembers alike that cleanup was not easy. Afterward, I sat down on the cafeteria bench, took off my pumps, and rubbed my sore feet.

"Told you that you should've worn your sneakers," Joshua whispered in my ear.

"Oh, leave me alone." I waved him away and laughed.

Later, Joshua, Lilah, and I hopped into the Navigator and headed to the Benning's house for dinner.

While we were riding I wondered what antics of Mother Benning's we would face this time.

There was always something going on with that woman; like nothing I did ever pleased her. It was a mystery to me how Bishop Benning managed to stay married to her—and managed to stay sane at the same time. I sighed and put on a fresh layer of lipstick so I could start out on the right foot.

When we arrived, Mother Benning met us at the door in a charming gold-colored shoulderless dress. I didn't recognize the fabric, but it looked very expensive. Her shoes were gold colored also. Probably Steve Madden I guessed since she'd once declared that he was her favorite brand.

"Merry Christmas, darlings," she said, hugging Joshua and I at once.

"Merry Christmas, Mother Benning," I said.

Joshua gave his mother a peck on the cheek. "Merry Christmas, Mother."

Then Mother Benning reached down and picked up Lilah. "Come and give your Big Mommy a kiss."

I hated when she said that. "Big Mommy" stole all the momminess away, and there was none left for me. I smiled and watched the perfect loving interaction between Lilah and her grandmother, secretly hoping that one day I'd have a part in it.

Mother Benning smelled of raspberries, and I wondered if she had been baking a raspberry pie. Looking at her glamorous outfit, it didn't seem likely. She wasn't the domesticated type. In fact, I was pretty sure that Angelina, the cook, had prepared the entire meal.

"Big Mommy. Big Mommy," Lilah said.

"How is my beautiful granddaughter on this Christmas?" Sister Benning hugged Lilah tightly. Then she led us inside to the formal dining room where she had the table set. A swan-shaped crystal vase full of fresh orchids sat in the center of the table. Huge, original African paintings lined the walls, along with various African artifacts gathered from her many mission trips to the continent. Somehow, I had trouble picturing Mother Benning on any mission but her own. One of the paintings captivated me because the eyes of one of the African warriors were so piercing. It was as if he could see me looking at him. The collection was quite impressive.

Everything else was exquisitely elegant and tasteful; the gold-plated dishes, the selection she played on the grand piano, the vegetable-stuffed honey-roasted turkey, everything except Mother Benning's attitude, which eventually became funky, of course.

Mother Benning tilted her head to the side. "Why, Alex, dear, have you done something different with your hair?"

I immediately felt self-conscious since my hair was only tucked back in a ponytail, and hers hung flawlessly around her shoulders. "No, ma'am, I haven't really done much with it at all, to tell the truth."

"Oh, I see," she smirked.

"Joshua, have you given any more thought to taking over Kingdom House and blessing your parents' hearts?"

Joshua had a slight smile on his face. "I'd love to bless your heart, Mom, but no, I haven't changed my mind."

"Well, I guess you want us both to die then," she said.

Joshua clapped his hands and laughed. "Come on, Mother. Please stop with the drama."

"Oh, I'm just getting started," she smiled.

Eventually, Bishop Benning came downstairs and joined us at the table. He looked frail, barely spoke, and practically stumbled back to his room as soon as he had finished eating.

All in all, it wasn't the worst visit I had with Joshua's parents. However, it was my first Christmas dinner without my sister, and it really began to affect me. When we were children, Christmas was always big in our house, even when we didn't have many material things. Mama always made us a big dinner with whatever she had, and it wasn't always a traditional Christmas dinner either. It didn't matter to Taylor and me as long as we were all together. Mama usually cranked up the radio really loud as the stations played all the Christmas favorites. If she were in a really good mood she would even play "Silent Night" on her guitar while Taylor and I gathered around to sing. Yes, Mama played the guitar and used to be in a band when she was younger. That explained some of her wild side.

She was very talented. Sometimes Aunt Dorothy would come over with our cousins Nehemiah and Jeremiah. They were terrors, but we still had fun playing together. Even one Christmas when our power was off, we went out to eat at McDonald's, celebrated with candles, and went to bed early. Mama never complained about anything during Christmastime. Instead, she'd always say, "It's not about us. It's about Jesus." Then she would find someone who was in a worse position than she was in and help them. Even during her roughest times, that was what Mama did, helped people. I missed her during this time of year most of all.

Taylor was having dinner with Keith, Aunt Dorothy, and Dad. I missed them all, but I was grateful to be having dinner with my new family.

The evening was long and not the most festive, but we survived it and came out shining.

The very next day, unfortunately, we received a frantic call from Joshua's mother. She was crying and begging us to get to the hospital fast because Joshua's father was having heart pains and was having trouble breathing. She feared that he was having a heart attack and they were on their way to the hospital in an ambulance.

"Oh, Lord, please let Bishop Benning live," I whispered before grabbing my purse and heading out behind Joshua. One quick stop to drop off Lilah at Mrs. Johnson's and we were on the road.

When Mother Benning called to announce that her husband had been rushed to the emergency room, Joshua and I immediately began to pray. We knew his condition was already fragile and that we would need divine healing power to get us through this ordeal.

As we arrived at the hospital, we ran into Pastor Martin in the lobby.

"Hello, Pastor Martin," Joshua and I said in unison as if it were planned.

"Hello, Josh. Alex." Pastor Martin hugged us both with one of those quick church hugs, the kind where none of your body parts touched, except, of course, arms touching back. "Your mother called me, and I came right over. I just left your father's side. Good thing I was already in the area."

"Yes, it's a good thing," Joshua said. "We've been praying the whole way over here."

Pastor Martin's eyes narrowed. "I know what you mean. Your father is a good man and Satan had better know we're not going to give him up that easily."

I smiled. "Thank you, Pastor."

"Yes, thanks." Joshua tried to hide it, but he looked worried.

"I'll be going now because I've got another emergency on the other side of the city, but I'll be back tomorrow." Pastor Martin put on his hat and headed out the door. "Good night."

"Good night," Joshua and I said, again in unison.

We walked over to the front desk where a tall Jamaican lady gave us directions to the ICU. We took the elevator upstairs in silence. The fluorescent lighting illuminated the plain white walls, as well as carefully placed instructional signs. I didn't like hospitals at all, not since Mom died in one. It was too quiet, and way too gloomy.

As soon as we turned the corner, Mother Benning walked over to us. "Joshua. Alex."

"Hi, Mother," Joshua said.

"Hello, Mother Benning." I reached out to hug her, but she walked right past me.

Mother Benning threw her arms around Joshua. "Thankfully, it was only a false alarm and not a heart attack, but they're going to keep him overnight. His doctor wants to watch him closely because he's so weak."

Mother Benning led us to his room. After spending a few minutes with Brother Benning, a doctor came in and asked us to leave the room so he could be examined. Since his vital signs were better, we were allowed back in but not before the doctor spoke to us briefly about his condition. The doctor explained that the prostate was a walnut-sized structure that made up the man's reproductive system and the problem was that it was wrapped around the urethra, which carries urine out of the body. It was amazing to me that one body part out of order could cause so much trouble. It was just like Taylor always said, "You gotta start taking better care of yourself."

I remembered Mama and how cancer ate up her body. She used to call out for Taylor and me all the time during her last days. All she wanted before she died was to know that Taylor would soon give her life to the Lord and get back in church. That was all she ever asked about and all Taylor did was say, "Yes, Mama." Then she'd slip away to go to some party or to hang out with some loser while our mother's life ebbed away. I wanted to strangle her back then. I wanted to hurt her for her selfishness until one day while I was sitting by Mama's bedside, Mama helped me to realize that Taylor was hurting just as much as I was.

Mama, in all her fifty-five years of wisdom, told me that since Taylor wouldn't trust God, her wild behavior was just her way of dealing with the situation. She clubbed until she couldn't club anymore, and there was nothing anyone could do to stop her. Not until, of course, God intervened, and her life of partying became her prison. I swallowed hard as the pain from the memory faded.

The doctor talked about the radiation oncologist and the results of his treatments so far.

It was a very technical discussion, and I must admit that I tuned out most of it. About two minutes later, Mother Benning started in on us.

"Joshua, I hope you've reconsidered your position, especially since we almost lost your father today." Mother Benning looked directly at Joshua.

"I'm sorry, Mother, but I haven't," Joshua said. "I can't."

Mother Benning stood directly in front of my husband. "Can't? Are you telling me that even seeing your father here in the hospital, you're still not willing to help out?"

"I told you that I'd help out in any way I can, any way other than pastoring KingdomHouse of Prayer Church. I will be too busy pastoring my own church."

"Oh, please." Mother Benning waved him away with her hand. "You're barely out of seminary school."

"Mother, that was just a formality anyway," Joshua said. "The school didn't call me. Jesus did."

"You were always so stubborn—just like your father."

Bishop Benning tried to sit up in bed. "Get off the boy, Mirriam. Let him be."

"Are you all right, dear?" Mother Benning ran over to his side.

"I will be when you stop badgering our son." Bishop Benning, obviously in a lot of discomfort, strained to get out his words.

Mother Benning stroked her husband's hair and didn't say a word. She continued to watch Joshua from the corner of her eye.

I sat and watched my husband look helpless. Not at all the strong-minded man of God I'd married. He looked like a little boy, Mirriam's boy. And I didn't like it not one bit. I liked to think of myself as a strong woman, and I needed my man to be strong, especially against the wiles of the devil. Not that his mother was the devil, but sometimes I thought she let the devil use her more often than any of us wanted to admit.

I mean, none of us had perfect relationships with our parents, and I certainly had my own ups and downs with mine, but I believed in a mother letting her child grow up and live life without constant interference. And that's what Mirriam Benning was—constant interference.

I sighed because fate had me in an uproar again. By the time Joshua and I stepped out of the room into the private waiting area, Mother Benning came charging in behind us. I could see her twisted eyebrows a mile away. Was this the first lady whose job was to co-watch over people's souls? I winced at the irony.

Mother Benning bent her lips into an awkward smile and spoke slowly. "I have a proposition for the two of you." She rubbed her diamond-clad hands together.

Joshua shook his head frantically. "Mother, I—"

"Now just hold on. Since you obviously have made up your mind that you want to start a little ministry of your own, and that's okay too . . ." Dressed in an all-white wool pantsuit with three-quarter length sleeves, Mother Benning fondled an eye-catching diamond bracelet as she spoke.

Joshua sighed. "Nice of you to acknowledge that."

She took a deep breath. "Anyway, your father and I could help you with that. We could—"

"Oh no. You can't buy me, Mother."

"Really? Weren't we funding your little international adoption venture? I didn't hear any complaints about that."

"That's different. That's not a venture. It's a child's life, a human soul," Joshua said.

"Well, this is your father's life and our life together. Don't you care about that?"

"Of course, I care, but I've explained to you before what I've been called to do. It's been clear for a while now."

"Oh, I know. I know. That's your calling, you say, to be a little minister in a little local church, to tear down the walls of hypocrisy . . ." Mother Benning threw her slim arm into the air. "I've heard it all before."

"Right." Joshua sighed. "I want to build my church from the ground up. That's what God told me to do."

"It's very commendable, son, but not very realistic. Can't you see how desperate we are?

We didn't expect your father to retire so soon. Can't you do both? I mean, have your little church and run Kingdom House at the same time?"

"Mother, please," Joshua started.

Mother Benning continued. "I can get people to help you, to volunteer, of course, and then you'd be free to—"

Joshua sighed and rubbed his forehead. "To do what it is you and Dad want me to do?"

"Yes, I'm afraid so," Mother Benning said.

"I'm sorry. I can't do both. I can help out, but I've got to stay true to the vision that's in my heart."

Mother Benning poked out her full lips. "Does that vision include your little international adoption?"

I immediately remembered the day Joshua told her that we wanted to adopt Kiano.

Since Joshua was still paying for school along with mounds of debt accumulated by his deceased wife, Mother Benning knew he wouldn't have the extra money necessary to pay all the expensive legal fees. So she stood up boldly and volunteered to help with the cause, saying she'd love to have an addition to the family. She said Lilah would enjoy having a big brother, and that being a grandmother was the best job in the world. Apparently not. All her words—lies—swirled around in my head.

Joshua looked her directly in the eyes. "What are you saying?"

"I'm saying that if you won't take over for your father, we'll have to hire someone else,and then I'll be forced to withdraw my financial support for your Kenya project."

"Mother, you wouldn't." Joshua put his hands on top of his head.

Mother Benning took out her checkbook and waved it around in his face. "I would. I'll do what I've got to do."

"I thought this was about doing God's will," Joshua said.

"Don't tell me about God's will. Was it God's will for your father to fall sick like this? Was it God's will for me to miscarry what would've been your older brother? Maybe he would've been the one to be concerned about his father."

Joshua looked like he was choking. "Don't do this."

"I'm just protecting my husband's legacy." Mother Benning didn't hesitate.

"This is blackmail," Joshua said.

"Call it whatever you like." She became louder. "You and your little Mother Theresa wife over there don't have a clue about what it takes to build a ministry."

"Mother Benning—please don't do this," I said.

Joshua stepped in. "You can't do this to an innocent kid who we've already told that we're adopting."

"My hands are tied." Mother Benning put the checkbook away.

I couldn't believe what she was saying. I couldn't believe a woman of God could be so heartless. "We're not just going to sit back and watch you mess up a little boy's life."

Then Mother Benning's hand went up again in my face. "Sweetie, you're already way out of your league. Stay out of this."

I sat down, not out of defeat, but out of respect for Joshua.

"Mother, you can't be serious." Joshua's eyes filled up with tears.

"I'm as serious as a heart attack." Mother Benning took up her mink coat and walked to the door. "This is about survival of the fittest and may the best man or woman win."

Chapter Seven

Joshua

The awkward silence in the small off-white waiting area made it seem like a tomb. There were other concerned families in there sitting on the soft gray chairs and waiting, some grieving. Mother seemed oblivious to them all. She seemed to only care about herself, and her agenda.

I was more hurt than angry. "She crossed the line this time." I couldn't believe that she had all but ignored me up to this point, then threw this mess in my face, threatening me. And even brought up who would have been my older brother in order to guilt me into doing what she wanted. Now that was low, even for Mother. I had to put a stop to that.

"Give her more time," Alex whispered to me, trying to hold me back.

When Mother returned, I cornered her. "Hasn't this gone too far?"

"On the contrary, son. I'm a winner, so I'm taking this all the way to the finish line," she said as she walked away.

So that was my life ever since I could remember. Mother would either pout or strong-arm my father into getting whatever she wanted, even to the detriment of everyone else. But it didn't matter. Mother used to say nothing mattered except for the vision. *Vision* is what she called it, and she used it to her advantage, at home and in the political arena also.

I looked over at my beautiful wife slouched over in the waiting-room chair.

She looked so sad. Maybe she was worried about me. I wanted to put my arms around her and take away her pain, but I couldn't. To be honest, I couldn't even handle my own.

Why couldn't Mother just accept the vision God had given me? Why did things have to always go her way? *Does God favor women over men?* I wished that I could depend on my father for backup, but he was too weak. In his very fragile state, I wondered how badly I'd hurt him when I said no to taking over the church. I knew my mother had probably poisoned his mind against me like she always did. She always knew how to pull his strings.

I was too close to having everything I ever wanted. I was married to Alex, was about to adopt an under-privileged child, was finally an ordained minister, and all I needed was a biological son to make it all perfect. I wasn't going to let Mother's selfishness destroy me.

Mother was always serious, but committed to her family in her own controlling way. I knew she loved me, but sometimes I really wondered if she liked me. She had a no-nonsense kind of strictness, yet she wasn't old-fashioned at all. The daughter of attorneys, she believed in change, and sometimes change at all costs. My father, although he himself was a judge and was the son of ministers, he was more laid-back. He was the one who attended all of my high school and college basket-ball games, while Mother *ran* the community. Although my father was a very powerful man, I knew my mother was the stronger of the two. Even now that he was in his hospital bed, I didn't worry that mother would be fine without him, but I didn't know if my father would be fine without her.

When we got home, I just wanted to be alone, but Alex wouldn't let it go. She followed me around the room. "What are we going to do, Joshua?"

Just like a woman, always nagging. I mean, we hadn't been in the house two minutes and Alex was already whining. I didn't have all the answers, and I hated that. So I disappeared into the kitchen where I had left my financials sprawled across the table.

I plopped down in the vinyl chair and buried my head in my hands. Before I could lift my head I heard the sound of Alex's gentle footsteps.

"I don't think we can do it. There's just too much going on," I said.

"Too much going on? Do what?"

"The Kiano thing." I threw my hands into the air. "Where are we going to come up with the money for the adoption, along with paying for my last quarter in school and all these bills De—" I stopped before I went any further.

"No, go ahead and finish. It won't offend me. All these bills Delilah left you. That's what you were going to say, right? And shouldn't she have had life insurance to cover some of her debt anyway?"

"Believe it or not, I did use some of it for that, but most of it went toward her funeral and moving expenses. Plus it took me a minute to find a job here in New York City after Lilah and I moved."

"I understand all of that."

"I just don't know if we can swing this international thing anymore. It's very expensive." I cringed at the thought that my own mother had added to this pressure.

"It was always expensive," Alex said.

"And you know my mother won't help us with the adoption expenses anymore, not that she should have to . . ."

"I know she doesn't have to, but she promised." Alex blinked her eyes to hold back tears.

"We promised too."

"I know, and I'm sorry."

"Sorry? You should've been sorry when Delilah was using up all your money buying her authentic Gucci wardrobe." Alex's piercing stare made me uncomfortable. "Look, I apologize. I don't want to be mean. It's just that Kiano means a lot to me, and I made him a promise. *We* made him a promise. We can't go back on that now."

I stood up and pulled her close to me. "Alex, you're right, and I am sorry. I never wanted to bring you into this mess. I should've paid all my debts off before we even got engaged. It's just that when I met you, my whole world changed, and I didn't want to wait for my finances to change too."

"I know."

"No, you don't know. After Delilah, I wasn't sure I could love again . . ." I was holding back so Alex wouldn't see how weak I really was.

"It'll be okay. Maybe I can do some overtime, take on more hours for a while or something." Alex smiled and patted me on the shoulder. "Who knows?"

"No way. Not my wife."

"But Joshua . . ."

"This discussion is over." I left the room while I could still stand myself.

It hurt my heart to hear my wife talk like this when all I wanted was to be a good provider, a good husband, and father. And I really wanted Alex to stay home and be a good mother. It was just this whole money thing turned upside down. It was bad enough she had to even work part-time, but the thought of her having to work extra hours really made me upset. I was supposed to take care of everything so she could concentrate on carrying my baby. I needed God to help me get a grip on things. I needed a grip fast.

Chapter Eight

Alex

The next morning the sunlight streaming through the blinds woke me up. I jumped out of bed before Joshua, took my shower, and then slipped back into bed with him. Normally, Joshua would have been up praying at 5:00 A.M., followed by his Bible reading and meditation. When I touched his shoulder, he just groaned and turned the other way.

I could tell Joshua was especially depressed because of what happened with his parents last night. It was all so emotionally draining, his father's illness and his mother's aggression. I suggested that he take a day off from work, but he dismissed that idea quickly enough. Joshua never liked to take days off from work unless it was absolutely necessary. I guess he could be classified as a workaholic since that was pretty much all he ever did. In fact, the only real recreation Joshua participated in on any kind of regular basis was watching basketball games.

Yes, he loved to follow LeBron James's career during basketball season. And he even enjoyed shooting a few hoops every now and then, but this was rare.

Finally, Joshua climbed out of bed as if on his last bit of strength. He showered, dressed himself in one of his many pin-striped suits, and was ready to go off to work. He didn't even want his usual bagel and tea for breakfast.

"Everything will be all right," I said, walking him to the door. But I could tell he had so much on his mind.

Lilah was still asleep since we were both officially on Christmas vacation.

"I'll call you later." He gave me a dry kiss and walked across the hall, disappearing into the elevator.

I went to check on Lilah, saw that she was sleeping soundly, and then sat down at Joshua's desk. I wanted to open and read some of the Christmas cards we had received from the church. I opened one and it was a beautiful nativity scene from Sister Marguerite. Then I started to open another when a stapled group of bills caught my eye. There were old credit card statements dating back from three years ago. They were different cards with different large balances; five thousand, seven thousand, ten thousand.

"Wow," I said to myself. There were purchases from Macys, Lord & Taylor, Neiman Marcus, Victoria's Secret, Gucci, and Tiffany's. I knew these had to be Delilah's purchases.

It must be nice to have such expensive taste, I thought to myself. No wonder my husband was stressed out about money and could barely afford the life *we* wanted together. His first wife had buried him in debt. There was hardly anything left for me.

I looked at the thin tennis bracelet on my arm that he had given me for Christmas, and suddenly I was upset, envious, I guess. Did I have to walk in a dead woman's shadow? Couldn't I have some nice things for myself too? Why did I have to be the wife to make all the sacrifices?

Be not envious of sinners. The Holy Spirit calmed me down quickly, and I walked away from the desk, grateful for what I did have, and mostly grateful for my husband.

He had been through so much already with Delilah that I was determined to make him forget about her. I was determined to be a better wife to him than she had been.

Later on in the day, Lilah and I headed out on an adventure of our own.

"How would you like to go ice skating?" I asked her.

"Yay!" Lilah started jumping up and down.

"All right, then, let's go," I said.

First, I whipped up a batch of strawberry pancakes and bacon for Lilah and me, which I knew I would regret whenever I visited the gym again. Then I picked out a cute little jeans outfit for Lilah and one for myself. Mine was a little rough getting over the hips, but I'd have to work that out with myself later. In any case, we were matching in pink denim and ready for action. I took her hand, and we walked through our eclectic Brooklyn neighborhood to the nearest train station one block away.

I could see the excitement in Lilah's eyes as we boarded the train. This was our first real outing alone since I'd been married to her father, so I needed it to be special. Lilah talked the entire time about how she had seen ice skaters on Sesame Street and how she knew she would have so much fun on the ice. I hoped so because I wanted more than anything to really connect with her. Since Lilah had been so used to getting pretty much everything she wanted from her grandmother, this was not necessarily an easy task.

Finally, we arrived at the ice rink at Rockefeller Center in Midtown Manhattan. It was just as beautiful in person as it had been on television. There was a huge Christmas tree decorated with glamorous lights and the famous Prometheus statue in all its bronze glory. Lilah's eyes were big with anticipation, which made me smile on the inside and out. We rented skates and were told before starting that we should walk on the rubber matting, keeping our skate guards on. It sounded like good advice.

Since I had never been ice skating before, this was a challenge for both of us. I had wanted to go ice skating with Joshua once, but he showed no interest in it at all, so here I was with the four-year-old making it happen despite myself. I used my knowledge of roller skating to help me navigate this new world. First, we walked around the edge while holding the wall, trying to get a feel for the ice. *Please, Lord, don't let me fall.* Eventually, I began to bend my knees and lean forward as I watched the techniques of the skaters who glided around the rink. Before long, Lilah and I were moving, falling, and then moving again. Getting up wasn't easy because the ice was so slippery, but one young man stopped to help and give us advice.

"Get on your hands and knees and put one foot between your hands," he said.

"Okay," I replied, happy that I hadn't split my pants.

"When you want to stop, place one skate behind you with the toe facing away from you. Then drag it behind you until you stop." He smiled. "Oh, and another thing, take longer strokes."

"Thanks." I looked up at him. "You sure are a lifesaver."

"Well, I wouldn't say that. Take care now," he said as he disappeared into the lively crowd of skaters.

"You too," I replied.

I was so grateful for this information. *Thankfully, there were still nice people left in the world,* I thought as I watched everyone else circling around us without even a glance. Lilah and I laughed and took off again.

This time we tried to take longer strokes, whatever that meant.

I wouldn't exactly call it skating, and I wouldn't necessarily call it fun, except that we were together, an unlikely stepmother and stepdaughter forged together by unfortunate circumstances. Lilah did seem to enjoy herself though, and begged to come back again when we were leaving. I promised her that we would.

Afterward, I took her to eat at Angelos between Fifty-third and Fifty-fourth Streets. I remembered that they were nearby and had some of the best pizza that I'd ever tasted. Needless to say, Lilah and I left tired but happy. I hoped I was successfully building a real relationship with the little girl who refused to call me "Mommy."

Chapter Nine

Alex

It was an average winter day for New York City. Now that Christmas vacation was over and we had welcomed the new year, I was glad to finally return to work. It gave me something to focus on besides my fertility issues. There was the usual office banter between coworkers and administration on how the holidays were and who received what for Christmas. The holidays had become so commercialized that I could hardly stand it sometimes. There were new students starting new classes, and lots of exciting new plans to look forward to, plans that could preoccupy me for a few hours per day. Missionary had been given a generous donation in order to expand its library. I was excited that a whole new wing was being built in honor of the benefactor, Dr. Joseph Calholm. Then there was talk of a commercial and a new Bible radio show headed up by Dr. Harding himself. That would really put a new spin on Missionary.

Marisol didn't seem to be interested in either. She was too busy watching for tall, eligible bachelors on the registrar's list. And I do mean that she was seeking them out literally.

There should've been a law against what she was doing, and, in fact, there probably was. I stayed clear of her and her plans.

Marisol came over to my desk with the registrar's list in her hand. "Here is one registered for a full-time credit load, studying for his master of divinity, and he paid his tuition in full."

"Go on with that foolishness, Marisol. You shouldn't be digging through people's personal business."

"Oh, please, it's my job," Marisol said.

"No, it's your job to check for certain items on the list. Not to scrutinize people's lives."

"Okay, whatever." Marisol put up her hand. "Either way, I'm going to be seeing the same information."

"But not to use for your own benefit."

"All I'm doing is keeping my eyes open, that's all. You never know who I might run into."

"Marisol, you're a mess." I shook my head. "Now get off of my desk with your work before we both get in trouble."

Marisol hunched her shoulders, gathered her papers, and left with a smile. "I'll catch up with you later, *chica*."

"Not if I see you first," I laughed.

Marisol nodded and pointed at me as she was leaving. "Oh, so it's like that. Okay, I got you, girl."

With all the work we both had for the new year, we never did catch up with each other.

By the end of my shift, I was tired.

After work, I drove down the highway with the wind in my hair, noticing the snowcapped trees and the icy walkways. I hated driving in that kind of weather, especially when I was in a hurry. An old coworker of mine lost her life because she skidded into the side rails on the highway one winter evening. I was determined not to fall into that trap, so I prayed for God's divine protection over my life, and I kept my speed to the bare minimum.

I was almost late for the meeting with Mr. Bowman, the business attorney who filed my not-for-profit status for Giving Life Ministries. Surprisingly, parking turned out not to be a problem, and I caught the elevator going up just in time. Mr. Bowman and I completed our business in a timely manner, and I was on my way with all the paperwork I needed.

Up to now, the group and I had been meeting at the church, but in a few months when the renovations to Taylor and Keith's fitness center were completed, our group would be holding our meetings there. At least that was the plan until Joshua and I started our own church.

The whole project was scheduled to culminate at the Push It Fitness Center's official grand opening. Since Taylor and Keith had purchased the center from its former owner, they had kept everything the same, both the décor and the policies. The much-needed changes would give them the opportunity to show off the new management and the new ideas they would soon implement.

I was just grateful that Giving Life Ministry could come along for the ride and could be separated from Missionary. It wasn't that I didn't love Missionary, but I needed this separation for two reasons. The first was so I'd be able to qualify for the donations and grants necessary for my programs by having a 501(c)(3) of my own. The second reason was that my vision was big, and I knew we'd already outgrown Missionary's place for us. Pastor Martin was generous enough to put me over the program, but I knew he had no idea what he was getting himself into.

I was still amazed that I was delivered and was now able to help other girls who were struggling with the abortion and/or fornication issue. I wanted to catch them before they made these mistakes and teach them about their true worth. I wanted to emphasize the importance of purity before marriage, and the special gift of giving oneself to one's own husband. I wanted to teach them about starting over and abstaining from sex, even if they'd already been involved in a sexual relationship. Oh, how I wished I had known that sooner.

It would have kept me free from so many meaningless relationships. I wanted them to know that Jesus could cleanse them from all unrighteousness and that they could be clean again, no matter what they'd done. I wanted to talk about how to fall in love with Jesus, and so many other valuable things I'd learned over the years. There were so many young girls who just fell through the cracks and ended up broken. With God's help and mercy, I wanted to rescue them all.

Just thinking about the ministry made me tingle. It was as if I were born for this task.

By the time I returned from the meeting, stopped at the grocery store, and picked up Lilah from Mrs. Johnson's place, it was almost time for Joshua to get home from work. I scurried around the already posh apartment, fluffing every throw pillow and neatening the tablecloth, making sure everything was perfect. I set a pot of water on the stove to boil so I could make spaghetti. Then I proceeded to let the seasoned ground beef simmer in the skillet as I continued to slice green peppers into it. Lilah sat at the kitchen table quietly playing with her doll until we heard the front door open.

I lifted Lilah into my arms, and we went to greet her father at the door. "Hi, baby."

"Daddy, Daddy," Lilah squealed as I plopped her down in front of him.

"Hi, you two." Joshua looked tired and tense. He gave me a quick kiss on the lips, and bent over to give Lilah a peck on the cheek.

I grabbed his arm and led him toward the center of the room. Lilah followed.

Joshua tugged at one of Lilah's thick, wavy ponytails. "Something smells really good."

"It's your favorite," I said, still holding his arm.

Then he loosened himself from my grip, went to his desk, took out his checkbook and bank statements, and started hitting the digital calculator. I didn't dare bother him, but I knew he looked worried. Whatever it was I wished he would've shared it with me. Lilah ran over to hug her father. He scooped her up in his arms, and I could see the joy on his face. He really did love children, and I felt a little sorry for him. I was sorry I couldn't easily give him the second child he longed for. I walked over and hugged them both tightly. This was my new family, and I'd do anything for them.

Lilah giggled and ran off without a care in the world. Instantly, I remembered Kiano and the little mud huts from his village. I knew that a boy his age should be just as carefree as Lilah, but he wasn't. I decided in my mind that I had to get him out of there soon. Yet I didn't want to bother Joshua with my concerns.

I walked up behind my husband and threw my arms around him. With a look of surrender, he sat back and let me massage his back for a few minutes.

"Mmm, that feels so good," he said.

"You're so tight, Joshua." I squeezed his upper back and shoulders.

"Yeah."

I sat on his lap. "Are you sure you're okay?"

He kissed me on the forehead, pushing me gently off his lap. "I'm fine."

I knew he wasn't. I just couldn't figure out why he was acting so different. I went back into the bedroom, paced the hardwood floor for a while, then sat on the edge of my bed with my head in my hands. I wasn't sure what was wrong or when it had gone wrong.

Before I knew it, I had picked up the phone to call my dad. I hadn't had a serious talk with him since before the wedding. Sure, I had seen him, and we chatted a little, but still we hadn't talked like we used to.

Dad sounded like he had been sleeping. "Alex, is that you?"

"Yes, Dad. How are you?"

"I'm okay, but what's wrong?"

I sighed. "Nothing, Dad."

"Oh, come on, I'm your father. You can't lie to me. I can hear it in your voice." Dad cleared his throat. "Something is wrong. Now, what happened?"

"It's nothing, really. I'm just a little tired."

"Okay. How is Joshua?"

"He's fine, just very busy," I sighed. "Always working when he gets home."

"Oh, I see."

"He's just swamped with work this time of year, that's all." I couldn't believe that I was making excuses for him. *Love covers all things.*

"If you say so," Dad grunted.

"Why do you sound so skeptical?"

Dad chuckled. "Because *you* called *me*, remember?"

"I know, and I'm sorry." I paused before continuing. I had to take time to organize my thoughts and speech. "I guess neither of us has been acting like ourselves lately."

Dad coughed, a consequence of his previous years of smoking. "Maybe the two of you are working too hard at everything. Maybe you need a little break, Alex."

"Maybe you're right," I said.

"Are you sure you're all right?"

I hesitated for a moment before I decided not to go deeper. "Yes, I am. I'll talk to you tomorrow."

"Get some rest. Good night."

"You too. Nite." I hung up the phone, feeling slightly foolish.

Was I that desperate that I had to run back to my daddy like a little girl? Mama always said I was a daddy's girl. Maybe she was right. In any case, I needed someone. I just wasn't sure getting my dad involved in my marital problems was the right answer.

Chapter Ten

Joshua

A draft came in from the hallway as I kissed my wife and daughter good-bye. Alex was wearing one of her old cutoff T-shirts that she liked to sleep in. The sight of her beautiful legs and thighs made me want to turn around and go back inside the apartment. Instead, I whispered something sweet in her ear and gave her a look that promised I'd be back. My wife was a beautiful, thick woman, and I loved every inch of her. I squeezed Lilah once more and ran out the door with my briefcase in my hand.

I still had my beautiful wife on my mind when I got downstairs to the parking garage and jumped into my Lincoln Navigator. Since I was on my way to work, I had to start thinking about business, banking business, because I never knew what challenges were ahead of me. Driving through Brooklyn streets didn't bother me as much as it used to when I first moved here from Rochester.

Back then, the streets here made me crazy. I prayed for God to deliver me from these wild drivers, honking their horns while giving me the bird or just plain cussing me out just because they're New Yorkers, but now I was used to it. I smiled as I saw a lady who looked like she was in her midtwenties crossing the intersection with a baby stroller. Immediately, I thought of Alex and our baby, or at least the one I was going to make.

These days I was on Alex so much I was tired, she was tired, and I didn't know how we were ever going to have a child this way. I just knew that we needed to have one. And the more I thought about it, the more I needed it to be. Alex mentioned that we might need to see Pastor Martin for counseling, but personally, I felt like I had everything under control.

By the time I arrived at work and got settled, customers were clamoring at my door to get the financial solutions they needed. I was happy to oblige. There were loans and more loans to approve and deny. That was my job, and I did it well. It gave me a certain satisfaction when I helped people with their banking matters. It was like I was inadvertently helping them get their lives in order. On top of that, numbers were like a game to me. Ever since I could remember, I'd play number games in my head, and banking was just an extension of that. I drummed my fingers on my desk, thinking about the money Alex and I had saved in our account. It was not enough for the down payment on a church property we needed or for the house we needed. Nor was it enough to pay off all the bills we had accumulated. It was only a tiny speck in the span of things, a sad representation of my commitment to my work and my family.

When I got the chance, I pulled Simon to the side and told him that I was really strapped with bills.

"That's too bad, Josh. Times are tough these days," he said.

I tried to remain optimistic. "They certainly are, but a raise would really help to stabilize my situation."

Simon adjusted his reading glasses. "Right, right."

He'd been promising me a raise for a while, and it was long overdue. Against my better judgment, I sat in Simon's office practically pleading my case while he sat back in his chair, thumbing through papers. Finally, he brushed me off by answering a phone call while I was still talking.

He held the phone away from his ear and whispered. "I'll get back to you later."

It was always the same story. Suddenly, I began to feel agitated, and I couldn't wait until the workday was over.

Besides work, Bible study provided just the escape from my problems that I needed.

Alex, Lilah, and I arrived at Missionary right on time. Alex helped me to straighten my tie, and then gave me a big juicy kiss on the lips before we went in. It made me love her even more.

After the initial hugs and handshakes from random members, we separated. Alex went to go sing with the praise team while I took Lilah down to the children's ministry. Sister Sarah greeted us at the door as I signed Lilah in.

"See ya later, Daddy," Lilah said.

"See ya, sweetie," I replied.

By this time I could hear the praise team singing "It Ain't Over" in the sanctuary. I clapped my hands to the beat as I walked upstairs. Just as I reached the top of the stairs and pushed open the door, I came face-to-face with Yvonne Johnson. She wore a short, clingy skirt suit with a plunging neckline and tall, black boots. Same cute, flirty Yvonne.

"Hello, Deacon Joshua." She walked over to me and touched my shoulder.

I sighed. "Hello, Yvonne."

She must've noticed that I tensed up at her presence because she smiled and stepped back.

"Don't worry. It's hands off for me now." Yvonne put her hands in the air.

"Right." I was a little thrown off by her comment.

"No, really. I never got a chance to apologize for how I acted last year."

"It's not necessary." I put my hand up, indicating that I wanted her to stop.

Her curly red hair framed her face. "No, it is necessary. I know better now."

"I understand," I said.

"I should've respected your relationship with Sister Alex. I knew you two were engaged, but I still . . ."

She was right about that. If she had respected our relationship, Alex and I would've never had to confront the jealousy issue along with our many other issues. I was never interested in Yvonne, even though I've got to admit the attention from a woman like her was flattering. She should've stuck to her own thing, whatever that was, instead of trying to mess up Alex and me. But I was over that now.

"No, really, it's okay," I said, backing away from her.

"It's just that I was new here and in a big city like this—you can get real lonely."

"I get it."

"I let myself get too carried away." Yvonne looked down at the floor. "I'm sorry."

I had to admit she was making me feel very strange. "I accept your apology."

Yvonne sighed. "Well, I hope we can be friends now."

"Sure. I'll see you around church," I said, turning away.

Yvonne walked away. "Right. Bye."

Her musky perfume lingered in the air. I had little doubt that Yvonne was trying to be sincere. Poor Yvonne. She looked embarrassed. I figured it must be hard to be in a big city with only her overbearing aunt by the name of Winifred. I hoped she had really turned her life around, and wouldn't try to come between Alex and me again. Either way, I walked into the sanctuary to find my wife. I didn't have time for Yvonne's issues. I had too many of my own.

Chapter Eleven

Alex

The new year was here, yet every day I went to work feeling more and more sluggish. I stepped into the lobby with what seemed like the weight of the world on my shoulders. An appropriate scripture popped into my head. *My yoke is easy and my burden is light.* Deep inside, I knew I'd have to give my worries to the Lord eventually, if I expected any peace at all. But being my determined self, I wasn't ready to let go of the sulking yet.

Marisol met me in the lobby with her usual super-bubbly personality, but I wasn't in the mood. Too little sleep and tension with Joshua had all but broken my spirit. Since my evenings were filled with ovulation tests, making sure my body temperature and the atmosphere were perfect for conception, I was burned out. The daily procedures took all the romance out of our relationship because we had to make it happen instead of being in the mood. The only thing left was a sense of hopelessness lingering in the darkness, hovering over our bedroom. Then, of course, there was the frequent bickering because we were under so much stress. I wondered when the cycle would end.

I was always so exhausted because I had problems getting to sleep. I kept wondering what would happen if I couldn't have Joshua's child? Would he grow to re-

sent me or stay with me out of obligation? Then I told
myself, no. The Lord said be fruitful and multiply so
this was His will. Not mine. I just couldn't accept my
barrenness without a fight. Joshua was up all hours of
the night, looking like a madman, pacing around the
living room, mumbling to himself, or sitting slumped
over his desk, punching those stupid calculator keys.
What could possibly be so important? I wondered, but
I didn't dare ask. Joshua made sure he told me that
our finances were off limits for discussion at the present time, and that it wasn't up for negotiation. Typical
male arrogance was how I summed it up. How dare he
not let me know what was going on with *our* money. I
wasn't tripping though, at least not yet because everything appeared to be paid on schedule. Everything except Kiano's attorney fees, that is. And that was bothering me more and more every day.

I settled in at my desk with my bottle of orange juice.
I booted up my computer, then went through the files
in my inbox, yawning.

Dr. Harding walked in and set a stack of files in front
of me. I looked through them and realized that one of
them was on the Mercy Group Home, the orphanage
that Kiano lived in. It appeared that the group home
would be closing down by the end of the year and splitting up the group, sending the children to other loca-
tions. They cited a lack of funds as the main reason, but
the dilapidated conditions of the building, if you could
call it a building, was the other reason.

Immediately a lump began to grow in my throat as I
broke into a cold sweat. What would happen to my poor
Kiano? Then I started to get angry. We should have had
him with us by now. He should've already been in our
apartment, warm and comfortable, playing with Lilah.
The tears came without warning, and I found myself

wiping them away with Kleenex. I was still crying on the inside though for my child who was lost in Kenya, and for the one who was lost in me. I didn't know how either of them were going to make it home, but I knew I had to hold on. I knew that I couldn't give up on either of them, that if I kept the faith, they'd both be mine.

I dialed Joshua's number on my cell phone. "Oh, Josh."

"What's wrong? You sound upset."

"I am upset. It's the Mercy Group Home in Kenya. They'll be closed by the end of the year."

"That's terrible." Joshua sighed. "What happened?"

"I just ran across a file a few minutes ago. Money and bad conditions of the building and . . ."

Joshua's voice was sad. "It'll be okay."

"How will it be okay? What about Kiano? I feel so bad for him. What are we going to do to make sure it's okay?"

"Look, I'm about to go into a meeting now, but we'll talk about this when I get home."

"All right then, bye." I let him go now, but I knew we'd have it out later.

"Bye," Joshua said.

That evening our heated conversation about Kiano was interrupted by a call from Sister Winifred down at the church. I wondered if her snake of a niece, Yvonne, had put her up to this.

In any case, she needed Joshua's help with a few administrative issues and since the pastor and assistant pastor were both out of town, Joshua was next in the line of authority. So I watched him throw on his jacket and walk out to play hero at the church while I wondered if he would ever be a hero at home.

Chapter Twelve

Joshua

Good ol' Sister Winifred is what I thought when I pulled up beside the church and parallel parked. She stepped out of her old station wagon, clutching her purse to her body, and looked all around her with those thick glasses. Although I wasn't looking forward to dealing with her, I was glad to be called away from that mess at home. Alex just didn't seem to understand what I was going through, and I was tired of arguing. All I ever heard was complaints about Kiano and the adoption. Didn't she realize everything I was trying to hold together already? Didn't she know that a man could only take so much without reaching his breaking point?

I took my time before going inside the building. Sister Winifred met me at the front door with her walking cane and her cotton white hair glistening in the artificial light. "You're late, Minister Joshua."

"I'm sorry, ma'am, but I got here as soon as I could," I said.

She looked me up and down. "Well, I guess it will have to do, won't it?"

"What exactly seems to be the problem?"

"Well, it seems that we have a cutoff notice for the water and a few other things that should've been done." Sister Winifred twisted her lips. "Somebody is slacking around here."

"I'm sure it's just an oversight, really. Pastor has a lot on his mind. I'll take care of everything."

Sister Winifred frowned up her wrinkled face. "Folks shouldn't be just running in and out of town when their business ain't in order."

"With all due respect, Sister Winifred, I'm sure there is an explanation for all of this. I'll get Pastor on the phone first thing in the morning."

"Humph," Sister Winifred said.

When I was done with the few matters at hand, I decided to grab a broom to sweep the lobby area. I was in no hurry to get home and back to the Kiano issue.

Instead, I started daydreaming about the day when God would release me to start my own little urban contemporary church. I thought about the programs we would start, the mission trips we would take, the Word I would preach, and the lives we would impact with the gospel. A few of the members started coming out of the sanctuary when I realized they'd had a choir rehearsal.

I greeted each one in between my sweeping duties. Then Brother Jameson came up to me.

He gave me a hand shake and a pound. "What's up, man?"

"Oh, nothing much. Just cleaning up a little since I'm here, that's all."

"Cool," Brother Jameson said.

"I haven't seen you around for a while." I put the broom down. "How have you been?"

"We've been good," Brother Jameson grinned. "I had an out of town assignment for a couple of weeks, and my wife and baby went to stay with her mother while I was gone."

"Okay, because Alex and I have been looking for you around the church."

"How is Sister Alex anyway?"

"She's fine," I smiled, proud to be married to my beautiful wife.

"The last time I talked to you, you all were trying to have a baby right away. How has Dr. Henley been working for you two?"

I let out a deep breath. "Well, we're still believing, but I've got to be honest; it hasn't been easy."

"Hold on, man." Brother Jameson shook his head. "It'll happen for you guys when you least expect it."

"I know," I said.

"That's how it happened for us, man." Brother Jameson's face became very serious.

I listened carefully. "I know."

"Remember, it was three long years before my wife became pregnant. All those tests and stuff were driving me nuts, and then one day, *bam*. Just when we'd almost given up hope . . . God blessed us." He shook his head. "But I'm not gonna lie. Those were some rough times."

"Yeah, it's rough on us right now," I said.

Brother Jameson scratched his short beard. "At least you already have one child."

"That's true, and don't get me wrong. I'm grateful. But I'd just like to have at least one child with my wife."

He nodded as if he understood my pain. "I know what you mean, man."

"It would be nice to have a son to carry on the Benning legacy."

"Legacy?" Brother Jameson laughed. "Now you're really tripping, bruh."

"Nah, I mean, I'm not saying that a daughter can't preach or run a church. I'm just saying I come from generations of preachers. My dad and granddad were both pastors, and it would be nice if my son could be the fourth generation."

"Yeah, I get it," Brother Jameson said.

"We're gonna keep trying."

"God willing, you'll have what you want," Brother Jameson nodded.

I thought of Alex becoming pregnant with my child. "Then everything will be perfect, back on track."

"I'll keep praying for you two."

"Thanks, man." I grabbed his hand and pulled him toward me fast. "God bless you."

Brother Jameson slapped me on the back. "God bless you too, brother."

I watched him walk away, thinking what a cool guy he was. I'd like to hook up with him again soon to shoot some hoops, if I had any time to spare.

Before I could blink, Sister Yvonne appeared from around the corner.

"Hi, Joshua," she said.

I grabbed the broom and started sweeping again. "Hi. What are you doing here?"

"I'm here helping my aunt."

I looked down at the floor. "Oh."

"You look a little down. Are you all right?"

"I'm cool." I faked a smile.

"I'm sorry, but I couldn't help but overhear your conversation with Brother Jameson."

I sighed. "You were eavesdropping?"

"Oh, no, I just happened to be passing by." Yvonne fluttered her fake eyelashes.

"Right, passing by," I mumbled to myself.

"No, really. I mean, something you said caught my attention, but I wasn't—"

I shook my head. "It's all right. Don't worry about it."

"It's just that I'm sure that fertility specialist of yours is highly recommended, and the Jamesons did have a baby, but three years is a long time to wait, though."

I squinted my eyes at her. "What are you getting at, Yvonne?"

"Well, just that there are other options still."

"Excuse me?"

Yvonne used her hands to express herself. "I mean, I have a friend who does that."

"Does what?"

Yvonne leaned toward me like she was telling me a secret. "She helps couples have babies."

"What?"

"She helps couples have babies," Yvonne whispered again.

I looked around to make sure no one else was listening. "Helps them how? Is she a doctor?"

"No, she is a professional surrogate."

"A surrogate?" I started shaking my head and my hands to indicate a definite no. I had heard a few things about surrogacy over the years, but unfortunately, everything I knew was far from good.

"Yes, she does that for a living, and she's had five babies for other people so far."

Yvonne stepped closer to me, and I could smell her flowery perfume.

"Sounds very interesting, Yvonne, but I want to have babies with my wife, not some stranger."

"I know what you mean, but she can carry your baby for you just in case Sister Alex can't."

Now I was offended. "Who said my wife can't? I would never ever accept that unless God Himself came down from heaven and told me."

"Whoa, wait a minute now. It's not me saying that. I mean, you never know, just in case."

"Just in case?"

"Yeah, just in case things don't work out the way you want. You two can use her eggs or Sister Alex's. It doesn't matter to my friend at all. She gets paid either way."

"So it's all about money for her?"

"Hey, don't judge my friend. She's just doing a service like everybody else in business.

It's all very clean and legal."

I swallowed hard at the thought that Alex might not be able to conceive. Then I snapped back. "Thanks for the offer, but we've got it under control."

"Okay, but if you ever change your mind, here's my new cell number." Yvonne handed me a card with her name and number on it. "I'd love to help."

Then at the sight of me sweeping furiously to avoid eye contact, Yvonne walked out the front door. I was angry now at how she had approached me and at how I had let her foolishness get in my head. Although I brushed her away, and I didn't even want to think the unthinkable, after the next few disappointing attempts Alex and I went through, I couldn't help but remember Yvonne's words.

Chapter Thirteen

Alex

The next morning, Joshua was up early praying as usual. When he was done, he seemed to stay far away from me, quietly getting ready for work. I fixed breakfast and got Lilah and myself dressed. Joshua and I hardly talked or touched at all. Our hands did touch once as I reached to tighten his tie. He mouthed the words "thank you," and then disappeared from the bedroom. Normally I would have followed him into the living room, but my mood was different too.

My mind was on Kiano and the other children in his village. I wondered what they would do when their orphanage closed. I pictured all of the children piling into one small building miles away, crying and smeared with mud. I remembered all the hardships those children had to face on a daily basis, and it almost broke my heart. Two trips to Kenya had been enough to settle what I needed to do. Still, I didn't say anything. I just watched my husband play with his privileged child, Lilah, at the breakfast table.

Kiano didn't sit at a table like this or have a breakfast of oatmeal and bacon like ours. He didn't have parents to play with him or hug him before he went off to school. In fact, his village barely had a school, if you could call that raggedy one-room shack with one teacher and a few books a school. When I thought about the living conditions for him over there compared to the kind of home we could give him here, my spirit cried out to rescue him. But I couldn't do it alone. I blinked away the tears that were welling up in my eyes. Still, I refused to start an argument this morning, so I kept my mouth closed.

I watched Joshua in his model father role lift Lilah into the air, hug her tightly, and wave good-bye. He kissed me hard on the lips, and I closed my eyes to savor the moment, to pretend that everything that was out of order could be set straight with a kiss. My spirit didn't rest, however.

Once he left for work, I took Lilah across the hall to Ms. Johnson, hopped into my pink car, and sped off. I hoped that another busy half day at work would at least occupy my mind.

Thankfully, it did just that until the dynamics of the workplace changed.

I couldn't believe my eyes when I saw Seger coming out of Dr. Harding's office.

They were shaking hands, and I was more than just a little curious about what Seger was doing here at Missionary Bible College. Seger, in all of his dark manliness, towered over Dr. Harding. I took a deep breath before I walked over to them.

"Seger, what are you doing here?" I asked.

"Happy New Year, Sister Alex. It's good to see you." Seger gave me a quick hug as I patted the strong muscles in his back.

"Happy New Year to you. I'm surprised to see you here." I looked back and forth between him and Dr. Harding for an explanation.

Seger laughed. "I'll let Dr. Harding explain."

"Brother Seger has agreed to be our new assistant director of admissions," Dr. Harding said.

"Oh, I see. So he'll be replacing Brother Jacob?" I avoided eye contact with Seger while I processed the information. I didn't want Seger to notice my uneasiness, but a million things were running through my mind at once. I kept smiling.

"Yes, and I have complete confidence that he will do an excellent job," Dr. Harding said, patting Seger on the back.

"Thank you, sir." Seger gave us both a big smile.

"Welcome aboard, Seger," I smiled back. "I'm sure you'll be very happy here."

"Yes, I'm sure I will." Seger held his gaze on me a minute too long in my opinion.

I had to get out of there and figure some things out. Sure, Seger was my missionary buddy, and sure, we shared a common interest in ministry, and even a common bond with the Kenyan orphans, particularly Kiano. But was this friendship thing we were nursing worth the headache I knew I was about to have? As I walked down the hall I couldn't help but go through a myriad of emotions. I was excited that Seger would be working with me, yet skeptical about what my husband would think when he found out.

I went back to my desk a little frazzled. Why did Seger have to get a job here of all places? Why couldn't my life be simple? Why did complication after complication keep arising?

It just didn't seem fair.

Later that evening I made Joshua his favorite dinner and set out caramel-scented candles.

I brought home a special Dora video for Lilah. Then I bathed in my lavender bath oil and slipped into Joshua's favorite outfit of mine, a silky, hip-hugging, low-backed black dress. This was the dress that always got me what I wanted. I used my curling iron to do

spiral curls, pinned up the back, and only left the few
hanging down in the front to frame my face just right.
I sprinkled Joshua's favorite perfume, Obsession, behind my ears, on the inside of my wrists, and on my
inner thighs. I looked at myself in the mirror, spun
myself around, and despite the slight bulge in the waist
area I couldn't seem to get rid of, I was pleased. I had
to tell him about Seger in the right atmosphere, when
he was happy and secure.

When he came in he kissed me quickly and kissed Lilah who ran into his arms. He then immediately settled
in at his desk with his briefcase and his computer. He
looked deep in thought when I approached him.

"Sweetheart, I'm sorry, but I've got some serious
work to do, if you don't mind." Joshua took my hand
and kissed my palm.

I watched Lilah skip back and forth to her room,
dragging two of her dolls behind her.

"I know. I was just hoping we could spend some real
time together this evening." I kissed him on the neck. I
secretly hoped he didn't misconstrue what I said, but I
knew he probably had.

"Oh, don't worry. We're going to spend some time
together, believe me." Joshua patted me on the bottom.

I became sick to my stomach at the thought that he
was only thinking about conception. I stepped back
away from him. "No, I mean, time to talk."

"Oh, okay." Joshua put his arms around my waist
and laid his head on my stomach. "As soon as I look
over these numbers you can have me all to yourself."

"Promise?"

"Promise."

So after dinner, and after I put Lilah to bed, I put on
soft music, lit a few candles, and pampered my husband.
When the mood was right, and I had him all wrapped

up in my arms, I told him about my day, and I told him about Seger. That was when his mood changed instantly, and he slipped from my arms as easily as he had come into them, blew out all the candles, and laid down Joshua's law. He said that I could no longer be friends with Seger, and that he didn't even want me working at the college anymore. He didn't even want me mentioning Seger's name.

And I had never heard it put down so sternly, the "you are my wife and you will do as I say" speech. I took it all in although I was rebelling in my heart. Under my breath I swore I'd be friends with Seger whether he liked it or not.

Since the next morning was Saturday, and since Saturday was typically when I went down to the gym to see my sister, I woke up early, showered, and dressed in my least fashionable workout clothes. I didn't care what I looked like because I was still upset about the confrontation Joshua and I had the night before. Feeling defiant, I headed out the door before Joshua even woke up. I put a baseball cap on my head and kept it moving as I drove over to the Push It Fitness Center anxious to talk to Taylor. I walked past the front desk, waving at Jasmine, the bubbly receptionist, and went straight into Taylor's office.

It was half decorated in turquoise blue and red with all contemporary furniture. One wall was only partially painted. Taylor sat behind her desk in her wheelchair, wearing a white and blue workout outfit and matching headband. Her hair was pulled back in a ponytail, and when she looked up, I could tell she was surprised to see me.

"Hi, girl," Taylor smiled.

I plopped down in one of her red vinyl chairs. "Hey, the renovations are really coming along."

"Yeah, I guess so," she said.

"I like it." I looked around the room, nodding my head. "It's really beginning to look like you and Keith in here and not like the old management."

"Thanks. It'll be really nice by the time of the grand opening."

"Oh, yes." I clapped my hands. "I can't wait to get all the Giving Life girls out here. It's going to be a lot of work, though."

"We're used to it," Taylor said. "So what's up?"

I spit it out. "Joshua wants me to quit my job."

Taylor pushed her neck all the way back. "Quit?"

"Yeah, quit."

"Are you crazy? You've already gone down to part-time." She rolled her eyes. "What else does he want?"

"I don't know. I guess he just wants me away from Seger. Period."

"Hold on." Taylor put her hand up for me to stop. "I missed something."

"Seger is the new assistant director down at Missionary."

Taylor nodded. "Oh, now I see."

"No, you don't see." I put my head down on her desk. "My life is a straight mess."

"Oh, come on, it can't be that bad." Taylor stuffed a stick of chewing gum into her mouth. "Why is he so jealous anyway? I never figured preacher boy to be the jealous type."

"Yeah, well, you were wrong. He's convinced that Seger wants me," I said.

"Why would he think that?"

"I don't know. Something about the way Seger looks at me."

"Hmmm. That sounds hot." Taylor used her hand to fan herself.

I pushed her. "Taylor."

"What? It's not my fault that some dude is hot for you."

"Oh, come on. The only one hot for me is my overly zealous husband."

"So what's the problem then?" Taylor sucked her teeth. "You can keep your little job and be happy."

"You don't understand. Josh is very serious about this, and I need my job. First of all, we need the money. And second, the short hours will work well with my grad school schedule, and Lilah and—"

"And the new baby, right?"

"Yes, and the new baby," I sighed.

"If you ask me, you're doing too much at once." Taylor bent over to take a protein drink out of her mini refrigerator. She waved it at me as if it were a warning. Then she spit her gum into the trash can and began drinking.

"Taylor, whose side are you on?"

Taylor frowned. "Girl, please. Ain't nobody talking about you. I'm just saying. Why don't you stop letting him push you around?"

"He's my husband, and he's not pushing me around." I wasn't sure I believed it myself, but I had to save face before my man-bashing sister ate me alive.

"Really? You're the one in here stressing about quitting your little job. And what was it last week? Whining about how you're tired of this whole baby thing."

"I was not whining, just frustrated, and I do want Joshua's baby," I said.

"I didn't say you didn't, but what's all the hurry?" Taylor sucked her teeth. "You two haven't even been married a year yet."

Now I was on the defensive. "So what?"

"So I ain't babysitting, that's what."

"Taylor," I said, with a hint of a smile.

"You're the one trying to be super mommy, not me," Taylor said.

Indeed, I did want to be super mommy with all my heart. I'd never in my life wanted anything more than I wanted to be that.

"I know, but Joshua just wants a baby so bad." I felt the tears bursting from their ducts and running down my face.

Taylor rolled over and put her arm around me. "All I'm saying is this madness has gotta stop."

"If I stay at the job, Josh will be furious."

"Well, what's most important to you, your job or your marriage?"

I grabbed a tissue from the box on Taylor's desk and blew my nose. "Easy for you to say."

"That's right, it's easy for me because I'm not caught up in this marriage mess." Taylor rolled out of the room in her wheelchair. "Probably won't ever be."

She said it with a smile, but I could tell from her eyes that she was hurting. I hoped it didn't have to do with her not being able to walk on her own yet. She was adamant about being able to walk down the aisle, without assistance, on her wedding day. I wondered if that was the issue or if something else in her engagement to Keith had gone wrong. I just wasn't sure if now was the right time to ask about it. But I would and soon.

Chapter Fourteen

Alex

Sitting in Dr. Henley's mint-green office, trying various fertility techniques, enduring disappointment after disappointment, was seriously taking its toll on us, emotionally and financially. We practically kissed each of Joshua's paychecks good-bye as we embarked on this painstaking medical journey. Personally, I knew I was just going through the motions with my body while my mind and heart were in limbo. I knew we needed a real break from all the routines that had become our life. So after much convincing, Joshua and I agreed to plan a trip away for the weekend.

Sadly, we couldn't even agree on the specifics of that. I wanted to go to a romantic lodge in the Poconos, to ski, swim, and to soak in a heart-shaped tub, but he wanted to go to Miami to see LeBron James play with the Miami Heat. I wondered if it was just me or did women everywhere go through this? In the end, we settled on a three-day weekend trip to Atlantic City in New Jersey.

Clearly, it was nothing like our honeymoon trip, but I decided to make the best of it. We drove down to Atlantic City, chatting lightly about upcoming events like Missionary's Women's Conference and Kingdom House of Prayer's Anniversary Banquet. Then there was Lilah's upcoming birthday, and we decided on a party in Prospect Park. Since the ride didn't take too long, Joshua did all the driving so I wasn't too worn out from the trip.

We arrived at the hotel on Friday night, checked in, freshened up, and went out to dinner at a local restaurant. Nothing fancy, just filling the stomach, and I was a little disappointed.

Even more disappointing still was my husband falling asleep on me watching a basketball game on television.

The next day, however, we woke up late, grabbed some of the complimentary continental breakfast that consisted of fresh fruit, bagels, orange juice, tea, and coffee. We both dressed in faded jeans, a T-shirt, baseball caps, and sneakers. I put Ambi daily moisturizer on my skin, put my hair up in a ponytail, and I was ready for the day. Then we went to the Ripley's Believe It or Not Museum and enjoyed the various displays. I was finally able to laugh and be myself, someone I hadn't been for a long time. We had lunch and later on in the day we saw a dolphin show at the IMAX theater. I thought that it was really cool how three dimensions made me feel like I was really out on the ocean, riding the waves. Not that I was crazy about the ocean or anything, but it did remind me of being at the beach.

I smiled as I decided to let my mind go with whatever it could get. *After all, beggars couldn't be choosers,* I thought. Saturday night's dinner was a little fancier because I insisted.

So we basked in a nice Italian restaurant eating Veal Parmigiana and Shrimp Alfredo. We stared into each other's eyes on occasion but not so much that we would start thinking of our problems.

We had both agreed not to do that, not this weekend. Once I thought I even caught a glimpse of something mysterious in his eyes, something like guilt. Since I couldn't figure it out, and since I was banned from the subject of "us," I put it out of my mind.

On Sunday, we visited a local church for its early morning service and did a little shopping. Nothing serious. We just bought a few souvenirs for the family, mostly T-shirts and postcards. We did buy a cute little Atlantic City tote bag for Lilah. By late afternoon, we toured the Absecon Lighthouse, even though it was too cold to really be out on the water. The grand finale, though, was when we went on a sunset cruise. There, we had a tantalizing salmon dinner on board and danced in the moonlight. Now that was romantic. When we returned to our hotel room, Joshua started going on and on about how he regretted not purchasing a particular T-shirt in the gift shop for his mother.

"There was only one left in her size," Joshua said. "Would you please go and get it for me while I take my shower?"

"Why me?"

Joshua used the remote to flip through the channels. "That way you can double-check the size thing and make sure it would fit her."

"What do I know about your mother's size?"

"Oh, come on, please," Joshua pouted. "Do this for me, please."

"Can't it at least wait until tomorrow?" I was so tired, but he insisted, and seeing his drooping lips gave me the burst of energy I needed to go downstairs. "Oh, all right. I'll go."

By the time I came back to the room with the shirt, I practically fell through the door. It had taken the salesperson too long to assist me, and I now I was annoyed.

I noticed there was soft music playing, and I recognized the selection was "This Must BeHeaven," one of my favorite oldies but goodies. Joshua was wearing only his boxers, sporting his semimuscular chest and strong bow-shaped legs. I squinted as I saw a trail of rose petals from the bed to the bathroom. He led me into the bathroom without saying a word. There, I found rose petals from the door leading up to the tub and floating on top of the water. Scented candles were lit around the room everywhere enveloping my senses.

I was shocked. "Joshua, how did you do all of this?"

"It wasn't easy, but I did have some help. Didn't you notice that the cashier took an extremely long time downstairs with the shirt?" he laughed.

"He sure did. Wow, he was in on it too this whole time?"

"Anything for you." Joshua began to kiss the nape of my neck. He peeled off my clothes and lifted me into the tub of lavender-scented water. Then he quickly climbed in with me, whispered in my ear, nibbled on my lips, made me remember and cherish that I was his wife. Then I remembered why I loved him so much, and why I wanted to have his baby, despite the grueling process.

Afterward, Joshua wrapped me in a soft, fluffy towel, and caressed my body with shea butter until every nerve stood on end. That night he was mine and I was his. No amount of marital stress could disrupt our magical union.

Chapter Fifteen

Alex

The week after the vacation, life went back to being stressful. As soon as we returned, we had messages from his mother about his father's condition, messages from the church about the various tasks that needed to be done, and worst of all, messages reminding us of Dr. Henley's appointments. Needles, consultations, and timing ovulation. I felt like my whole world was spinning out of control. Couldn't a sister just savor some of that sweetness from Atlantic City?

Didn't I deserve that? I never expected things to turn dry so soon. Don't get me wrong. Joshua tried to be attentive, but it was more about his motives than his actions. I knew that all his tenderness was just to get an heir out of me. A healthy, hopefully baby boy to carry on the traditions of his stuck-up family. And yada, yada, yada, I thought to myself. To tell the truth, I was so fed up, I wasn't sure I even had it in me anymore.

On a better note, work kept me too busy to focus on myself. There was one thing I knew about working at a Christian college or theological seminary, since I had worked at Missionary for so many years; there were plenty of opportunities for learning. I had access to professors and their curriculum, whether it was in Christian counseling, Christian theology, divinity, Bible, youth ministry, or many other areas. And sometimes if I was really diligent, with all the Word going forth through books and papers, I could get a revelation from the written Word. Now that I was at a crossroads in my life, I needed more than just the written Word. I needed a *rhema,* a word *directly* from God.

One afternoon, Marisol and I went out for lunch. I bundled up in my pink shearling jacket, and Marisol threw on her long goose down coat. Complete with hoods on heads and gloves on hands, we walked two blocks over to a little café we liked. When we finally reached the storefront, we ordered two cappuccinos and two club sandwiches.

We sat down in a corner booth and waited patiently for a waitress with a Mohawk, six earrings in each ear, two in her nose, and a tattoo around her entire neck to bring our order.

Marisol wasted no time before she said exactly what was on her mind. "So I've got to stop dating all these losers and get me a husband like yours."

I twisted my lips. "Don't rush it, girl. Marriage is a lot of work."

"Yeah, but it's also a lot of fun, isn't it?"

"It has its moments."

"I'll bet," Marisol winked at me with her fake eyelashes.

"I'd say just let it happen naturally." I remembered the short courtship that Joshua and I had before our engagement, and suddenly, I wished it had been longer. Maybe then, I would've known my husband better.

"I'm just checking out my options, you know."

"Look, you're pretty, funny, and smart. Any guy in his right mind would be honored to get with you," I said.

"Yeah? Maybe you should tell *them* that." Marisol threw her head back, laughing.

The waitress delivered our meal, and I devoured it like I hadn't eaten in months. I felt like such a pig minutes later, watching Marisol's dainty eating habits. That explained why she was able to maintain her size six figure, and I was always stuck teetering on the edge of the plus sizes. Why did I get so carried away at the sight of food? *Emotional overeating again.*

Marisol took a sip from her cup. "I mean, if a guy isn't marriage material, then why would I want to date him in the first place?"

"Right, right." Only the Lord knew how many times I had made that mistake before.

"I mean, I already have all the male companions I could ever want. I don't need any more friends. I'm looking for a mate, and I'm serious about that."

"Well, just remember that the scripture says '*he* who findeth a wife findeth a good thing.' Just make sure you're in a good position to *be found*," I said.

"I hear what you're saying. Sometimes when I'm lonely though, I try to help God out a little."

"Uh-uh. Wrong move, girl." I laughed.

At that moment, the door opened and in walked Seger with a tall, exotic-looking young woman. I put my cup down and stared. The woman looked like she was about twenty-five years old, with an oval-shaped face, high cheekbones, and dark, catlike eyes. She was so pretty she made models for Covergirl look ugly. She wore what looked like at least three-inch stilettos and a white body-hugging dress that accentuated her smooth dark chocolate skin tone. The dress came way above the knees, showing off her endless legs. Her hair, which didn't appear to be weave, hung to the middle of her back where Seger's hand was resting, by the way. She was clearly a high-fashion model, and I wondered what she was doing with Seger, a devout Christian missionary. Maybe it was his sister I thought at first, but when I saw the way she grinned at him and put her hand on his, I knew they weren't related.

It was none of my business anyway, but I couldn't even concentrate anymore. I couldn't stop staring either.

Marisol started staring too. "Now she's beautiful. I'll bet she can have any man she wants."

"Nonsense. So can you, Marisol. It just has to be the right one, that's all. She doesn't even look like his type," I said, trying to suck in my pudgy stomach.

"I don't know about all that. She looks like any man's type, if you ask me."

I started fluffing out my hair, which had been matted down from the hood. "You know what I mean, Marisol."

Seger opened his briefcase and took out what looked like a portfolio. He looked at it, and then at the young lady with obvious admiration. I squinted and tried to figure out what it was, but I couldn't see. My eyebrows remained raised the entire time.

"I know. I know." Marisol looked away from them, and said very matter-of-factly,

"Maybe they're working together on a project or something."

I snapped my fingers. "Yes, that would explain it; a project."

"Yeah, maybe or maybe not." Marisol hunched her shoulders.

I put my cup down and frowned. "What do you mean by that?"

"Seger did mention to me that he was looking for a wife," Marisol said.

"I'm sure he did but—"

"But what?" Marisol put her hand on her hip. "You don't think he wants to get married?

We talked about it just the other day in the break room."

"I do but surely not to someone as young as her." I sucked my teeth. A sister had to always be concerned about her looks and about her age while brothers just relaxed and let things happen. All my life I'd been told to watch my weight, fix my hair, straighten up my clothes, and get it together so I could get a man. And for what? So I could be semi miserable the way I was now? That wasn't fair either. I never saw men worrying about their waistline, a bad hair day, or blemished skin.

"Hey, you never know what's going on in a brother's mind." Marisol squinted her eyes.

"That's true, but this brother happens to be a good friend of mine," I said, nodding.

"So what? He's a friend of mine too. That doesn't mean we know what he's thinking or planning every moment of the day."

"I didn't say that."

"Maybe Seger is looking for someone young, someone like her." Marisol glanced over at them.

"I don't know, maybe. It's none of our business anyway." Now I was really annoyed.

The entire time we were eating my mind was gone. Was Seger really interested in this woman romantically? And why was I so interested in what was going on at his table, anyway? I was utterly disgusted with myself at this point. Was I jealous that a woman had Seger's undivided attention, or was I just concerned for his welfare? I finally decided on the latter, and with that thought, I stopped staring. As we were leaving, we waved at Seger, and he politely waved back. The young woman never even looked our way. Now that was confidence.

Back at work I was annoyed for no apparent reason. A slight headache crept in as I settled down at my desk. Usually, I only worked four hours per day, and would've been gone already except that I promised to help Dr. Harding get some specific office matters in order.

Even though I no longer felt up to the challenge, I couldn't go back on my word. I made one call to Joshua to explain that I would be getting home an hour later and one to Mrs. Johnson who was keeping Lilah. Then I dove into the pile of extra work that Dr. Harding had for me, trying hard to keep my mind on my work and not on the conversation Marisol and I had earlier.

As I was about to finally leave for the day, Seger ran into me in the hallway. He put his hand on my shoulder. "Alex, I'm surprised you're still here."

"Yeah, I'm a little off schedule today," I said, rocking back and forth on my sore foot.

"Right, so am I. I had to meet with that young lady you saw me eating lunch with. She's from Paris, and I've been assigned to show her around the city."

"Assigned?"

"Yes, she's a foreign exchange student and she's also a model friend of my sister's."

"Oh, okay . . ." I said, waiting for an explanation.

"Thanks to Dr. Harding, she'll be doing a commercial with Missionary. She's not just a pretty face, but she's a professional."

"I'm sure she is, but I've really got to go." I stepped away from Seger and waved. "Bye."

The funny thing was, for some reason I felt relieved.

Chapter Sixteen

Joshua

It was Saturday morning. The sweet aroma of pancakes and beef sausage arrested my senses as I came out of the shower. By the time I threw on my jeans and a polo shirt, I heard Alex calling me.

"Breakfast is ready, husband."

"Thanks, babe," I said as I entered the newly decorated kitchen. Alex had gone out of her way to change the accessories. We had brand-new stainless steel pots and pans, a new lacquer table set with white chairs, and beautiful orange and white curtains. Even our toaster was orange. I didn't know how she came up with that idea, but it did brighten up the room, so it was cool. I smiled because my wife was brilliant, and she was all mine. Fortunately, she made all these purchases with our wedding gift money, and she did so before I laid out the budget.

Lilah came running out from her room, fully dressed in a purple sweat suit, and hopped into my lap. "Hi, Daddy."

"Morning, sweetie," I said, balancing her on my knee and giving her a peck on the cheek.

I stood up to put Lilah into her own seat, said grace, and we began to eat.

"Lilah and I are about to run out to do some shopping this morning," Alex said. "Want to come?"

"No, thanks." I stuffed a sausage into my mouth. "I think I'll run a few errands of my own."

Alex gave me a sweet kiss, but I could tell she had a lot on her mind. Before long, she and Lilah were gone, and I was left alone with my thoughts.

No matter how hard I tried, I just couldn't stop thinking about Yvonne and what she'd said about her friend who was willing to be a surrogate mother if we needed her to. Thanks to Dr. Henley, we had already discussed in vitro fertilization as an option, and I wondered if Alex's body was really up to the challenge. So I decided to set up a meeting with Yvonne at an obscure little Cantonese restaurant in the village. I assured myself that the information was just to be used as a last resort, kind of like insurance.

I arrived a few minutes early just so I could scope out the scene. Just like I remembered, it was dark and quiet. Everyone looked like they were minding their own business, which was the kind of environment I wanted. I hadn't been here since Alex and I first started dating, when I discovered that she didn't care for Cantonese food.

A few minutes later, Yvonne pulled up in Sister Winifred's station wagon. She didn't look like herself today. Her curly hair was pulled back into a ponytail, and she wore an African print head scarf on top of it. I'd never seen her look so laid-back, but that wasn't the point. I was anxious to get down to business—baby business.

I looked over my shoulder. "So what have you got for me?"

Yvonne slid a big manila envelope over to me. "This is her profile, name, address, and even the agency she goes through."

I felt like some kind of spy. "Agency?"

"Oh, yes. I told you it's all very legit."

I picked up the envelope. "I hope so."

Yvonne rolled her gum around on her tongue. "You'll see."

"I don't know, Yvonne. I'm just getting information. I didn't say I—"

She smiled. "Don't worry. I'm not judging you, honey. I'm just sayin'—"

"I'm just checking out everything before I get with Alex on it." My restless fingers tapped on the table in front of me. I was trying not to look nervous, but I knew it was probably obvious.

Yvonne smirked. "You might have a fight on your hands knowing Sister Alex."

Alex's possible reaction flashed in my mind. "Maybe."

"Probably."

I kept my eyes on her. "My wife is very strong willed."

"Humph. You could say that."

I began contemplating how I would tell Alex about this. "I just have to convince her that this is just something to consider."

"Well, good luck with that. I'm just here to give you some options." Yvonne grabbed my hand and squeezed it. Her hands were soft and smooth. "Consider it my good deed for the month or whatever."

Since I knew meeting with her behind my wife's back was wrong, I tried to push that detail to the back of my mind. It was all for the greater good of having a child, our child, the one we both wanted and prayed for. Or at least that's the story I told myself to justify my actions.

Of course, when I arrived home, I had to avoid any eye contact with Alex because I was afraid she would see right through me.

Chapter Seventeen

Joshua

Ironically, during church, Pastor Martin talked about keeping secrets and lies. He preached about sins of the mind as well as the flesh. And he talked about renewing the mind so we might overcome the tricks of the enemy. At this point, I was sure the enemy was myself. I found myself sneaking toward the restroom behind Yvonne to ask more questions about her friend. I had even been making secret phone calls to ask the same questions over and over again.

"Are you sure she can help Alex and me, just in case? Are you sure?" Man, what was I becoming?

When service was over I couldn't wait to get out of church. The guilt was just too much for me. Instead of driving straight home afterward though, where Alex and I had to face each other, I remembered that we still had a basketball in the trunk from the last time I'd played a few weeks ago. So I decided to stop at the basketball court for a little one-on-one. Surprisingly, it was empty. At first, my wife thought I had lost my mind, but after she saw me moving around, flailing my arms around in my suit, she and Lilah jumped out to play too. Since Alex used to play in high school, and I used to play in both high school and college, hitting the courts was good for us. It was the first time in a long time that there was no tension between us. My wife was good on the court, even in boots and a wool dress. No one would ever know my wife had skills by just looking at her. She was definitely a girly girl; soft, curvy, and sweet, but she was fierce with a basketball in her hand. She shot right past me and leaped into the air. I grabbed her and swung her around. Then I lifted Lilah high into the air so she could put the ball into the hoop. "Slam dunk," I said.

"That's not fair," Alex said. "You cheated."

I leaped into the air. "Who says so?"

Alex put her hands on her hips. "I say so."

"Prove it," I said, dribbling the ball away from her.

"Never judge a book by its cover." Alex managed to get the ball away from me and ran to make the shot. Unfortunately, she slipped and fell down.

I ran over to her side. "Are you okay?"

Alex reached up and pulled me down. Lilah jumped on top of us, giggling. They were my family, and I loved them, no matter what it looked like.

Later that evening things weren't as much fun. I was on the Internet reading an article about the dangers of surrogacy just to make sure I had every angle covered when Alex snuck up behind me with a kiss. My heart jumped.

"Woman. Why?" I said.

"Scaredy-cat," Alex teased.

"Alex, I don't have time for games now." I turned my back to her. "I'm busy." I quickly clicked to another tab on my computer screen.

"Oh, I'm sorry." Alex poked out her bottom lip.

"Just not now, baby. Not now."

I watched her walk away, looking defeated, but I didn't know what to do about it. I was working on making things better for all of us. She'd soon see.

Chapter Eighteen

Alex

I woke up to a bright light shining in my eyes, and it wasn't the sun. Joshua had turned on the ceiling light in order to find his notes. It was early Saturday morning. Needless to say, my sleep was broken, and I was ticked off. Couldn't a sister get any sleep around here anymore?

Did a brother have to turn on the big overhead light at five in the morning? I mean, really.

Joshua looked over at me. "I'm sorry, baby. Did I wake you?"

I wanted to throw something at him. "Yes, you did."

"I'll hurry and turn off the light," he said, smiling. "I just found what I was looking for."

"Great," I said, dipping back underneath the covers.

Luckily, it was the weekend of Missionary's Annual Women's Conference, and this year it was out of town. I was actually glad to be leaving for a couple of days, and the funny thing is, I'd never expected it to be that way so soon. When we were first married, we were inseparable, and I couldn't have imagined it being any other way. But the truth was that Joshua and I, after only a few precious months of marriage, could use the time apart. I wanted to breathe, to have conversations that weren't about babies and body parts. I also wanted to just be me, not the patronizing minister's wife me, but the real me. The one I wasn't sure Joshua was even interested in anymore. It was funny how he changed once I became his wife. Or did he change?

Maybe it was always there, but I missed it, or maybe it was just the pressure-pressure to do the marriage thing and do it right. That meant babies, and money, and submission to one's spouse-pressure.

Since I couldn't get back to sleep, I decided to take advantage of the extra time to get ready. I chose to put on a new pair of flare leg jeans, a candy-red sweater, and my flat red boots. I released my curls from the head scarf I was wearing, grabbed my purse, jacket, and overnight bag. I knew I wouldn't have to worry about makeup because Taylor would bring enough for both of us.

Lilah woke up eventually and came into the bathroom, yawning. "Is it time for your trip yet?"

"No, sweetie. Not yet. I'm still getting ready. Then I have to pick up Auntie Taylor."

As soon as I said "Auntie Taylor," I wondered if Lilah really regarded Taylor as her aunt when she didn't even acknowledge me as her mother.

When I was done getting myself ready, I went into the kitchen to make Cream of Wheat, scrambled eggs, and toast. The three of us had our last meal together for the weekend, and I was on my way.

"I left a fresh pair of pajamas for tonight, a church dress, and a play outfit for tomorrow afternoon. Her snacks are all labeled in the fridge. Oh, and don't forget to give her a vitamin in the morning."

"Okay, okay. Thanks, Supermom."

"Joshua, are you going to remember all of this or should you be writing this down?"

"Babe, don't worry. We'll survive," Joshua said. "I've got this."

"All right. I know you're used to doing things your way, but things are different now."

"Not that you're the woman of the house?"

I put one hand on my hip. "You know it."

"I promise to do everything just like you would've done it," he laughed.

"Thanks." I smiled because I liked what he was saying. "I love you."

"I love you too." Joshua pulled me to his chest. "Are you sure you don't want me to do

something for you?"

"Just take care of Miss Lilah for me," I said.

"We'll take care of each other, right?" Joshua ruffled Lilah's already unkempt hair.

"Yes sir, Daddy." Lilah skipped around the living room.

I pulled Lilah into my arms and squeezed, praying that she would feel my love one day. Then I reached for my husband and gave him a gentle kiss on the lips. I wanted it to be special, but because I was already so burned out, I didn't have much left in me. Joshua hugged me like he didn't want to let me go, and that was comforting, but I had to get out of there.

Suddenly, the situation was suffocating me.

Once I brought the car around front from the parking lot, Joshua and Lilah waved good-bye to me from the window. I waved back until I turned the corner. Then I hit the gas.

Taylor was ready when I arrived. I helped her come downstairs with her two bags filled to the brim with clothes and accessories.

I laughed. "Where in the world are you going with all of this stuff?"

"Girl, you know how I roll." Taylor snapped her fingers and rolled her neck.

And indeed I did. Ever since we were little girls, Taylor had been the diva of the two of us. People expected me to be the same way because we were twins, but I'd always been more of a plain-Jane. Fashion, however, was my sister's unofficial MO. Shopping, shopping, and more shopping was the game. She read *Vogue,* and she knew all the designers by name as well as style before she was sixteen years old. Whether it was a party dress, business suit, or her daily workout gear, Taylor just liked to look good, no matter what. Always had.

I smiled as I loaded her bags into the trunk of my car. In the process of rearranging, by the time I fit her bags in, there was hardly room for mine. So I shook my head and placed mine in the backseat, along with Taylor's leg braces and walker. Thank goodness both of her walking aids folded neatly for carrying. Then off we drove, and we were at Missionary within minutes, where we loaded on to a charter bus for our trip to Maryland.

Taylor's bags were so stuffed I was barely able to squeeze them in the overhead. "This is so embarrassing."

"Oh, get over it," Taylor said, smacking her gum.

We settled into seats on the sixth row, which was just close enough to reach the front door in case we needed to get off quickly, but not too far away from the restroom in case the sodas I was about to consume wouldn't wait until we arrived. We were sitting right behind my aunt Dorothy and Sister Trudy. They had been friends for years since they were both widows, and both a part of the hospitality ministry. Behind them First Lady Martin and Sister Lakesha Swanson sat together. Sister Lakesha was married to Brother Jacob, and was one of the lead singers in the choir. Her voice was so fierce, the entire congregation rejoiced when she sang. A few rows back sat miserable Sister Winifred and Yvonne. They were the only two I didn't care for sitting so close to. Sister Winifred was a busybody and her niece was a man stealer. Not a good combination at all.

The seats were nice and plush with thick comfortable armrests and a huge flat-screen television with a DVD player upfront. We even had a female bus driver, a heavyset woman named Miss Cathy who told us that since God was the real driver and she was just His assistant, that we would have to pray if we expected to get there safely and on time. Now *she* was an interesting character.

After the bus driver made a few brief announcements and First Lady Martin had taken the roll for the trip, we were on our way. Everyone started talking and laughing, excited about the conference. A short while later, Tyler Perry's movie, *Diary of a Mad Black Woman,* came on the big-screen television, and everyone became quiet. Throughout key scenes in the movie, laughter erupted throughout the bus as we enjoyed both each other's company and the comedic genius of Tyler Perry. We stopped twice for a quick restroom break, but other than that, it was a straight ride to Maryland. It was a pleasant ride, and one that reminded Taylor and me of the bus trips we took as children growing up at Missionary. Yes, Missionary used to be famous for its bus trips, but we hadn't taken one in a while.

Between the movie and texting Joshua, I was totally occupied the entire time. At one point during the ride, Yvonne squeezed by to give something to Sister Trudy. I closed my eyes and tried to block her out. We were never friends, but ever since she tried to pull that stunt with Joshua last year, she was definitely off limits. I'd smile and be polite, but I was always watching her. Never could trust her as far as I could see her.

"Girl, don't even worry about her," Taylor said.

"Believe me, I'm not," I replied.

It was funny how twins could always sense each other's pain. It was as if we were each living through the other, knowing what was in each other's hearts, and reading each other's minds. Even when we were little, Taylor would know what I was thinking even when that didn't necessarily benefit me. And sometimes she'd use it to her advantage, without me knowing it, until I found out later. Sometimes it was good, and sometimes it was not so good, but we always felt each other's pain. Even though we didn't always agree with each another, we always, always had each other's back.

Once we arrived at the Sheraton Inner Harbor Hotel and checked in as a group, we had only an hour before the first service of the conference, which was being held right at The Baltimore Convention Center adjacent to the hotel.

"Okay, Taylor, we've only got an hour so . . ." I started.

Taylor tilted her head to the side. "Are you trying to say I'm slow?"

"No, just thorough."

"Thorough? Uh-huh." Taylor smiled. "All right, I guess I can accept that."

"Didn't expect that one, did you?"

"Nope."

Taylor started throwing clothes all around the room, sitting in front of the mirror, adjusting weave, putting on eyeliner and eyelashes. By the time she was done, I hardly recognized her. All I did was freshened up, combed my hair, and changed into a blue and black pantsuit with navy blue pumps. I hoped my ankles wouldn't get cold because I didn't bring my boots. Afterward, we still had a little time so we went to grab something to eat before the first session. Nestled in the heart of downtown, the convention center seemed to be walking distance from nearly everything. Since Taylor had the walker, we took a cab to The Nest on Pratt Street. There, I gobbled down a burger, fries, and a Coke while Taylor had a salad and water.

"You make me sick," I told her. She was always showing out with her healthy eating habits.

"Gotta stay healthy. And you gotta start taking better care of yourself," she said as she bit into her crisp garden salad with Ranch dressing. "This body is the only one I have."

"Tell me about it," I said. "I wish I had a new one right about now."

Taylor twirled her lettuce around on her fork. "One of these days you're gonna have to stop eating so heavy."

"Yes, one day, girl, but not today," I said as I swallowed the last of my soda.

Once we were at the conference the staff greeted us with a warm welcome, door prizes, gift bags, and a purple and white conference T-shirt. There was a whole committee of Missionary's women. They had been in Baltimore since yesterday, and were working the floor. I was glad that for once, I wasn't serving, and was able to sit back, relax, and enjoy the Word.

The guest speaker, Dr. Elizabeth Durrant, was a ministry powerhouse, known all over the world for empowering women through God's Word. She was a pastor, a gospel singer, a spoken Word artist, a prolific speaker, and a liturgical dancer. I had read a couple of her books before, but I absolutely loved to hear her speak. I mean, when God was handing out gifts, she must've gotten double doses.

She was a woman of medium stature in height and width. She wore a simple light gray and white dancer's costume with white and gold dance shoes. She wore her hair in a small curly Afro, had dark, even skin, and she wore very little makeup at all, yet she was gorgeous. Her understated gold hoop earrings and matching gold beads accentuated her beauty. There was something in her eyes, in her movement, in her entire demeanor, that mesmerized me. She was the essence of woman, and she carried that persona out into the spotlight.

She started off by gliding across the stage like lightning, swirling and bending to my favorite praise song, "Yes." *Would your heart and soul say yes?* It was as if the woman floated on air, she was so graceful. After a beautiful dance routine, she wiped her face and took her place in the pulpit, waiting for Sister Martin to introduce her. Then the crowds applauded and cheered.

My soul says yes. My heart began to beat faster. I realized I was already touched before the woman even opened her mouth. The song had opened the gateways to my heart. It always did.

Then Pastor Martin gave her the microphone, stepped aside, and let her take center stage.

"I want to talk to you today about the superwoman syndrome that a lot of us overachieving women have. We've got to be careful not to overload ourselves with the cares of the world. We're out there trying to do one hundred things at once. We've got our families and many of us are neglecting them. Yes, neglecting them because we've got our careers, our hobbies, and sometimes even our ministries. But like the Proverbs 31 woman, we've got to submit them all to God. We've got to have our house in order, and by house, I not only mean the one our family lives in, but I also mean our body, which houses our spirit. Some of us are out there trying to rule the world, judging the world, and yet we're not even submitted to our own husbands. That's right;

if you're not submitted to your spouse, then you're not really submitted to God. Ephesians 5:22 says, 'Wives, submit yourselves unto your own husbands, as unto the Lord.' So even though he's got a commandment to love you and be right, so do you likewise have a commandment to reverence him and be right.

"You see, there is an order to this thing, and a lot of us are just out of control and out of order on every level. I'll even go as far as to say that some of us, even in the church, are buck wild and can't be stopped. But spiritual matters must be in order before we try to jump out there on the water like Peter. We say we're anointed and we want to conquer the world. I say if your house is not in order and you jump out, you'll sink. I've got forty-two years of marriage under my belt, five kids, two global ministries, and a number of companies that have my name on them. At the end of the day, my husband is still the head of our household. There is protection in the order of God."

I looked around and wondered if she was talking to me directly. Admittedly, I'd had a few challenges in this area, but this was no longer the fifties, and women had certain rights I wasn't about to give up. I mean, wasn't I already giving enough? Did I have to lose my whole sense of identity for my husband to be happy? It wasn't like I was some ultramodern woman who had a problem with cooking, cleaning, or having kids. I just wasn't a roll-over-and-play-dead-like-back-in-the-day woman either.

Dr. Durrant kept talking while her audience remained captivated. "That's why God said, seek ye first the kingdom of heaven, and then all things shall be added unto you. It's the seeking we have to do first. The seeking before the doing. Do you remember this day in the Bible when Jesus was talking to Mary Magdalene and Martha, but Mary was the only one listening? Jesus reprimanded Martha because what she was doing wasn't as important as the listening. Not that what she was doing, the natural things, weren't necessary, but that she was out of order.

"I say to you today, my sisters, put spiritual things first. Then the natural things will come. Seek God's will first and get your life in order. Get your prayer life right. Get your heart right, because out of the heart comes the issues of life. I'm telling you, my sisters, if you get your heart right, the issues will shrink up and die. They'll shrink up and die. Issues can't survive without you feeding them negativity. If you keep on feeding on the right stuff, God's Word will get rid of your issues. Prioritize your life, your time, your issues. Put Him at the top of your list, not your position, not your promotion, not your desires, not your need for success. Superwomen, put His will first, and watch God work. Watch God work in your home, in your marriage, on your job, in your circumstances."

The audience screamed. A lady sitting two seats down from me fell to her knees. Taylor and I clapped our hands and shouted as the word came forth.

"But we won't surrender it all to Him. We want to keep a little bit of power we think we have for ourselves. We want to keep it for ourselves, and God can't help us until we turn it all loose, 'til we turn it all over to Him. He's waiting, ladies, and so is our destiny.

"We say we're tired, burned out, and forgotten. God hasn't forgotten us, but we've forgotten Him. And we've forgotten His will for us. Come back to what should be first place in your life. Come back to number one, numero uno . . . Seek His face. Come after Him with a passion in all you do. Do nothing without Him. Submit your projects and your decisions to His will, and if He ain't in it, let it go. I say, if He ain't in it, let it go."

"Amen, sister. Amen." The woman sitting right next to me shouted continually and waved her hands in the air.

The audience roared with excitement. There was music and women dancing at their seats. I had to admit, Dr. Durrant's words stung a little as the truth rang true in my heart.

Taylor touched my shoulder and whispered, "Now you know that's the truth."

"Humph. Wasn't a lie in it," I said.

"That lady is something else," Taylor chimed in.

"Anointed." I nodded my head in agreement. "That woman is anointed."

By the time she was finished, I felt renewed and convicted at the same time. The rest of the day was spent in various workshops bonding, learning, and growing closer to God. There were workshops on health, beauty, being a single woman, being a single mother, how to be a good wife, how to raise godly children, how to get prayers answered, how to worship, how to be a good children's ministry leader, and the list went on.

In the evening, Taylor, a bunch of ladies from the church, including Aunt Dorothy, and I went out to eat. We discussed the message, ate, and laughed about the situations, good and bad, that characterized our lives. We all vowed to make changes.

Back at the hotel, I called Joshua to say good night. He sounded a little tired, but glad to hear from me nonetheless. Then Taylor and I had our own little slumber party, watching television, polishing our nails, and staying up all hours of the night, giggling. We hadn't done this in years, and I had missed it.

The next morning, we hardly wanted to wake up because of our late-night antics, but we had to catch the nine o'clock prayer breakfast and then the last service with Dr. Durrant. I threw on a plain beige sweater dress while Taylor put on a jazzy black ensemble with a jazzy black hat. I always wished I had her flair for style, even half of it.

"Oh, come on, that's so boring," Taylor said, staring at my outfit.

"What?"

"Let's liven this outfit up a little." She reached into one of her bags and pulled out a big burgundy leather belt. "Put this on."

"All right, all right. Is it that serious?"

"When you're out with me, yes, it is," Taylor laughed.

I wrapped the belt around my waist, and it really did give the dress a new look.

"Now, just put this around your neck, put on these burgundy shoes, and we're good."

Taylor handed me a burgundy and beige silk scarf and burgundy wedge heeled shoes.

Thankfully, we wore the same size shoes, even though her feet were a little slimmer than mine.

Before long, we were sitting in the service, listening to Dr. Durrant's prophetic words.

She issued us all the challenge of change, and I embraced every word.

After we were dismissed, we had time for sightseeing. Taylor wanted to go to the aquarium, but I didn't, so she went with a group of women from the church while I stayed with Aunt Dorothy and Sister Trudy. We went to the Inner Harbor and to the Baltimore Museum of Art. Then when Taylor returned, she and I went to Harbor East, Baltimore's premiere waterfront entertainment spot. There, we saw a collection of the area's best restaurants and retail stores, but we didn't do any shopping. We did buy sandwiches to take back with us on the bus though. On the way back, the movie we watched was *Blindside* with actress Sandra Bullock. It was a good movie, but, of course, with the theme of adoption, my mind turned to Kiano.

When I returned Sunday evening, Joshua met me at the door with a big hug and kiss. I could smell the pine-scented aftershave lotion on his skin. It was very masculine.

"I missed you so much," he said, not letting me go.

"I missed you too." Although I had fun with the women, it felt good to be back in my husband's arms.

Lilah was already asleep so I had lots of uninter-rupted time to tell him about the conference. Although I was a little tired from the trip, my mind was well rested, and for now, that was enough to get me through the night.

Chapter Nineteen

Alex

The next day, Joshua and I got into it again early that morning over a request for payment from the attorney handling Kiano's adoption. It was the same old story. Mr. Nyuoso had asked for his portion of the money, as well as the corresponding filing fees. God knows, if I could've written a blank check, I would've. I wasn't trying to start in on Joshua again, but it bothered me every day that we couldn't get Kiano. Once I had set my mind to something I usually couldn't rest until it was done. Not only were the adoption wheels no longer in motion, but the wheels had fallen completely off the wagon. We were at a stalemate, and I didn't know where to go from here.

"How can I get you to understand how serious this is?" I pleaded.

"I already know how serious it is," Joshua said.

"I don't really think so. If you did, you'd put more of an emphasis on it."

"Emphasis?" Joshua sounded like the word stuck in his throat.

"Yeah, I don't even think you're trying to come up with a plan. And this poor little boy is just sitting overseas waiting on us to save his life."

Joshua looked at me as if I were crazy. "Save his life?"

"Yes, save his life. Mr. Nyuoso said that everything could be done as soon as six months."

"Come on, Alex. We're not God."

"I didn't say we were, but we have the ability to help his situation, and ultimately, save his life." I fought back tears as I spoke.

"Okay, kill the drama, please." Joshua walked out of the living room.

Now I was really annoyed. How dare he walk away from me while I was making my point. I knew we were overwhelmed with all the fees associated with the international adoption, the travel fees, legal fees, and other expenses, but still I couldn't just give up. There was so much to pay for and so little time. My head had begun to spin at that moment I realized I no longer had any control over Kiano's destiny.

Then I clearly overstepped my boundaries, but I didn't care. I was angry. "Am I the only one concerned here?"

"What else do you want me to do?"

"I want you to *care*, Joshua." The tears began to fall. "As far as I'm concerned, Kiano is already a part of this family, and I want you to care as much as I do."

"I do care." Joshua turned around. "What about you? I think you care more about Kiano than having our own baby."

"Is that what you think?"

"Sometimes you act like you don't want to have my baby. Maybe *that's* what's wrong.

Maybe *that's* what's holding up the process." Joshua nodded his head.

"This is not a *process*, Joshua." I took a deep breath and tried to compose myself. "This is our child we're talking about. How can you say that? You know I want this baby."

"But not more than Kiano. Maybe if you'd stop stressing about him, you'd be pregnant by now."

"Oh, so now it's all *my* fault. Maybe if you'd stop stressing me out, talking baby for breakfast, lunch, and dinner, I'd be pregnant by now."

"Okay, so it's on me then." Joshua walked away in a huff.

"Well, if we could afford to just finish the adoption, that would end all of this extra stress." I didn't want to really go there about our finances, but he backed me into a corner, and I came out swinging.

"I'm doing the best I can." Joshua stormed out of the house without even saying good-bye.

All of a sudden I felt like we hadn't made any progress in the past weeks. I felt like our little second honeymoon was in vain and so was the women's retreat. How could I be so confident while I was there and so doubtful now that I was back? I felt like giving up, but the only problem with that was that I knew better. *Do not be weary in well doing.* I had a Savior that died on the cross to work everything out for me, and I had to have faith in that, no matter how hard it was. So I picked up my Bible and searched the scriptures for the balm that would make my pain go away.

During lunchtime when I was at work, Joshua called to apologize, but I was numb. I was tired of arguing over the same funky old issues, and I was confused about the real source of all his anger. Then there were the little disappearing acts lately. Even when he was with me, he wasn't really with me. I didn't know where he was going or what he was doing, but I knew something had to give soon. So I decided to stop by to see my sister after work.

As I walked into Push It, I heard easy listening music playing in the background, and I smelled a hint of potpourri. Taylor must've been cleaning again. Whenever she did, the scent would linger in the air for a while. I saw Keith working out near the front. I walked over to him.

"Hi, Keith," I said.

Keith gave me a big bear hug. "Hi, Alex. How are you?"

"I'm good, thanks." I tried to look happy. "Where is that crazy sister of mine?"

"Yeah, crazy is right." Keith pointed, but he didn't smile. "She's over there."

"Okay, thanks." I watched him get back to his weight lifting as I walked toward Taylor.

"Come on," Taylor said.

As soon I approached her, I couldn't hold it in any longer. A tear ran down my face, but I wiped it away with my sleeve.

"Uh-oh. What's wrong now?" Taylor sat on a machine diligently working out her upper body.

"I'm starting to suspect that Joshua is having an affair. He's moody and sneaking around; secret phone calls, frequent unexplained disappearances, and he has hardly laid a hand on me in two weeks." I jumped on an exercise bike and began to pedal hard.

"Sounds like stress to me." Taylor continued to exercise.

"I hope you're right, but he won't talk to me. He's just in and out, and he's so angry with me."

"Angry with you about what?"

"About me working, about Seger working at my job, about money, and Kiano and this baby we're trying to make." I threw my hands up. "I don't know . . . everything."

Taylor stopped what she was doing. "There has got to be more to it than that. He shouldn't be pressuring you like this over something you have no control of. The baby will come in God's timing."

Sweat ran down my face and neck. "Oh, look at you calling out God's Word."

"So we've got jokes . . ."

"I'm kidding. But really, I don't know what to do. He has stopped communicating with me."

"But what about your little weekend away? Wasn't that good?"

"It was really good, but it's like ever since we came back, he's even more secretive and aloof. He's sneaking around, and I just don't know."

Taylor shook her head. "That ain't good."

"I don't know what's up with him. I mean, one minute he acts like he's happy. The next minute, it's like he doesn't want to be bothered. I'm tired of it."

"That doesn't sound like him."

I stopped pedaling. "Tell me about it."

Taylor put up one French manicured finger. "Humph. Mood swings, disappearances. Maybe it's substance abuse."

"Taylor, Joshua doesn't touch any abusive substances."

"Are you sure?"

"Positive. The only substances going on in our house is food, and I'm the one that needs to push myself away from the table, not him."

"Okay, okay. Maybe something is going on at work."

"It could be something down at the bank, but why wouldn't he tell me?" I thought about that for a moment, and then dismissed it. There was no reason for him not to confide in me if something were going on at work, unless, of course, it was something I disapproved of.

Taylor put up her finger. "Unless it's a woman at the bank."

"You're not helping," I said.

"Sorry, but you started it. You're the one who came in here with 'my husband is sneaking around,' so I'm trying to help you unsneak him." Taylor continued to push herself on the machine.

I shook my head. "I can't believe this is what my life has come to."

"You've got to find out what's going on," Taylor said.

"I know, I know."

"I'm good with men who sneak around." Taylor cracked her knuckles. "I'll help you catch him."

"Oh, believe me, I intend to," I said.

"So what are you going to do?"

"I'm not sure yet, but I'll figure out something. Believe me, I'll find out what Mr. Joshua Benning is hiding."

Chapter Twenty

Alex

I knew from the moment I walked in on them that it was going to be bad. Yvonne had her chair pushed up close against Joshua, and they were huddled close together. Imagine coming all the way down there to a Cantonese restaurant in the village to find my husband dining with another woman. And not just any other woman, but the same church sister that already tried to steal him away before. I started breathing harder the more I saw and the more I thought about it.

Joshua knew I hated Cantonese food, and that I'd never come down here without a good reason.

This was supposed to be a safe spot I guessed. Too bad for him that I had overheard a telephone conversation and knew he was meeting someone here. I just didn't expect it to be man-stealing Yvonne; not this time.

I stood back and watched for a moment. She ran her brightly colored fingernails across his arm. I couldn't believe she was touching him. I could only see their faces from an angle, but I could tell they were looking at something on the table. Suddenly, I heard laughter, saw Joshua throw his head back, and Yvonne pat him gently on the back. That was enough for me. I hadn't seen him look that happy in months.

I charged toward them. "Joshua Douglas Benning!"

"Alex?" Joshua turned to me with his eyebrows raised and his mouth wide open. He looked like deer staring into headlights.

"Yes, it's me—your *wife*." I stood over him. "Remember me?"

Yvonne seemed to be amused by the whole thing because she stood up with a smirk on her face. "Sister Alex, how are you?"

I looked her up and down. "Girl, please."

"Sweetheart . . ." Joshua still looked like a deer stunned by the headlights. "Yvonne and I were just working on something."

"Oh, I can see that." I took a stance with one hand on my very ample hip, and the other ready to throw the first blow if I had to. She wouldn't be able to make it to the door. *Lord, help me.*

"No, really. We . . . I . . ." Joshua stammered.

I patted my foot and prayed silently. *Lord, please don't let me show out in this place.*

Please keep me in your Spirit. "I'm waiting. What were you two working on that I don't know about?"

Joshua reached across the table and handed me a manila envelope.

"I can see that you two need some time alone so I'll just go." Yvonne straightened out her fitted skirt and walked away.

I wanted to snatch every curl out of her little red head. "Yes, please just go." I opened the envelope and pulled out the contents. There was a picture of a young woman with medium brown skin and long black hair. There was also something that appeared to be a medical file.

"What is this?"

"Let me explain," Joshua said.

"Go on."

"Please, have a seat." He held out a chair for me.

I took my time sitting down. "Are you going to tell me what's going on now?"

"I will."

"Who is this?" I held up the picture of the woman.

Joshua swallowed hard. "I don't know her."

I wanted to lunge at him. "Then why do you have her picture?"

He hesitated. "She's a friend of Yvonne's."

"Now that doesn't make any sense." I knew that this wasn't going to be easy, but it was clear that all he could do now was to come clean and suffer the consequences. And I did mean *suffer*.

Joshua swallowed, then said, "She works with an agency."

"What kind of agency, Joshua?" I was tired of playing games.

"She helps people."

"Helps people with what?" I was getting more tired by the minute. "Get to the point, please."

"She helps families who want kids."

I wasn't expecting that one. "Oh? How does she help with that?"

"She's a professional surrogate." Joshua dropped his head.

First I thought that I heard wrong. Then I thought I'd strangle him. "Excuse me?"

"She's a surrogate mother," he whispered.

"*What?*" I pushed my chair back and stood up.

"Please sit back down." Joshua grabbed my hand.

I pulled away from him. "No, why should I?"

"Come on. I'm sorry. I was just getting some information."

I was furious. "For what? Are you *that* desperate for another child, Joshua, that you would plan for one and leave me out of the equation?"

A waiter walked over to me. "Ma'am, I'm going to have to ask you to lower your voice, please."

"Oh, I'm sorry," I said, sitting back down in my chair.

Joshua spoke very low. "I told you I was just getting information. I'm sorry . . . I . . ."

I couldn't believe what I was hearing. I wanted to run away and hide. "You humiliated me." My voice began to quiver.

"I'm sorry. I wasn't leaving you out. I was just covering all the bases."

"And with the likes of Yvonne, of all people. She never wanted to help anyone a day in her life." I stood up again.

Joshua stood up and looked at me with pleading eyes. "Alex, wait—"

"No, you wait." I put my hand up to my heart, but my voice remained low. "You've gone behind my back and told our business to Yvonne."

"No, I've told her nothing, no details."

I looked around to make sure no one was able to hear me. "Then *how* would she know we were trying to conceive?"

"She only overheard a short conversation I had with Brother Jameson, and she offered to help," Joshua said.

"I'll bet." Tears of anger ran down my face. My heart raced as I contemplated what Joshua had just told me. I couldn't believe what I was hearing. Perhaps I was mistaken. Surely I wasn't hearing right. Not from my Joshua who promised to love me till death do us part. This wasn't love. I wanted to lash out at him, but I waited.

"No, I was skeptical at first, but as time went on I . . . I . . ."

"You became more obsessed with having this child, so much so that you're desperate to do anything to have him, even if it's not in the will of God."

Joshua stuttered. "I . . . I . . ."

"Joshua, I love you, but I don't know." I took a deep breath. "You need help."

"You're right." He pulled me to his hard chest. "I see that now, and I'm sorry."

I pushed away from him. "I'm sorry too, but right now, I don't want anything to do with you," I said as I left him standing there.

When we finally got home I went straight to our bedroom and locked the door. I didn't want to see Joshua or even be near him. Touching me was definitely out of the question. So I had made my bed with Joshua, but did I really have to lie down in it? I mean, obviously, I didn't know what I was getting myself into when I let that man put a ring on my finger and I said, "I do." I didn't know he'd turn into the baby-obsessed madman I was living with today. I mean, who knew?

After a quickie shower, I slipped under the cool covers alone. Joshua would have to make do on the couch for tonight. I remembered my mother's words, "Sweetie, don't be a fool for no man." I wondered what she would think of me if she were alive. After all, had I ever listened?

Nope, I hadn't listened with Ahmad, my long-ago lover with buttermilk skin and charm to match.

I certainly hadn't listened with my husband either, but did that give him the right to humiliate me?

When I found myself unable to sleep, instead of praying, I walked over to the window and looked outside. I didn't want anyone to look up and see me though. As if I could be seen from the fifteenth floor, as though a random passerby could see through my soul and maybe they could see through me; that's just how raw I was.

Chapter Twenty-one

Joshua

I spent the night on our leather sofa so when I woke up my entire body ached. I couldn't believe I had gone as far as I had gone. I let my desire for a child get the best of me. No, I wouldn't ever go that far again. *Lord, I'm sorry*. It would have to be His way or no way. I had upset my wife, which is the last thing I wanted to do. Alex woke up, did her morning routines, and left the house before I did. That wasn't like her at all, so I knew she was still mad. I knew I had to get it together, or I'd lose everything I wanted so badly.

The phone rang. I picked up the phone and put the receiver to my ear.

"Good morning," Aunt Dorothy said.

"Morning." I knew I sounded bad.

"May I speak with Alex for a minute, honey?"

"I'm sorry, but Alex isn't here." At that moment, I regretted answering the phone. I sighed heavily.

"Are you doing all right? You don't sound too good."

"No, I'm okay," I said.

"That's strange. I wanted to catch her before she left for work. She doesn't usually leave home this early."

My headache was getting worse by the second. "Nah, not usually."

"Well, all right then. I'll catch her on her cell phone."

"That's a good idea." I was about to hang up.

"Are you *sure* you're okay?"

"Yes, Aunt Dorothy, I'm fine."

"Well, I'm gonna be praying for you anyway, 'cause something ain't settled right in my spirit."

Her words were slipping past me, and I didn't care what she was saying. "All right. I've got to go now."

"Bye, Josh."

After I hung up the phone I started to get ready for work. I missed Alex being there to help me. She always added a special touch to my morning, whether she knew it or not. When I went into Lilah's room to wake her up, I saw that Alex hadn't forgotten to lay out Lilah's clothes for the day. I quickly helped her to wash her face, brush her teeth, and get dressed.

Then I poured her a bowl of Crispy Crunch cereal and watched her eat it while my stomach growled. Alex had left me a toasted bagel on the counter, but I didn't feel like eating, not when it felt like my whole life was falling apart.

Once I dropped Lilah off at Ms. Johnson's, I took the long route to work. I was early, and I was in no hurry to deal with the next set of problems.

At the bank, my cherry wood desk was covered with papers and files. I finally figured out that small amounts of money had been taken from the bank periodically. I leaned back in my executive chair and stretched my legs. If my calculations were right, someone had been stealing.

Not a lot, but stealing, nonetheless. I was sure money was missing unless there was some kind of computer glitch or some other crazy explanation that only Simon could give. I was not sure what happened so I decided to confront Simon right after lunch.

Immediately, Simon, the president, denied that anything was wrong or missing. He told me I was mistaken, and that he'd personally check into my claim and clear up whatever had possibly gone wrong. He assured me again and again that it was no big deal. After a while, I began to think that maybe I was tripping. After all, I did have too much on me lately. Maybe, just maybe, Simon was right. We'd been working together for the past ten years, and he'd never been wrong before.

Later on that evening, I brought home a dozen red roses for Alex. She was wrapped up in her big flannel robe with her bunny slippers, and she had big pink curlers in her hair. Not exactly what I was hoping for, but I had to make the best of it.

I came in slow and handed her the flowers with my head hung low. "These are for you."

Alex rolled her eyes. "Thanks, but it'll take a lot more than flowers for me to get over this."

"But I'm sorry, baby." I lifted my head.

"No, Joshua. I don't even want to hear the word 'baby.'" She turned her back to me. "I feel so betrayed."

"I know. I know." I was so mad at myself. "I messed up."

"Big time," Alex said.

Then she turned to face me. She just stood there staring at me, not talking, not even blinking.

"Big time," I said.

She walked up to me and put her finger in my chest. "I don't understand. Why would you do that to me?"

I grabbed her finger and put it against my face. "I was desperate."

"Why were you so desperate?" Alex jerked her hand away.

"I was crazy."

"Why were you so crazy?" She lunged at me but began to cry. "What if, Joshua?"

I didn't understand. "What if what?"

"What if I can't give you a child?"

I shook my head. "No, don't say that."

"But I have to say that because what if I can't, *then* what?"

"What do you mean, then what?"

She leaned against the wall. "What happens if I don't bear your child?" By now, she was trembling, and I felt bad for her. I wanted to hold her, but I knew she wouldn't let me.

"Don't say that."

"What will happen next? Will you leave me if you can't get what you want? Will our marriage really be able to survive it, or will you just move on to the next fertile soul?"

"No, never," I said.

"Really? What if I don't believe you? What if I decide to leave you before you leave me?"

"I'd never let you leave me." I pulled her to my chest. "I love you more than you know."

She pulled away. "Apparently, it is more than I know because I don't know anything anymore."

"Please, Alex," I said.

She kept walking away from me so I had to keep moving and cornering her.

"Please what? You were willing to let another woman carry our child as if that's the way God intended it to be. So I just don't know anymore."

"I'm sorry. I just kept playing it over and over in my mind, and the more I did that, the more doubts came in."

"Okay, so doubts came." Alex stood there nodding her head and sucking her lips.

Since she stopped moving and started listening, I kept talking. "And the next thing you know I couldn't stop thinking about having a child."

"Couldn't stop thinking about it, huh?"

"Yeah, and it got out of hand."

"I thought we'd agreed on God's will," Alex said, balling up her hands into fists.

"I know." I was so ashamed. I wanted to hide my face, to bury this mess I had made.

Unfortunately, I had to face up to it, no matter how painful it was.

"I thought we were supposed to be confessing that God would multiply us. Not multiply you with someone else. I mean, that is so Abraham, Sarah, and Hagar to me."

"I know, baby, but I didn't see that then," I said.

"Don't call me baby," Alex said, with cloudy pink eyes. "How could you not see that? Is that what you want us to have, an Ishmael?"

"No, I do not want an Ishmael." This time I walked away, ashamed.

"Are you *sure?*" Now she followed me.

I sighed. "Yes, I'm sure, and I'm sorry." I sighed because I didn't like hearing it, but I knew I deserved every bit of it. So I took it like I used to take castor oil when I was a kid.

"But at least Sarah knew what was going on. *I* didn't even know." Alex paced the floor, flinging her arms wildly. "You should've been meditating on the Word, praying, or something. But instead, you were meditating on surrogacy."

I pleaded with her. "I know that now, and I'm sorry. I got carried away."

"How do I know you won't get carried away again? How do *I* know I can really trust you with my heart?"

I took Alex's hand, kissed it, and then put it on my chest. "Because I'm trusting you with mine."

Chapter Twenty-two

Joshua

It sure wasn't a good time for Alex and me to be fighting, not with my father having another relapse and fighting for his life. His red cell count was very low. He had lost an extreme amount of weight, was very lethargic, and his doctors feared the worst. Thankfully, I knew a healing God. It was bad enough that he had the most common form of cancer in American men, but why did it have to be my father? He was such a good man. He had raised me up to love God.

He had built up the church, and he had dealt long and hard with my mother. And for that alone he deserved a medal.

We sat across from each other in the waiting room with angry stares all around. Mine, Alex's, and Mother's. What did a brother do to deserve this? Two women against one man, and both of them looked like they were enjoying torturing me.

Mother walked around the room glaring at me from the corner of her eyes, huffing and puffing as if she wanted to pick a fight.

"Mother, if you keep this up, you're going to give yourself a stroke." I tried to smile to break the tension.

"And you would get great satisfaction from that, wouldn't you?" she snapped.

Joshua frowned up his face. "Why would you say something so mean?"

She walked right up to me. "Well, since ignoring sick parents seems to be your thing, if I do have a stroke, then you'll be two for two, won't you?"

Joshua shook his head. "Oh, you're a real gem, Mother."

"I try to be," she said.

Then I saw the hurt in her eyes. "It will be okay. Dad will be okay."

"And how did you decide that?"

"I just know it in my spirit." I reached out to touch her hand.

She withdrew her hand from my grasp. "Oh, I see. Young minister out of school less than a year and you have a prophetic word?"

"Yes, Mother, I do. 'Touch not mine anointed, and do my prophets no harm.'" I walked out of there. I'd had enough of her badgering. I had to leave before I said something I'd be sorry for.

Alex came out after me and put her hand on my shoulder. I could feel her warmth and it brought me back to my right state of mine.

"Joshua, don't let her get to you," Alex said.

"I don't want my father to die while everything is in such a mess."

"But your father's life is not in a mess. Ours may be, but his is not." Alex ran her fingers over my back. "Try to take some comfort in that."

I closed my eyes tightly without turning around. I didn't want my wife to see how vulnerable I was. So I stood up straight, cleared my throat, and deepened my voice to answer her.

"I appreciate that." That was all I could get out without stirring myself up too much. I was a man, and I had to be strong for everyone—my wife, my father, and most especially for my mother. I knew she needed me more than ever even if she was too stubborn to admit it.

I turned around to grab Alex's hand. She prayed for me, which gave me the strength I needed to go back inside and face my mother.

Another long night at the hospital drifted into another long day. The doctors spoke of hormonal manipulation with medication and an alternate treatment called proton therapy instead of the usual radiation in order to insure a better quality of life. My parents and I listened carefully, not fully understanding all the implications of changing treatments. My mother, being a very smart woman, said, "Thank you, Doctor. We'll consider it in prayer." I smiled because that was the mother I knew and loved.

Chapter Twenty-three

Alex

After a couple of weeks Joshua and I were on fairly good terms again. He promised that he would slow down his efforts to impregnate me by any means necessary, that we wouldn't keep secrets from each other, and most especially, that he would leave the "Sister in everybody's business Yvonne" alone. Period. Now that was a biggie because I'd had quite enough of her antics for a lifetime.

"So you mean you just let him off the hook just like that?" Taylor rolled her mascara-covered eyes. "No, it couldn't be me."

"What did you expect me to do, kill him?"

"Now *there's* an idea," Taylor said.

"Taylor."

"I'm just sayin'. A brother was trippin' with that one, but hey, if you're okay with it . . ."

"You know I'm not okay with it. That was one of the most embarrassing things that has ever happened to me. Imagine having to confront my husband in front of Yvonne while she basically laughs at me under her breath because she knows what's going on the whole time."

"Right, and I'm sure she loved it too."

"She did. I could see it on her face. But just the thought of how I made a fool of myself because of Joshua's nonsense makes me mad all over again," I growled.

"Girl, I know. I can't say what I would have done if it had been me."

"Oh, trust me, I was upset. It took the Father, the Son, and the Holy Ghost to hold me back."

Taylor fell over with laughter. "I know that's right."

My sister would always help me bring humor into a situation and see the silly side of things even when she wasn't trying to. I guess that was the dynamic of our relationship. I'd rescue her with reason, and she'd rescue me with straight sista girl advice, which always made me laugh.

Meanwhile, as my life seemed to be getting back to normal, Michelle Harris, Minister Harris's daughter, just showed up at my job one day. Perky little Michelle, the teenager I had helped to rescue from making an irreversible mistake last year, walked into my cubicle during the afternoon. She had baby Elijah with her, and she immediately put him in my arms. All of my hormones stirred as I smelled his fresh baby skin.

"How are you?" I hugged her, while holding her son tightly.

"I'm good. I'm here to register for a faith class."

"Oh, I see. That's great." I couldn't stop being emotional as I remembered all we had gone through together last year.

Michelle pushed her medium-length weave braids out of her face. "I'm taking college classes too while I work, of course."

"Right. I'm so proud of you." I motioned for her to sit down.

I could see a little fatigue in her face, but I also saw joy in her eyes. Then I remembered that the joy of the Lord was our strength. Michelle had been away from the church for a while, despite Pastor Martin's rebuke of the church concerning their judgmental behavior. Since the big scandal over her pregnancy last year, her parents, Minister and Sister Harris, thought it was best that they all took an indefinite leave of absence. I hadn't seen them since.

"Anyway, we're back to stay now." Michelle pulled up a chair and sat down in front of my desk. "My family and I went to stay with my grandmother up in Vermont for a while."

"Oh," I said.

"It was kind of nice, a small farm town. Lots of land and fresh air for me and Elijah.

My dad says he was able to hear a word from God up there."

"And Sister Harris?"

"My mom just rested 'cause it was real peaceful," Michelle said.

"What about your siblings? Weren't they in school?"

Michelle stretched out her legs and leaned back in her chair. "Nah. My mom started homeschooling them so . . ."

"I see. Well, it's really good to see you and to know that you're back." I paused.

"Michelle . . ."

"Yes, Sister Alex?"

"No one should've ever pushed you away from the church in the first place. It wasn't fair." I shook my head.

She tried to smile. "I know."

"You repented of the fornication, and there is no sin in carrying and mothering a child." I stood up, reached across the desk, grabbed her hand, and squeezed it.

"I know," she said.

I let go of her hand and sat back down. "I just hate that things went down like they did."

"It's okay. Believe it or not, I think we just needed time away to recuperate after everything happened."

"I can certainly understand that."

Michelle gave me a thumbs-up. "Yeah, that's old news."

"It still bothers me that people in the church treat that particular sin differently than all the others. That's why I continue to work on the Giving Life Ministry."

"Thank God for people like you, Sister Alex." Michelle took her son. "It's all right, though. We're okay now."

"Good," I said. "We'll be meeting at The Push It Fitness Center in a couple of months."

"Really?"

"Yes, with the official grand opening. My sister is busy renovating the building now."

"Oh, okay." Michelle nodded. "Cool."

"Stop by and join us sometime," I said.

Michelle stood up. "I will."

I hugged her and hoped all the love I had inside would spill over to her. People say that misery loves company, but in my case, misery feeds off other people's joy because seeing Michelle made me happier than I'd been in weeks. And that happiness carried over into that evening when I saw my husband and shared that happiness with him.

Needless to say, Joshua was excited that I still loved him.

A few weeks later, I was eating a bowl of homemade tapioca pudding with Lilah, just enjoying life, when, without any warning, I began to feel nauseated. After throwing up on the bathroom floor twice, I decided to schedule an appointment to see my doctor.

Even though I had been through this time and time again, that didn't stop me from having the jitters that morning when I walked into Dr. Henley's office. I hadn't even told Joshua where I was going that day because I didn't need additional pressure. I just waited until his schedule was good and full, and then slipped away without hardly being noticed. Lilah was spending time with her grandparents so that made this task a little easier.

Here I was sitting in the waiting room, hoping this wasn't a false alarm like the last time.

I didn't know how long I could stay on that roller-coaster ride, which was my life.

"Mrs. Benning," the nurse said.

I stood up and smiled. "That's me."

"How are you?" The nurse smiled at me and continued walking.

"Very well, thanks." *Enough of the small talk,* I thought to myself. I was in no mood for pleasantries. I had to know what was going on with my future.

I followed the nurse into Dr. Henley's office as I had so many times before. It was a midsized room with pastel blue furniture. I remembered from psychology class in college that blue was a soothing color, yet *calm* was the last word I'd use to describe how I felt. When the doctor entered the room, I immediately stiffened up as if I were about to endure a pap smear or something. Realizing this, I quietly summoned my body to loosen up as the doctor took a blood sample.

"All right, Mrs. Benning, we'll have the lab results in just a few minutes."

He was in and out just like that, yet, I was left shivering on the table. I wasn't cold. I was just anxious to know those results. I needed to know those results for Joshua's sake, and for the sake of our already shaky marriage. *Maybe this time, Lord.*

Soon, Dr. Henley returned. I held my breath when I heard his deep voice. "Mrs. Benning, He did it again."

My heart beat faster. "Pardon me?"

"God did it again," he said.

I took a deep breath. "I'm sorry. I don't understand."

Dr. Henley laughed heartily. "Another conception. God did it again. You're pregnant."

I put my hand over my mouth, and then the tears came. "Oh my goodness. Thank you, Dr. Henley."

"Don't thank me. You know who to thank." Dr. Henley nodded his head and smiled.

"Oh, thank you, Lord. And thank you for all your encouragement."

"Congratulations. Go home and celebrate with your family, and I'll see you in my office for your first examination in a week."

The moment I reached my car, I dropped my head down and prayed. "Thank you, Jesus," I shouted.

Beyond my greatest longings came this second chance from God. Over the years, I'd heard these horror stories about poorly done abortions causing sterility and other malfunctions.

I'd been able to bury that fear up until I started dating Joshua—the only man I ever truly wanted to have children with. Then the doubts started coming up again, the doubts that I could actually conceive a child without complications—or at all. Now that I was able to give Joshua a child, he could fulfill the Benning legacy, and I could fulfill my destiny as a mother.

Chapter Twenty-four

Alex

Cold is not even the word for how bitter it was. The February snow had turned to ice, and after a day of being walked and driven on, it was now a dull gray. In some areas salt was already sprinkled on the ice to prevent slip and fall injuries. As I walked down the sidewalk I was careful not to lose my bearings, though I was wearing my sole-gripping suede boots. The wind whipped my already wild hair, and I threw my hood over my head to protect what decency I had left. I'd tried to call Joshua before I left Dr. Henley's office, but he was in a meeting so I had to wait to share my good news.

In the meanwhile, I did my usual runs to the supermarket and to the dry cleaners to pick up Joshua's suits. As I walked down the aisles squeezing mangoes and tomatoes for ripeness, I couldn't stop thinking about carrying Joshua's child and about how my life would change.

Maybe, just maybe, this baby would end all the tension.

It was about two o'clock in the afternoon when I finally pulled into my parking space. I turned off the ignition, hopped out of my car, and continued walking happily toward the elevator.

Once again, I tried to reach Joshua. I was put on hold. A million thoughts ran through my mind as I listened to the classical music that was playing. I managed to get all the way up to our apartment before I actually reached him. So I settled in on the couch, took a deep breath, and waited for my husband to come to the phone. I couldn't wait until he got home from the bank.

"Hi, baby," Joshua said.

I giggled." Hi, Daddy of the Year."

"What did you call me?"

I playfully pretended to cough and muffled my voice. "I called you Daddy of the Year."

"Okay, why? What's going on?" I could hear the curiosity in my husband's voice.

"I figured you're such a great dad already and since you're going to be a dad for the second time that—"

"A second time?"

"Yep, a second time," I smiled.

"What are you saying?"

"We're going to have a baby, Mr. Benning."

"Yes!" Joshua let out a big breath. "Oh, I'm so happy, Mrs. Benning."

"I'm happy too, Mr. Benning."

"Wow. God is so awesome," Joshua said.

I paused to think about the truth of his statement. "Yes, He is."

"How . . . I mean, when?"

"I just saw Dr. Henley, and I couldn't wait to tell you."

Joshua whispered, "Thank you, Lord." Then he was silent for a minute.

"Are you okay?"

"I'm better than okay, baby," Joshua said, chuckling.

"Good." I was so happy I could deliver this news to my husband. We had survived all these months of trying, praying, and confessing. I was so grateful that we didn't even have to do in vitro fertilization, which was the next step on our list. We were actually scheduled for that procedure two weeks from now.

"This is the best news I've had since you agreed to be my wife."

I could hear the relief in his voice. "For me too." I was so full of emotion I could hardly speak. Mostly, I just held the phone and let the reality sink in while Joshua talked, and laughed, and planned.

Needless to say, he was ecstatic. This was what we had been praying for since the first week we were married. I was just so grateful to have gotten to that point by God's grace.

My second call was to my sister, who was very excited about becoming an aunt, and we planned to meet for lunch soon. My next round of calls were to Dad, Aunt Dorothy, and Marisol.

Then I went across the hall and knocked on Ms. Johnson's door to get Lilah.

Once back at home, I made us two huge bowls of cherry chocolate ice cream.

After all, I was eating for two now, and we had a lot to celebrate. We had decided to wait until Joshua came home so we could tell her together, but judging by the look on Lilah's face, I was sure she knew something was up.

There was so much to do. I went over to the desktop computer and started researching maternity clothes and supplies on line. Before I knew it, hours had gone by. I hoped the joy I felt during this time would never end.

Two days later, Taylor took me out shopping to celebrate. I picked her up at her apartment building. She came outside with her leg braces and propped herself in the front seat of my car.

Although she was still a little wobbly, this was progress, and I hoped she recognized it as such.

One day she'd walk again. I was sure about that, but in the meantime, would all of us still be able to stand her sometimes bad attitude? That was the real question.

She turned off the soft praise music I was playing and popped in her own gospel rap CD.

"This is a new group. Keith introduced me to them, and they're hot."

"Yeah, this sounds all right."

"All right? This is hype. What are you sayin'?"

"You're right, it's hype." I started to bop my head to the beat. "If you love Jesus, Jesus, Jesus."

The words were catchy, and the tune was cute, so we danced in the car like we were teenagers, giggling and enjoying the music. Their style was kind of Kirk Franklin—like which,

I thought was cool. When it came to music, Taylor really had good taste. I made up my mind that I'd have to borrow this CD from her later.

We drove down to Macys on Thirty-fourth Street, although we had to park a few blocks over.

"Let's go down to the maternity department first, 'cause you can't roll with me for the next few months with that tacky wardrobe of yours." Taylor shook her head and put her hand in my face.

I slapped her hand away. "Oh, come on. Let's go."

When we searched the racks, I looked for comfort and affordability while Taylor looked for style and designer. It was definitely a battle of the minds, but I managed to select a few outfits that we could agree upon. I chose one simple pair of denim stretch pants, a pair of black dress slacks, two pretty blouses, one in green and one in pink, and a lovely black party dress.

After we paid for these items, along with nursing bras, support pantyhose, and comfortable cotton underwear, we were ready to go to the children's department.

Excited about getting started on the nursery, Joshua and I had already decided to paint the small room yellow. Of course, we really planned to move to a bigger place by then so we would have more than enough room for our growing family, including Kiano. Yet, for now, he or she would have to bunk with Lilah because we only had two bedrooms. When the time was right, we'd have to move, hopefully, into a house with a backyard.

In the meantime, I browsed the clothing section for Carters and Disney's Winnie the Pooh Collection. I listened to Taylor rave about Baby Gap before I purchased several packs of plain white gender infant onesies, a yellow duck towel set, a colorful infant gym, a yellow tub, and several neutral gender infant toys. This was the most happiness I'd experienced in a long time. I just hoped it would last.

Chapter Twenty-five

Alex

Surprisingly, a few days after Mother Benning found out about my condition, she invited herself over. Bishop Benning was still in the hospital so he wouldn't be there to referee. Joshua and I were on our own. I made sure that everything in the apartment smelled and looked fresh and clean. I dusted every corner, every crack, and every crevice. I rewashed every dish, and every eating utensil. I deodorized the entire living room, dining area, and kitchen. I swept and mopped, scrubbed windows, and cooked. Then I even changed into a cute, long black dress so I'd look smaller. By the time she arrived, I was done.

"Hello, dear." Mother Benning hugged me, and I was taken aback.

"Hello, Mother Benning." I led her inside and took her jacket.

She looked at Joshua. "Hello, son."

"Hello, Mother." Joshua gave his mother a peck on the cheek.

Lilah ran into the room and landed in her grand-mother's arms. "Big Mommy."

Mother Benning smiled. "Big Mommy's little sweet-heart, how are you?"

"I'm fine. I missed you," Lilah said, pouting.

"Awww. Big Mommy's poor baby," she said in a soft, sweet tone while smoothing Lilah's hair. "I missed you too."

When Mother Benning was talking to Lilah it was almost like she was another person.

Joshua and I just stood back and watched in awe as she let her gentler side shine through. She was never harsh with Lilah, and I'm sure Joshua wondered why she couldn't be that way with him. Or us. She kept interacting with her granddaughter, uninterrupted, for about ten whole minutes before she acknowledged either of us again.

I hoped I didn't still smell like floor polish when we sat down at the dinner table. Joshua helped me to serve his mother so that everything would go quicker. We had a mildly amicable chicken dinner before she settled in for the kill.

"Well, thank God there is one more Benning to carry on the Benning legacy."

I was so tired of hearing that. Legacy of hatefulness, I wanted to say, at least if Mother Benning had anything to do with it. How dare that woman go on and on like the sun rose and set on her family only. Like legacies were more important than human beings. I was disgusted with the whole premise, but I kept my mouth closed and listened while my mother-in-law snapped her jaws back and forth. She rattled on and on about honor and heritage.

"Now, Joshua. You see, this is even more of a reason for you to do what you need to do, because now, you've got another child depending on you," Mother Benning said.

I could see Joshua's jaw tightening.

"I'm already doing what I have to do," he said.

"Not quite, son."

"How is that, Mother?"

"You know what you should be doing for your family, Joshua. You know what is expected of you." Sister Benning cut her eyes at me. "You used to not have a problem with that."

I didn't dare say a word. I just excused myself from the table and started clearing away the dinner dishes.

"No, that's before I knew what God wanted me to do with my life specifically," Joshua replied.

"So, are you saying God wants you to break your parents' hearts?"

"No, just that He doesn't want me to pastor Kingdom House." He picked up his Bible from the center table.

Mother Benning remained calm. "But you're a minister, so is that so far-fetched?"

As usual Joshua held his own. "It's far-fetched for me because I haven't been given those instructions."

"So God wants you to be a pauper all your life, disappoint your entire family, and bring ridicule to the Benning name?" Mother Benning stood up, walked over to the leather sectional, took a tissue out of her pocket, wiped off the seat, and then sat down. I mumbled to myself about her nerve.

Joshua shook his head. "Mother, why must we continue down this path? You know I've been told to build a new church, to build a different kind of ministry."

"Right. A different kind of ministry, one so different it's right off the pages of the Bible."

Mother Benning pursed her lips.

I didn't know how Joshua was going to handle that one. Her mouth, like the Word, was sharper than any two-edged sword.

"Now you know that's not true," Joshua said.

"All I know is that every day I have to look at your poor, weak father and know he can't rest because his only son, who is a minister, refuses to help out."

Joshua almost looked defeated, with his head held low and his bottom lip even lower. "I never refused to help out."

Mother Benning was not moved by his countenance. "Well, there is a gap in the system somewhere, son, because we still need help."

"You've got an interim pastor at the church now, and I'll always help out just as long as you and Dad both know any ministering thing I do at Kingdom House of Prayer is just temporary."

Mother Benning rolled her eyes. "God's work is *not* temporary."

"But me working at Kingdom House is." Joshua raised his voice slightly to emphasize his point.

"You're stubborn, just like your father." She grabbed her coat from the coatrack.

Joshua looked up to the ceiling. "Oh, so I'm stubborn like my father?"

Mother Benning walked toward the door without looking back. "Are you implying that *I'm* the one that's stubborn?"

"Listen, can't we just have a truce?" Joshua held up both hands. "I don't want to fight with you. I just know what I have to do."

"Well, let me know when you change your mind." She turned to face us.

Joshua didn't blink. "Change my mind?"

Mother Benning tilted her head slightly. "I serve a powerful God, and my prayers are worth a million."

"Then I need you on my team," he smiled and kissed his mother's cheek.

Mother Benning seemed to soften a little. "I guess this baby may just bring us all together." She lightly touched my stomach before she headed through the door.

I smiled at the possibility that we might be a family after all.

Chapter Twenty-six

Joshua

I sat slouched out on the couch watching basketball with Brother Jameson. His first name was Robert, but no one, including me, called him that. Peace and relaxation. No women or girls in the house at all. Just hot wings, roasted peanuts, nacho chips, and cheese dip, and lots of soda. Just watching LeBron score without interference. Now *that's* what I was talking about.

"Oh, did you see that jump shot? Bruh, did you see that?" Robert jumped off of the couch with his hands in the air.

"Man, you know I didn't miss that," I said.

"A brother could score with his eyes closed." He put up his hand.

I slapped him five. "All day long."

Suddenly, a Missionary Bible College commercial came on with a tall, exotic-looking model in it. The young lady reminded me of Delilah. I remembered her mood swings, how she'd walk out whenever Lilah was crying. What kind of mother walked away from her crying infant?

Apparently motherhood was just too much for her. All she ever wanted was money and fame. How could I have been so stupid that I thought I was enough for her, that I could make her happy? Instead, I was more like a plaything for her—a temporary toy for her amusement.

It hurt me to know that Lilah and I were never more than that.

This rang a particular chord with me today because it was Lilah's fifth birthday. I couldn't help but think of Delilah when I looked into Lilah's deep dark eyes or when I touched her thick, wavy hair. She looked more and more like her mother every day. I'd be lying if I said it wasn't still painful because it was, but it was less painful than it used to be. And by the grace of God, it was getting better every day.

Alex and Lilah were gone and wouldn't be returning until the late afternoon. She informed me beforehand that they'd be doing some birthday shopping before the main event.

Then we'd go out as a family to celebrate Lilah's birthday at The Prospect Park Zoo.

So we sprawled out on the couches in the living room, making the kind of mess I knew my wife would be upset about. But it was okay because she wasn't here, and by the time she got back, I'd have it all cleaned up anyway. There would be no sign of how much fun I had without her. I had to smile at the thought.

By the time the game was over and Robert went home to his own wife, Alex and Lilah returned. While they walked to Lilah's room with hands full of shopping bags, I hurried to finish vacuuming up the crumbs so my wife wouldn't go off.

"You shouldn't be carrying all those bags," I said.

"Nothing is heavy," Alex yelled out to me.

Lilah ran out. "We bought a lot of good stuff, Daddy."

"All right, sweetie," I said, dumping the last of the soda cans into the trash.

When Alex came back, she kissed me on the forehead, shook her head, and proceeded to take the birthday cake out of the refrigerator.

"I can see that you and Brother Jameson had fun today," she said, looking around the room.

"Yeah, a little," I said.

Alex smiled before she put the cake in my hands. "Looks like more than a little fun to me." Then she grabbed the bags of juice, and the three of us headed down to Prospect Park for Lilah's party.

We invited ten of Lilah's little friends from the children's ministry. Most of them knew Lilah pretty well because they'd played together at church twice a week for the past two and a half years. Since Alex and I chose the barnyard theme for three- to five-year-olds, Lilah and her ten invited guests were able to feed sheep, play barnyard games, and pet an alpaca's nose while their parents looked on. Lilah fell in love with Aggie the cow and wanted to take her home.

Mother, Taylor, and Keith were there also. We served the cake, juice, and sang Stevie Wonder's version of "Happy Birthday." The zoo's birthday staff gave out the goodie bags, and everyone enjoyed the rest of their time at the zoo.

I was glad everyone was having fun, but my mind was actually on the five hundred-dollar price tag for this gig. We had discussed having this party a few months back, but that was before the money situation became tight and not right. With a new baby on the way, the fertility clinic bills, school bills, and Delilah's old debts, I was definitely strapped for cash. Still, I wanted to feel like I was a good father, so I let my daughter have the time of her life. Later on that evening, I stayed up after midnight with my calculator, trying to make right what I knew was wrong.

Chapter Twenty-seven

Alex

I was sick like a dog from the very beginning, throwing up constantly, getting dizzy, and even having sharp abdominal pains. So my first trimester was already wreaking havoc on my life. The nurses pulled so much blood during the first few months that I didn't know if I was dead or alive half of the time. I mean, the whole time I was being tested for this and that, my heart felt like it couldn't take it. I'd always whisper a prayer right before. *Please, Lord, let this baby be okay in Jesus' name.* And the baby always was okay, but that didn't stop me from holding my breath every time I had another appointment.

So despite the fact that I'd been sick at work all weeklong, it was time for Kingdom House's Anniversary banquet. This would be my first year attending as Joshua's wife. It would also be the first year that Pastor Benning would not be leading the ceremonies. Although he had been in and out of the hospital lately, I was glad he felt well enough to attend, though, because if he hadn't, the anniversary would have gone on without him.

Joshua was dressed in a black and white tuxedo with black shoes with white trim. I wore a little black evening gown, maternity-style, of course, although I was barely showing, and black patent leather pumps.

My sister had helped me put my outfit together so I
wouldn't make a fool of myself, not that I couldn't dress
or anything, but for this occasion, I wanted to make a
statement. A double rope of gold was around my neck,
and dangling gold earrings with a diamond in the center hung from my ears, compliments of Taylor. She
had an extensive collection of jewelry from all the big
ballers, shot callers she'd dated over the years. Lilah
was dressed in a simple lavender lace dress with patent leather shoes, and she had a lavender flower in her
hair. That too was a tip from Taylor, the bona fide diva.

When we arrived, both members and invited guests
aligned the walkway that led to the main entrance.
The church sat on ten acres of land that resembled a
college campus with its adjacent buildings and large
grassy rest areas. Kingdom House was a neotraditional
building with huge stained glass windows, and French
doors with brass handles. Inside the main lobby of the
sanctuary were cathedral ceilings and marble floors.
Once inside the actual sanctuary, I was overtaken by
the lights, cameras, thick jade carpet, jade cushioned
seats, a marble stage area, and the ivory pulpit. It was
quite a spectacle from my perspective.

Bishop Benning was there, although he looked very
weak. Mother Benning came up to the microphone,
greeted everyone, and introduced her son Joshua as
the master of ceremonies. Joshua then thanked his
parents for their twenty-seven years of service, thanked
them for allowing him to honor them by standing in the
pulpit, and congratulated them on Kingdom House's
anniversary. I was so proud of him standing there holding the microphone, a confidant man of God. When he
was done with his speech, the praise dancers took off
running across the stage, dressed in orange, peach, and
gold. It was so beautiful.

A Christian comedian named Joel Lee came forward next and entertained us with his clean sense of humor. He didn't look very much like a comedian when I saw him, with his three-piece suit, beard, and his slick goatee. But after hearing him tell jokes about the black family, though, I had to admit he was funnier than I thought he'd be.

Next on the agenda was a solo by Sister Kaelah Price, but she couldn't be found. First everyone scrambled to find her until they received a phone call saying she was still stuck at the airport. So Joshua insisted that I replace her on the program.

I punched him with my elbow. "No, Joshua."

"Why not? You can do it."

I shook my head. "I can, but I don't think—"

"Don't think. When it comes to God's will—just do," he said.

I knew Joshua was right, and the praise dancers would be done with their second act soon.

The solo was next on the agenda so I had to get ready. I took a deep breath before I started the song. I didn't know where the strength came from, but I found it somehow. I reached deep inside, stepped up to the microphone, and sang "The Best in Me." Inside my head I didn't know where God was going with this, but I let Him have control. It was as if I were floating outside of myself as I sang to His glory. I walked up and down the stage, shouting, "Hallelujah to the blood of the Lamb." As I surrendered everything, I felt burdens being lifted, yokes being destroyed, and I knew there was power in praise. Sure, I'd sung with the praise team for the past five years, up until the Lord placed the young women's ministry on my heart, but I'd never done a solo with such a large audience. Yet, the thick crowds applauded, cried out, and got caught up in the spirit. When I was done, I was soaking wet with perspiration, and I clearly felt God's presence. *Thank you, Jesus, for your anointing.*

I saw Mother Benning watching me from the corner of my eye. She walked over to me backstage, straightened a piece of hair that hung in my face, and looked into my eyes.

"That was very nice, dear," Mother Benning said.

Coming from my mother-in-law, that was the compliment of all compliments.

"Thanks." In a perfect world, my mother-in-law would adore me and I, her. We'd go shopping, call each other at least once a week, and plan all the family events together. But in my world, I was just glad to be acknowledged, on occasion, as Joshua's wife. I didn't dare hope for more than that, so I moved away from her quickly before she took it back. Lord knows she was capable of doing so.

Our own Pastor Martin was up next to speak, and his message was brief: Faith is the key to breakthrough. It was not a new revelation, but it was powerful nonetheless. If only I could tighten up my own faith walk.

By the time we were dismissed to the grand dining room, I was more than ready to eat.

Our plates of sirloin steaks and baked potatoes with sautéed mushrooms and green beans had just been served, but that baby in me was crying out for food like he or she hadn't eaten a day in his or her life. Then to make it worse, as soon as I sat down at our round table with Joshua and Lilah, I started to feel nauseated. *Oh no, not now.* I thought about this special occasion, my expensive outfit, and this elegantly set table in front of me, and tried to hold everything down.

Joshua saw the look of fear in my face. "Are you okay?"

"No, I'm feeling sick." I leaned over toward the floor.

"Let's go." He took my arm and quickly led me out to the ladies' room.

I made it into the stall just in time because I couldn't hold it in any longer. That was how my life rolled lately. I just hoped that with all that was happening, my life wasn't rolling out of control.

Chapter Twenty-eight

Alex

When I arrived at work that morning, Dr. Harding was already waiting at my desk for me. It wasn't that I was late or anything. Actually, I was never late to work. I took my job seriously, and I paced myself in the morning. Plus, with Joshua waking up at five o'clock every morning to pray, I never overslept. I always had plenty of time to get to work by nine o'clock.

Dr. Harding, being the visionary that he was, decided to add to my already overloaded job description. "Sister Alex, I wanted to speak to you about something important."

I tried not to look puzzled. "No problem, sir. Do you need me to come to your office?"

"No, it's nothing that serious. I'd just like you to team up with Brother Seger to work on the newest Missionary project, which is our radio show. It's going to be bigger than the commercial."

"Excuse me? Don't we have a producer for that?"

"Yes, we do."

I tried to look pleasant, even though I was nervous about his answer. "Am I missing something?"

"I've put Seger in on it also because he's got a lot of good ideas, and he helped secure our model for the commercial. That really helped us a lot. But now, we want to go a different route."

I couldn't believe what I was hearing. Was he kidding me? "A different route? A route where I'm involved?"

"Yes, I've been meeting with the board, and unlike the commercial, they want a radio show that's less trendy but more informative."

"Oh, okay," I said, trying to put the pieces together.

Dr. Harding pulled his graying beard. "I knew you would, Sister Alex."

I was still confused. "Okay, but why me? What do I have to do with all of this?"

"You did such an awesome job with public relations last year, I'd just like to see your ideas implemented in the show as well. It's cheaper to use the talent we have right here, rather than hire a special group for this project."

"I see." All I could think of was what this project would cost me—a lost night's sleep, bitter arguments with Joshua, or worse.

"You all will basically just serve as advisors for the producers," Dr. Harding said.

"I don't understand." I shook my head. "I don't know how I'll be able to help with a radio show."

Dr. Harding cleared his throat. "Sister Alex, you know this school like the back of your hand, and you also know what's in our best interests. I'd like you to be on board, ensuring that everything in the radio show will represent Missionary in its best light."

"Oh, I will, sir," I said.

"Good." Dr. Harding patted me on the shoulder.

"Well, thanks for the confidence in me." I forced myself to smile. "I'll see what I can do."

"No, don't see. Just do," Dr. Harding chuckled.

As one might imagine, when I told my husband about Dr. Harding's idea to team me up with Seger on the radio show, it did not go well. Joshua immediately said no, without hearing any of the details. And the moment he said no, unfortunately, was the moment I made up my mind that I would definitely do it. I was so dead set against having a man control me, so totally against it, that I was inadvertently sabotaging my own happiness. I wondered if this was a by-product of the anger my mother had for my once-wandering father or if me watching her single-handedly run things for all those years had changed my marital expectations.

"I won't tolerate it," Joshua said.

"Tolerate?" No, he did *not* say that.

"Really, Joshua?"

Joshua was calm, but I was seething. "Yes, tolerate. I am your husband, Alex."

"Yes, and I am your wife. Does that mean you have the right to always get what you want while I just sit back and don't say a word?"

Did it matter that Joshua was calling all the shots in our marriage, and that my dreams were being sacrificed for his? Or should I have spoken out more, as if I hadn't spoken, cried, and shouted enough? It was obvious that he just wasn't listening, that he had tuned me out as men do. What did it matter that I had given everything and had no more to give if my marriage was going to fall apart anyway?

It seemed that the more I prayed, the more we argued. And the more I read the Word, the more Joshua and I were at odds with each other.

I tilted my head to the side as if I weren't hearing correctly. "What do you mean I can't do the radio show?"

"I thought I made myself clear the first time," Joshua said.

"Surely you didn't think that just because you raise your voice and attempt to shatter what little self-respect I have left that you would get your way?"

"What?" Joshua frowned up his face. "Get my way? What way?"

"That I won't do anything at all with Seger, that I'll be too intimidated about what you'll say, that I'll sever the relationship, even though I've told you time and time again that we're just friends."

Joshua fixed his lips so that they barely opened. "And I've told you that I don't trust the man."

I fought back tears. "Okay, this isn't even about him. This is about me and my job."

"So?"

"So you can't just stop me from completing a project and expect me to keep my job."

"So quit." He shrugged his shoulders. "I told you to quit."

I walked right up on him and clenched my teeth. "Oh, you'd like that, wouldn't you?"

"Yes, I would."

I pleaded, "Aren't things tight enough as it is?"

Joshua swallowed hard. "You let me take care of things and worry about that."

"I *have* let you take care of things, and you're up all hours of the night doing just that—worrying."

Joshua bit his lip. "Oh, that's cold."

Tears of frustration began to run down my face. "Why can't you just let me be happy?"

"Happy? I didn't know that job was so important to you."

"I'm not saying that it is, but it does help with extra money, and we need that right now."

I put my hands on my hips. "Let's be real."

"Yeah, it helps, but not if everything else is in jeopardy. I want you home with Lilah anyway."

"You know we can't really afford that yet. Maybe when we get some things paid off first."

Joshua raised his voice. "I *told* you to let *me* handle that."

"I'll be on maternity leave soon anyway." I knew I was giving it to him plain, and I also knew he wasn't going to like it. Still, I had to say what I felt would free me.

"Exactly."

I was feeling more and more helpless by the minute. "Then why can't you just let me finish this thing out since I've committed to it?"

"Because I wish you'd just finish us, Alex. Forget about Missionary Bible Institute for a minute. Dr. Harding can get another desk clerk."

I nodded my head in disgust. "Oh, so now there is no value in what I do?"

Joshua looked up first, took a deep breath, and then looked down at me. "I didn't say that.

I need you to finish us."

"And what is *that* supposed to mean?"

"Harding can get another employee, but I can't get another wife."

I walked away from him. "If you don't stop trying to keep me in a box, you just might have to get another wife."

Chapter Twenty-nine

Alex

The August sun came through the windows and lit up the entire room. The brightness of the day warmed my spirit as I rubbed my own round stomach. Since I was now in the second trimester of my pregnancy, and we'd already had a sonogram, things became a little clearer.

This baby was taking shape in my body and in my mind. It wasn't one of my better days, even though it was my birthday. My belly felt like if it were swollen any tighter, I'd pop. Luckily, I knew this impending explosion thing was all in my mind. I wished I could calm my body down as easily, though. Then I remembered I was a child of God, so I prayed and commanded the enemy to cease in his maneuvers against me and my family, and in particular, over this child I was carrying.

I was well into my sixth month. Undoubtedly, the baby was getting bigger and stronger daily. We'd agreed that neither of us wanted to know the sex of the baby before it was time to deliver. But one thing we did know already was that it was a single child, not twins. How my heart longed for twins for so many years since I had given up my chance to mother my first set over ten years ago. It was only when I gave up believing that I could have children at all, that I stopped wanting twins. But I guessed it wasn't meant to be. At least, not

this time around. If I could just get through this pregnancy I knew I'd probably have the courage to do it all
over again. I needed God to show me I could still have
a baby, just once.

I walked over to the window, pulled back the curtains, and looked down to see the children scrambling
below on the pavement, hurrying into their various
buildings from school. I wondered if I'd be that type
of mother, always rushing to go here or there, like my
mother did. At this point, there was no telling. After all,
I wanted to hurry up to have this baby so I could really
get back to work and back to my vision for the women's
ministry. Then there was Joshua's vision, which I knew
I'd have to get behind soon. And building a church was
no joke.

Working with some of the ministers at Missionary
Bible School and being a devoted, always volunteering
member of Missionary Church, I knew firsthand the
work that was required.

It wasn't that I was ambivalent about Joshua's vision. It's just that I sometimes felt like his vision was
strangling mine. I still very much wanted to be friends
with Seger, adopt Kiano, and build a safe haven for
young women. Yet, all of that seemed to be buried underneath the many layers of plans Joshua had for *our*
family and *our* church. I wasn't exactly crazy about the
idea of being first lady yet either. Sure, it had its allure,
but when it came down to it, I knew there would probably be more sacrifice than satisfaction. Ultimately,
that was the story of my life. Give, give, and give some
more. Yet, I knew some things had to change, especially since I was now thirty-two years old.

At work, they gave me the usual store-bought-cake-
quick-delivery-special in the conference room, while
Dr. Williams played "Happy Birthday To You" on his

harmonica. The rest of the department sang along. That was how it went with office parties.

"Happy birthday, Sister Alex." Seger kissed me on the cheek.

I had been working closely with Seger two days out of the week on Missionary's radio show, despite my husband's attempt of putting his foot down. Who did he think he was anyway? He was my husband, *not* my master. Thankfully, that project was over, but the tension over the subject of Seger and my ongoing relationship didn't stop.

Marisol gave me a big hug. So did Dr. Harding. Then within minutes, we all scattered, settling in at our own workstations, trying to savor the cake and the camaraderie we sometimes overlooked.

After work, I drove to pick up Taylor and we went to the Too Hot Hair Salon.

When we walked in the entire salon smelled of hot wings. That wasn't necessarily a bad thing except that I was hungry. We signed in with the receptionist, and then sat next to each other, waiting to be called.

"Look, girl, remember the rule," I said.

"I know. I know. No talk of men, or jobs, or bills." Taylor laughed. "Like who would really want to talk about that lame stuff anyway?"

I definitely didn't want to talk about my problems, not today. I was tired of talking, and I was tired of being tired. "I know, right," I said, glad to have a break from the conversations that seemed to plague my life.

Taylor giggled. "What should we talk about then?"

"I don't know." I giggled too. "There is nothing else, is there?"

"Funny." Taylor shook her head. "There's food, fashion, and fun. Pick a topic."

"Well, since we're going out to eat next, I choose food."

"Girl, you're always choosing food," Taylor said.

"Very funny," I replied, shoving a red M&M into my mouth.

"No, but seriously, I want to get you on my nutrition regimen."

"Maybe one day, Taylor, but it's not happening—"

"Today." Taylor finished my sentence, knowing me all too well.

I licked my lips. "I can't wait to get my hands on a piece of that Junior's cheesecake."

Taylor snapped her fingers. "I'd leave that alone if I were you."

I gave her the look that said mind-your-own-business, and she left me alone.

All in all, we had a really good afternoon. We both laughed and enjoyed our meal, temporarily forgetting that we were anything other than two free-spirited sisters loving life.

Birthdays didn't really mean a whole lot to me except that God spared my life for another year. Don't get me wrong; I was grateful. I just wasn't one of those people who had to have a big bash every year to prove something. Taylor felt differently about this, of course. She considered her birthday just another day to indulge in extravagance. So we came to a compromise—a fancy lunch at Junior's and a trip to the salon for a new do. That was the best I could do, and she accepted because I was her sister. And not just her sister, but her twin. As long as she could spend money and look good, she was fine. And as long as I could eat a good meal, birthday cake or not, I'd be fine.

We decided we'd both get wrap sets so we could have a day of looking identical again. After we came out from under the dryers, our hair was soft, silky, and hanging to our shoulders. Then we had our nails done by Sheila, the nail technician. I received a simple French manicure and a pedicure. Taylor had her usual acrylics put on with silver and red nail art on top and had her toes done to match. That was just Taylor, the diva.

After we left the salon I drove Taylor home.

Later that evening, Joshua bought me roses and took me to a seafood restaurant for dinner.

"Happy birthday, baby," he said.

I told him thank you again and again. Joshua looked like he enjoyed his fish dinner, yet he was quiet the entire time, like he had a whole lot on his mind. I mean, he talked, but not about anything important, so I went along with him, playing the good little wife role. When we finally reached home and picked up Lilah, I was tired from the long day's events. I bathed and put Lilah to bed first. Then I took my own shower and smiled in the mirror as I got dressed. Joshua patted my big stomach and took his seat at his desk. Another year of my life had gone by, and thankfully, I was married and pregnant now. Otherwise, I would've really been depressed, because having my own family was something I always wanted, yet was always secretly afraid that I could never have.

I put my hands on my big round hips and turned myself around. I was happy with myself, for the most part, minus the extra pounds in the midsection I'd accumulated while carrying this child. Everything else was okay I thought, except that I could use more toning. My thighs told me that every day I took off my panty girdle. Still, all and all, I was pretty pleased with myself. I wasn't bad looking, had a great husband, even if I did want to kill him more than half the time, a beautiful stepdaughter, and one baby on the way.

Yes, I was blessed I decided. Best of all, I was a child of God, a true-to-life church girl, in love with God, and proud of it.

Yes, I believed wholeheartedly in the Bible, every letter on every page, and every demon in hell had to know I was serious about serving the Lord. And the key word here was *serve*.

Now, that was one thing Mama helped to instill in me—a love for the church and the things of God, something Joshua and I had in common. Suddenly, I had a warm feeling run through me.

I reached my hands under Joshua's collar and began to massage his neck. I knew I was going out on a limb, but I kept climbing anyway. "How does this feel?"

"It feels good."

"Good." Then I went in for the kill. "You know, I've been thinking that maybe we can get back to our plans of adopting Kiano after this baby is born."

Joshua folded his copy of the *New York Times*. "Is that all you think about? I don't think so."

"Not even if our financial situation improves?" I asked.

Joshua never looked up from his newspaper. "We might just have to postpone the whole adoption thing indefinitely."

"Indefinitely? Have you lost your mind? It's not an adoption *thing*. Kiano is a human being."

Joshua removed my hands from his neck and grabbed me by my wrists. "No, have you lost yours talking to me that way?"

Back in the day, those were fighting words. For a moment, my flesh wanted to take this argument in a whole other direction, but the Holy Spirit wouldn't allow me to go there.

A sista had come a long way. When I was a kid, my sister and I used to take words like that to the streets. I mean, Taylor and I used to fight like nobody's business at the drop of a hat. We loved a challenge, especially Taylor. All a girl would have to do was even look like she wanted to rise up on Taylor, and it was on. Then with the twin thing, it was always two against one. Most folk learned fast that picking a fight with one of us wasn't worth it. I never loved to fight like Taylor did, but I guess I felt like I had to be loyal. At least, that kind of loyalty was important to me up until the day I got baptized and really turned my life over to the Almighty God.

Unfortunately, I had a few instances of backsliding during my early twenties, but I finally got it right.

I put my hand up to my forehead as a headache started. "I'm sorry. It's just that I thought we wanted to do the international adoption thing—"

"No, *you* wanted to do the international thing, and I said I'd go along with it 'cause that's what you wanted," Joshua said.

"So, are you saying you didn't want to adopt Kiano, or did you not want to adopt period?"

Joshua clenched his teeth. "I didn't say that."

"No, but which is it?" I asked.

"Neither."

"Well, what exactly are you saying because I'm not understanding?"

"When I went to see you in Kenya, you were so happy, so content," Joshua said.

"Yes, I was, and then you told me you still wanted to marry me and said you wanted me back, the whole me."

Joshua sighed. "I did."

I tried to hold back the tears that were forcing their way out. "Well, the whole me came along with my dreams, and you knew one of those dreams was to adopt a child from Kenya. I told you that."

"Yes, you did, and I agreed," he answered calmly.

I was frantic. "But now you're saying something different."

"It was my mistake for agreeing to everything without being specific," Joshua said.

I couldn't believe what I was hearing. "Your *mistake*?"

"I'm just saying that we'll have to wait," Joshua said.

"Because of your selfish mother." I was so upset that I really wanted to say more but I bit my tongue for Joshua's sake. What kind of mother blackmails her own son? I didn't want to say that to him, but that was the whole of the matter. Mother Benning was using her money to manipulate us, and it was working because there were times I wanted to tell Joshua to just do whatever needed to be done. I just wanted to get that money out of Mother Benning's hand, but I knew that would be underhanded, and that I'd be stooping as low as she had.

"Now, you're out of line." The veins in Joshua's neck bulged up.

"Oh, I'm sorry again." I rolled my eyes. "I mean, because your mother will no longer be loaning us the money she promised she would."

"Look, I know it's a mean thing to do, but what can I do about it? Right now, I'm so strapped with bills from school, from the doctor's office, and from Delilah's old lifestyle, I don't know what in the world to do."

"I don't know. It seems like you should've cut off her spending a long time ago. You're in banking, Josh. There's no reason for your finances to be this messed up."

Joshua retreated. "You're right, I should've kept a level head."

"The past is the past. I'm not trying to bring your deceased wife into our conversation, but this is serious."

"Yes, it is."

"You made me a promise," I said.

"I know. I'm just postponing it, that's all."

"*Postponing* it? Can little Kiano hold on that long while we decide what sacrifices we can or can not make to get him?" I threw my hands into the air in disgust. "All he wants are parents. Besides that, the orphanage is going to close. You know that."

Joshua yelled, "What else can I do? What do you want from me, woman?"

"Nothing, Joshua. Nothing at all." I walked to my bedroom broken spirited.

A few minutes later, I heard Joshua's footsteps walking toward the front door. Then I heard the door slam.

This definitely wasn't how I pictured marriage would be. I had weathered the storms of abandonment by Ahmad, the twins' father, trying for years to forget him. At first, I rebelled, drowning my sorrows in and out of meaningless relationships, and then I finally surrendered to doing it all God's way. This spiritual commitment in me attributed to the four years I stayed celibate, longing and praying for a godly mate. I didn't realize that I'd be giving up a part of myself to become one with this mate. It was an eye-opening truth I was just beginning to realize.

Before I could stop them, the tears overcame me and I lay crying into my pillow. I must've fallen asleep because the next thing I knew I woke up with side splitting cramps, shooting up my whole front side and my back.

All of a sudden, I felt a discharge in my panties. I wasn't sure what it was. I went to the restroom to check and saw the bright red droplets and my heart raced. Yes, I was spotting.

I hopped back into the bed, bending myself into the fetal position, praying, "Jesus, Jesus, the blood of Jesus." Those were the only words I could remember to say as the worst pain I'd ever felt tore through my body, shaking me.

I thought about my husband who was well on his way to church by now. I thought about all we'd been through and everything that was at stake. I didn't want to lose him or to lose our dream. I didn't want to add to his worries. So I bit my lip in silence and vowed never to say a word about the pain that ravaged my body.

Chapter Thirty

Alex

Since my pains from last night subsided shortly after they began, I was confident about going to work the next day. Besides, how would I justify taking a day off anyway without explaining it to Joshua? The morning went by without any significant issues, just a little bloating. By midday, I began to feel really nauseated, and I felt that discharge again. First, I tried to ignore it. Then I started to pray when I realized it was serious. Soon, I started to feel dizzy.

Fortunately, Marisol noticed me about to topple over at the copy machine and slid a chair under me just in time. She called Joshua for me, and then she dialed 911.

Before I even knew what was happening, I was being carted away in an ambulance to Brooklyn Hospital. There was an oxygen mask over my face, an IV in my arm, and an ache in my heart.

The very first thing they did was strip me down to a thin paper gown and hook me up to the heart monitor so they could hear the baby's heartbeat. Then they slapped that sticky, cold jelly on my belly and did a quick ultrasound. Although I wasn't exactly sure of what was going on, I could hear the doctors and nurses mumbling about blood pressure, and about the baby's heart rate dropping. I was terrified. *Jesus, please save my baby.*

I guess I could say it went downhill from that point. I ended up in ICU with needles and tubes everywhere. The next thing I knew, I was sitting on a high table in stirrups being poked, prodded, and violated with every invasive procedure there was under the sun. Eventually, I was admitted and diagnosed with placenta previa.

When Joshua arrived about thirty-five minutes later, he was both devastated and apologetic. He stood at my bedside looking like a lost sheep. But I was no shepherd; I was ambivalent about his remorse. As far as I was concerned, he was not on my side.

Dr. Henley came in and explained that he feared placental abruption, and as a result, I would have to be put on bed rest indefinitely. It was one of the hardest days of my life, and I felt more vulnerable than I ever had.

"Bleeding in the second trimester of pregnancy is quite common. The greatest risk of placenta previa is bleeding." Dr. Henley seemed to look at both of our faces for our reaction.

I was sure he noticed the fear in mine, even though I didn't say anything. Joshua held me close to him, and I depended on his strength.

Dr. Henley continued. "Bleeding often occurs as the lower part of the uterus thins during the third trimester of pregnancy in preparation for labor. This causes the area of the placenta over the cervix to bleed. The more of the placenta that covers the opening of the cervix, the greater the risk for bleeding."

"Okay," I swallowed hard.

"There are other risks." Dr. Henley pulled his beard.

I finally managed to speak. "Like what, Doctor?"

Dr. Henley sighed, but didn't hesitate. "Abnormal implantation of the placenta, slowed fetal growth, preterm birth, birth defects, or infection after delivery."

"I see," Joshua said.

I started to cry, and Joshua hugged me close to him. I was only in my sixth month, and I was afraid.

"This is serious, but not impossible, not for God, that is." Dr. Henley came through again with his warm smile and his unshakable faith.

"So what's next, Doc?" Joshua asked, still holding me in his arms.

"I'll run some more tests, prescribe some pain medication, and we'll keep you under observation for a while. But until then, don't worry."

I nodded. Joshua took my hand in his. We prayed together, and we survived that day.

The next day went by slowly as I endured the many depressing hospital routines and contemplated my delicate condition. My doctor insisted that I remain in the hospital for further observation and tests, but I was restless. Never did like hospitals at all. The last time I had been in one was when I almost died from that infection over ten years ago, and that memory didn't help to ease my anxiety.

Later that evening, I looked up from my hospital bed and there was Seger, standing in the doorway. He was dressed in a two-piece brown suit, so I assumed he was coming straight from work.

"Sister Alex." Seger leaned over and kissed me on the cheek.

"Brother Seger. What are you doing here?" I'm sure my face lit up. "It's only four o'clock. Shouldn't you still be at work?"

Seger laughed. "And what if I'm playing hooky?"

"Ooh, I'm telling Dr. Harding," I said, playfully.

"I didn't see you at work yesterday so I asked Dr. Harding about you, and he told me you were in the hospital. So I had to come and see you."

"I'm glad you're here." Suddenly, I could feel tears building up in my eyelids. The pressure of this emotional ordeal threatened to make me crack.

"What's wrong?"

"Nothing." I swallowed the lump in my throat.

Seger came closer to the bed and gently touched my face. "No, really, what's wrong? I can see that you've been crying."

I tried to smile through my tears. "I've just been going through a lot, that's all."

"And the baby?"

"The baby is safe." I remembered the risk of placental abruption.

"Good," Seger said.

"I've just had a few complications from an injury I suffered some time ago." My mind briefly transported me back to that dark rainy day when I got the abortion.

"I see."

I sighed. "I'll be fine."

Seger put his finger up to my eyelid as if a tear were there. "I'm sure you will, but right now, you look so sad."

I whispered, "It's just that there is so much else going on."

"Do you want to talk about it?"

I considered what I would say before I answered.

Seger probed. "Problems at home?"

"No, it's nothing like that." I was careful not to give out information that Joshua and I would argue over later. "It's just that I wanted to adopt Kiano, and now . . . I just don't know if I can."

"But you've already started the process?"

"Barely started. Everything has just stopped," I said.

Seger looked like he was deep in thought. "And the orphanage will be closing soon."

Just the sound of it made me sad. An orphanage closing. It was like a sad ending to a long, heartbreaking movie. Unfortunately, Kiano was both the victim, and he had the starring role. Suffering was the theme, and self-preservation was our shame. I hated that we couldn't get him out of there for our own selfish, self-absorbed reasons. I mean, so what if a few bills fell behind, or if we had to cut back a little more? It would have been worth it just to see his innocent face finally happy and security in his eyes.

"Yeah, I know," I said.

"You won't be able to get him to the U.S. before the orphanage closes?"

"It's not looking too good right now."

"I see."

I had to explain more because I didn't want him judging us or looking down on Joshua.

"Everything was in motion, but we had to stop because—well, I was going to work more hours but . . ." I mumbled and sniffled.

"Hold on," Seger said. "I'm confused. More hours?"

"Yeah, I was going to try to do full-time again."

"Oh, I see. You wanted to work full-time hours?"

"Yes," I said.

"But I thought you were happy with part-time?"

"I am. I mean, I was." I closed my eyes and sighed. "The hours are great but—"

"What exactly is the problem?"

"I need the full-time pay." I dropped my head down in shame. "We can't adopt Kiano now because we can't afford it. It's just impossible now," I said.

Seger hardly blinked the whole time. "Nothing is impossible for God."

"Don't get me wrong. My husband is a very successful banker and a hard worker. It's just that we've got so much debt now with his college bills and a lot of previous expenses from his first marriage. And now with the new baby . . ." I wished so many times we didn't owe anyone anything. There were so many things I wanted to do concerning the ministry, but our debt, just like Pastor Martin said, was a form of bondage. I wanted to break loose and be free, but I was bound to those I owed. "Oh, it's a long story."

"Then keep it short."

I looked into Seger's dark eyes and sensed his genuine concern. "My mother-in-law originally promised she'd help with the legal expenses so we could make Kiano a part of our family."

"But now?"

"Now she's a little upset with us because Joshua won't take over his father's position as senior pastor of their church."

"Oh," Seger said.

"Since Joshua won't give up the idea of starting his own church, she has given up on us."

"I see."

I said it all so matter-of-factly, disgusted with the whole pathetic story myself. "His parents pastor this huge church downtown, and his dad is sick so—"

"Let me guess. The bishop wants his son to take over so he can retire, right?"

"Right," I answered.

"Messy situation," Seger said.

I shook my head, remembering the many disputes we had with Mother Benning over this issue. "Oh, you have no idea."

"What about his other siblings? Any brothers?"

"None. He's an only child."

"How unfortunate for him." Seger shook his head.

"Tell me about it."

Seger chuckled, revealing perfectly white teeth. "That's why we believe in having big families in Africa."

I fluffed my pillow and leaned back from exhaustion. "Keep the women barefoot and pregnant, huh?"

Seger chuckled. "I guess you could say that."

I snickered. "You're beginning to sound like my husband."

"Really?" I can see that Brother Joshua and I have a lot in common." Seger's eyes danced from my head to my toes.

I ignored his last comment. "In any case, that's where we are—nowhere."

"That's too bad."

I felt my eyes filling up with tears. "I don't know how we're going to break it to Kiano."

Seger looked like he was thinking. He scratched his head and focused in on my eyes. "What a shame."

"That's why I was hoping I'd be able to put in more hours or something and help us raise the money we need, but now . . . this."

"Oh, now I see the situation."

"So since I'm on bed rest and can't work anymore at all, there goes my shot at making extra money, or any money, for that matter." I dropped my head as I spoke.

"Sounds like you've been through a lot." Seger moved closer.

I could feel his breath on my face. "I have been, and unfortunately, it's been getting progressively worse."

"Remember that God is able."

"I know that." I waved my hand in the air. "He's the only one I'm holding on to right now."

Seger gently put his hand on mine and squeezed. "I'll be praying for you."

I looked into his kind eyes and was happy God had brought such a good friend into my life. When he leaned over to hug me good-bye, I became drunk with the smell of his cologne.

It was so masculine.

Just then, the door opened and in walked Joshua. "What are you doing here with my wife?"

Chapter Thirty-one

Joshua

After Alex was released from the hospital and I had her settled comfortably at home, I went to Big Willie's Barbershop on Fulton Street to get a haircut. It was a midsized shop with freshly painted blue and red checkered walls. A huge flat-screen television set was mounted on the wall. Men came from all around Brooklyn to get their hair cut, beard shaved, or their shoes shined. Not only would a man leave fresh and clean, but he would leave calmer too. Big Willie knew a lot about life, or at least that's what the local folk thought. He was a nice, older guy. He kind of reminded me of my grandfather.

While I was there, one tall, young man was talking about how his wife had left him for another man.

"Well, she never was really yours, was she?" Big Willie asked the man. "If she was really yours, she'd still be here. Let her go. You can't keep nothing that ain't yours."

I thought about it for a minute. Not exactly my grandmother's wisdom, but not exactly wrong either.

My jaws tightened as I thought about Seger Abasi. Trust was something I had to really work on and lately, it was wearing thin. Why was he so interested in my wife? Alex claimed he was friendly to everyone, but I still believed I saw something more in his eyes when it came to her. I couldn't stop thinking about his hands on my woman that day at the hospital.

Yes, I asked him to leave, and yes, I slammed the door in his face, but what was I supposed to do?

Was I supposed to ask him to stay and continue to push up on my woman? I didn't hate the brother, but I didn't want him to touch my family, not Alex or Kiano, or anything that was mine. I didn't trust that situation at all.

The last time I trusted a woman with my whole heart, she had destroyed it. I mean, she had wrapped me around her sneaky little finger, and then set me on fire. Delilah played me just like the Delilah in the Bible played Samson. What a fool I was the first time around.

I remembered the day the hospital called me to say Delilah had died on the operating table, trying to abort our child. And probably all for the sake of ambition, to save that miserable career of hers. It was hard to believe she loved her career more than me. Yes, it was the worst day of my life. Not only was she gone, but she had taken my unborn child with her, the one I never even knew about. I didn't know how to react or how to feel. It hurt more than anything, but how was a real man supposed to feel when my whole life had been stolen from me? Was I supposed to feel angry or suicidal? I didn't know. I couldn't talk. I couldn't cry. I couldn't read.

There were no books on it that I knew of. Sure, there were books on grief, but this grief was different because it was mixed with rage.

And how was I to tell my judgmental mother that the woman she had warned me about on several occasions not to get myself involved with had died and taken her second grandchild with her to the grave? "Was the child even yours, Joshua?" Mother had said, and

I cried out even more, even as I cursed the possibility. Had Delilah wanted to get rid of the child because it wasn't mine? I didn't know which thought was worse, but I knew she had taken the truth with her to the grave. I used to wonder if I'd ever get over it, if I'd ever trust a woman again.

I blinked away the memory as I sat in Big Willie's chair and listened.

I didn't have all the answers, but I knew I loved Alex. God blessed me with her, and even though I didn't want Seger anywhere near her at all, I wasn't willing to lose her.

When I arrived home, Alex met me at the door. She didn't look happy to see me, but she looked relieved.

"I'm sorry, so sorry about arguing with you," I said.

"I'm sorry too," Alex sighed.

Then I said all the things I imagined my wife would want to hear. I kissed her and caressed her. "I promise that things will get better."

She took me in her arms. "I know."

"I'm going to give you the life you deserve." I put my head against her breasts. "I'm sorry."

"It's okay," she said, but her body seemed limp, and so did her spirit.

I was grateful that I hadn't lost her. Yet I wondered what exactly I'd have to do to keep her, and as I looked into her vacant eyes, I wondered if it was already too late to try.

Chapter Thirty-two

Alex

After two weeks of unbearable tests, I was released from the hospital and put on bed rest.

I woke up smelling sausage and biscuits that Joshua made for everyone. It entered my nostrils and called me to the kitchen. There, the three of us ate a delicious meal before Joshua prepared to go off to work.

I sighed because it was another day at home on bed rest for me, and I didn't like it, not one bit. There was too much I wanted to do. I logged on to my laptop, working out all the plans for the ministry. At Joshua's insistence, Lilah left with him to go to Mrs. Johnson next door. She would stay there at least until after lunch. Then Mrs. Johnson would walk Lilah back across the hall. She would also deliver a freshly cooked meal no matter how many times I told her she didn't have too. Sweet Mrs. Johnson, complete in her long skirts and a wrapped-up head, belonged to that holiness church up the street. No pressed hair or makeup. Just plain old pale skin and a short, nappy 'fro. She seemed happy though, for whatever that was worth, at least happy enough since she'd put out lying and cheating Mr. Johnson.

After Joshua had gone, I began to put together the program for Young Women's Giving Life Ministry, incorporating all the areas I was concerned with: pregnancy, nonabortion options, prenatal care, counseling, postabortion counseling, childcare classes, workplace etiquette, abstinence, the dynamics of Christian dating, and women's health. The issues just kept flowing, and I was anxious to address each one of them. We were meeting once a month now, but I wanted to step it up to meeting on a weekly basis. Yes, I had a lot on my plate, but all of these workshops were needed. How could I possibly abandon my girls just because I had a little setback in my personal life? That was definitely not me. Give, give, and give some more. *That* was me.

So I pulled myself together and tried to stay as busy as possible, typing, calling, and planning for the ministry. Mrs. Johnson brought Lilah home on schedule, but minutes later, the doorbell rang again. I put my slippers back on and slowly shuffled to the door.

"Just a minute. I'm coming," I called out before opening the door.

It was Taylor. "Hey, girl. Let me in. It's burning up out here."

"Okay, okay. Come in. How are you?" I reached my arms around my sister.

"Hi, Ms. Taylor," Lilah said.

"Hi, kid. How are ya?"

"I'm good," Lilah said, skipping around the couch.

"She's just getting home from Ms. Johnson's," I told Taylor.

"Oh, I see." Taylor took off her coat. "How was your day, sweetheart?"

Lilah picked up her doll. "It was okay."

"I know. Why don't we all play a game?" I reached into the hall closet and pulled out the Uno cards.

Taylor pointed to herself as if my suggestion was a joke, then she gave in and said, "Sure, why not?"

The three of us played six rounds of Uno. It reminded me of my childhood and how Taylor and I would play games with our mother. I couldn't wait for Taylor to marry Keith and have kids. Then we'd really be a unit.

Afterward, I took Lilah to her room to watch *Dora* and led Taylor into the kitchen so I could start my stew. I began to cut up potatoes, carrots, and onions. "I've got to get this dinner started."

"Aren't you supposed to stay off of your feet as much as possible? Why are you cooking?" Taylor questioned.

"It's not that serious. I'm only throwing a few things into a pot with this beef. Then I'll sit down."

"Okay, but you look like a hot mess."

"Well, thanks a lot, diva." I thought about the fact that I was still in my pajamas, had just taken off my head scarf, and that I hadn't used any kind of skin cream in a couple of days.

"I'm just sayin', fix yourself up a little or something." Taylor started adjusting the collar on my robe. "If I had known, I could've brought my stuff and given you a make-over."

I slapped her hand away. "Oh, do I look that bad?"

Taylor put her hand in my uncombed hair and frowned. "You ain't looking good, if that's what you're asking."

I took a playful swing at her, and she ducked. "How can I look good, or even care, when it feels like I'm living in hell?"

"Well, you sure don't look like you're living in heaven, that's for sure." Taylor shook her head. "What's going on now?"

"It's Joshua. I just don't know what's happening with our relationship."

"Come on. It can't be so bad. You two are still newly-weds, really."

"Well, it doesn't feel like it. Feels like we've been married forever."

"Now that ain't a good sign."

"I just don't know. He's been so unapproachable lately. First, it was the fertility issue, and now that I'm pregnant, things are no better. I mean, were there warning signs before? Did I miss something?"

Taylor shook her head. "Nah, sweetie. You just did the unthinkable."

"And what's that?"

"You fell in love and got married." Taylor laughed uncontrollably. "Can't say I didn't warn you, but he's all yours now."

"I know, and I do love him. I just pray that things will change."

"I'm praying for you too."

Taylor stayed for half an hour longer, and then she called a cab to take her back to the gym. Push It Fitness Center was solace for Taylor, and I was glad she had something to keep her mind off her legs.

I continued to dice carrots and onions until I put them all into the pot to let them simmer.

After noticing the time, I also put a kettle of water on for Joshua's tea. It was so hot though, I really should've made iced tea instead. I had to hurry because I wanted everything to be ready when he came home. I really hoped he wouldn't come home moody like he had been lately. I hoped he was ready to talk, or at least ready to embrace me—like he had at the beginning of our marriage, not the way he did since we've been on this fertility ride.

My doorbell rang again, and I answered it, thinking that maybe Taylor was back for some reason. When I swung the door open wide, there was Seger looking down at me. I was a little hesitant to let him in, but I let my courteous nature overrule my good sense.

"Hello," Seger said.

"Oh, hi, Seger." I stood back and let him walk inside. Once he was in, I blocked him from going any further.

As if he sensed my hesitation he said, "I'll only be here for a minute."

"You didn't have to come all the way down here to—"

"Actually, I had some business to take care of downtown so . . ."

"You know I'd like to apologize again for by husband's attitude the other day at the hospital. I—"

"Don't. That's not necessary." Seger cleared his throat. "I understand. If I had a wife as beautiful as you, I'd be looking out too."

I paused. "It was very embarrassing."

"Don't worry about it," Seger said. "Listen, I don't mean to bother you, but I was thinking about your situation, and I think I may have a resolution."

"Really?" I was both curious and nervous at the same time about him being here. If Joshua knew Seger was anywhere near his house, he'd be upset.

"Yes."

"Well, don't tease me with it." I smirked at the thought that Seger might have an answer to my problems. "What is it?"

At that point, Seger walked past me and sat down in one of our leather armchairs. "I can give you the money you need."

"Oh no. We couldn't do that. We wouldn't," I said.

"Okay, then, a loan, perhaps?" Seger handed me an envelope. "Here is a formal proposal."

"You're very generous, but that's a lot of money, and besides, Joshua wouldn't like it."

"Talk to him about it and see. If he really wants to adopt Kiano, and that's the priority, then the rest shouldn't matter."

"It shouldn't, but it does." I sat on the arm on the couch facing him, nervously swinging my leg back and forth.

"Maybe he'll at least consider it." Seger leaned forward.

"Maybe, but I seriously doubt it," I said.

"Oh, don't doubt, my sister." Seger smiled. "You've got to have faith in order for it to come to pass."

"Look, I know that but—" I hopped up and walked over beside him as if I were ready to lead him to the door. "I don't think it's a good idea that you're even here right now, so thanks for the offer, but you've got to go."

Right on cue, he stood up and walked to the front of the room. "Your husband is a businessman. He can look at this as a business deal if he wants."

Seger sounded very convincing, even though I was almost positive that my husband wouldn't go for it. Maybe if he didn't already dislike Seger the outcome would be different.

"Well . . ."

"We can have contracts drawn up, and it can all be very official and professional," Seger said.

There was no need to hurt his feelings. "I don't know, Seger, but thanks again for the offer. It was sweet."

Seger stared at me. "You're welcome."

"No, really. I appreciate it." I touched his arm in a sisterly way and smiled.

"I just want Kiano to have the parents he deserves," Seger said.

Parents. That was such a big word. I thought about mine and how carelessly they raised me. How my father was not there for me much of the time. But I turned out okay, I guess. But really, what kind of parents did anyone deserve? The ones that would love them, take care of them, support them, and that teaches them about God. The list went on and on. I knew that Joshua and I had a lot of love to give despite our shortcomings. I just hoped that love was enough.

"Thanks again." I sighed, realizing Joshua would soon be coming home. "You really need to go now."

Seger walked slowly toward the door, and then turned to me. "Of course. Take care of yourself."

By this time I was holding the door open and ready to practically push him out of it. "You too."

"And don't forget to run this idea by your husband."

Again, I thought about what he was offering. "I don't think Joshua will like it."

At that same moment I looked up and saw Joshua standing in the doorway. "Joshua won't like what?"

Chapter Thirty-three

Alex

Okay, so it was official. Joshua and I were on serious cease and desist. By the time I finished explaining to him about Seger's offer, he was livid. Couldn't he understand how important Kiano's adoption was to me and that Seger was just trying to be helpful?

Joshua was pacing across the hardwood floors in our living room as I sat on the couch.

"First, you're out there working too hard, trying to help everyone. I mean, you knew this pregnancy was high risk from the beginning, but you insisted on continuing with these projects."

"What projects? It's one project, and that's the Young Women's Giving Life Ministry. You know how important that is to me."

"What about me? Aren't I important to you?"

"That's a stupid question, Josh."

"You're out there trying to help everybody else. You've got to slow down and help us, okay?" He stopped and turned to face me.

"I'm sorry." I avoided his eyes.

Joshua looked solemn. "I don't want to lose you or this baby."

"I'm sorry," I said.

"I don't know what I'd do if—" he snapped back. "You can't be sneaking around behind my back, making adoption plans and undermining my authority by talking to people like Seger about our marital problems."

"First of all, I'm not sneaking and doing anything. Not like you were sneaking around with Yvonne planning to meet with a surrogate mother. Second, I'm not trying to undermine you in anyway. And third, Kiano is not a marital problem."

"But it is our problem, and it's none of anyone's business. I don't need some African missionary—"

"Now, that's not nice at all. I'm disappointed in you." I couldn't believe he said that. Was he that insecure that he would resort to using ethnic slurs in order to tear down Seger? Was this *really* the man I married?

"I'm sorry, but I'm disappointed too—ever since you started this campaign against me."

"What do you mean against you?"

"You know I'm working as hard as I can to secure our future, yet you're out whispering about it behind my back, telling everyone how broke we are."

"What? Now you *know* that's not true." I put both hands on my hips. "Besides, we're not broke."

"That's how you make me feel, though. All I need now is your father on my back too."

"My father? Hold up, wait a minute. What does he have to do with this?"

"That would just seal it," Joshua said.

"Seal what?"

"Oh, come on, admit it. You know he never liked me anyway."

"That's not true." I didn't want to hear all of this.

"You know it is. I was never good enough for his precious daughter."

"It's not that." I wanted to throw out something mean. "He just doesn't like the way your family treats people, and me in particular."

There was a lot of bad blood between the Bennings and my father. He never did like their snobbish ways. When he found out that Mother Benning had hired a private investigator in order to discredit me to Joshua before we were married, that was it for him. My father told me, for the record, that God Almighty Himself would have to come down before he fooled with the likes of them again. Now my father was stubborn so I knew not to press for any family get-togethers or anything like that any time soon. Still, I hoped he'd calm down eventually, and that this new grandbaby would help to bring us all together.

"Well, I do apologize for their behavior," Joshua admitted. "They are too much sometimes."

"I apologize too," I said.

Joshua's forehead wrinkled up. "I just don't want my business out in the streets."

I softened. "I'm sorry, Joshua. That was never my intention."

"And that Seger person . . ."

"Seger is a nice guy, and he's just a friend. You know that."

Joshua's voice was unstable. "I don't know what I know anymore. I see the way he looks at you."

"Looks at me *what* way?"

Joshua's jaws tightened. "Like he wishes you two were more than just friends."

For a moment I had a flashback of Seger and me in Kenya, the time before Joshua came to claim me. He had been so compassionate with the children and generous with his advice about relationships. A devout missionary, he had shared more than his time, but also his heart with me.

It had seemed that he had a slight interest in me initially, but he had said nothing since he knew I was engaged again, and had certainly done nothing since I had been married.

Certainly nothing out of line since I was a married woman.

"Oh, come on. Seger is just friendly like that with everybody." I waved him away with my hand. "You're overreacting . . . again."

"I'm not."

"You're jealous." I came up behind Joshua and put my arms around his waist.

"I'm not." Joshua peeled my hands off of him and turned around to face me. He held my wrists tightly. "I'm just protecting my investment."

"*Investment?*" I jerked away from his grasp. "Mr. Banker, I'm *not* a piece of property."

Joshua let go of me, and I stumbled backward a little. "No, but you are my wife—or have you forgotten that?"

Chapter Thirty-four

Joshua

It's funny that my dad told me not to ever marry a hardheaded woman, that I'd have trouble for the rest of my days if I did. I wondered why he never listened to his own advice. Of course, hardheaded was only the half of it when it came to describing my mom. But this wasn't about Mom. This was about me and my wife. Why couldn't she just be the wife and mother she was supposed to be? And just be happy with that? Why did I keep getting mixed up with these women who wanted more? No matter how many times I tried, I couldn't get past the fact that Alex was disrespecting me. I mean, what did I have to do to be treated like a man?

Wasn't a husband who loved his wife and worked hard enough for women anymore?

I didn't even know. I hardly felt like a man of God, even though I knew I still was. *Lord, help me to be the man you designed me to be.* The pressure made me feel like I was losing it sometimes. I yelled at my wife. I slammed doors. I had become everything I knew I never wanted to be.

Granted, my parents didn't act like that, so where in the world did I pick this up from?

Then I remembered the summers I spent with my aunt and uncle up in Maine when I was young. Sure, they tried to cover it up, to hide it from me and my cousins. But none of us were blind. We could see auntie's black eyes even under the designer sunglasses. Besides, when our uncle would slip away for a few days where no one could find him, then finally trudge back to the house with roses and jewelry, we knew it wasn't because of love, but because of guilt. I pounded my fist against my hand because I wanted to be a better man than that. Sure, I hadn't hit her or cheated on my wife, but I had hurt her with my actions and even my words. Why was I so angry anyway? So, knowing God, and seeing the direction I was heading, I decided it was time to get outside help.

One call to Pastor Martin's office was all it took. His secretary made the appointment and I knew from that point on he would be willing to help as long as I wanted him to. Pastor Martin was a good man like that. He always took time out of his busy schedule to help the members of his congregation, and not just the members, but also visitors from the community as well. He walked the neighborhood encouraging people to vote. He carried food to those in need.

He went to personally visit the sick and shut-in. He organized soul-winning crusades and was first in line to knock on doors. And on any given day he could be seen cutting the grass in front of the church along with the deacons or fixing a leaky pipe in the church. Yes, he was a hands-on preacher, and I admired him for that.

I sat down in the soft leather chair in front of Pastor Martin. His sense of authority loomed over me before he even began to speak.

"To what do I owe this pleasure, Deacon, uh, excuse me, Minister Joshua?" Pastor Martin extended his hand.

The first time I counseled with him was last year after I had broken off the engagement to Alex. I was so stupid then, getting caught up in Yvonne's web of deception, and then discovering that Alex had been keeping a big secret from me. Imagine my surprise when I found out that my fiancée was hiding the fact that she'd had an abortion years ago. The same fiancée that listened to me bare my soul about my deceased wife and how she died butchering our own child. Yet, Alex never said a word about her own experience. I must admit that was a hard one to swallow, especially given all the trust issues I was dealing with. I got over it, though.

This visit was a little different. This time, my whole life was at stake. I smiled and shook his hand. "Pastor, there have been a lot of things on my mind lately."

"Things like what?"

"Sir, I've been keeping some things from my wife."

"Oh, is that all? Well, that's easily resolved. Just sit down with her and tell her what's on your mind."

"With all due respect, sir, how can I tell Alex what is eating me up inside?" I leaned forward in the chair and put my hands on his desk. "How can I get Alex to understand the seriousness of the financial hole Delilah, my deceased wife, put me in? I mean, she knows about the bills, but she just doesn't understand. She doesn't know what it's like for me to have promised to take care of her, and yet, we're barely getting by."

"So you have financial issues?" Pastor Martin leaned back in his chair. "Did something change?"

"Excuse me?"

Pastor Martin rubbed his forehead. "You didn't get a pay cut or lose your job, did you?"

"No, sir, nothing like that. It's just that we do have considerably more expenses."

"More expenses? Enlighten me."

"Like we had been seeing a fertility specialist before my wife became pregnant."

"A specialist. How did that come about?"

I remembered the day Brother and Sister Jameson told us about Dr. Henley, how he had helped them through their infertility issues. This conversation took place right after we were married, just as we had started trying. I listened carefully to the details, not because I expected Alex and me to have problems conceiving, but because the Jamesons were cool people, and I was really happy for them. The whole church knew they were trying to have a baby for years, so when it finally happened for them, it was no secret. It was a celebration.

"He was recommended by friends of ours when we weren't able to conceive on our own."

"Really? And who told you that lie?" Pastor Martin didn't play around. He said what he meant, and he meant what he said.

"Excuse me, sir?"

"Who told you that you couldn't conceive on your own?" Pastor Martin looked straight at me and hardly blinked.

"Well, no one, sir."

"I mean, you and Sister Alex are fairly young, and you haven't been married that long, so I don't understand the need to bring in a specialist."

"We wanted to start a family right away."

"I see."

"Anyway, it was very expensive." I loosened my collar.

"I can imagine."

I took a deep breath. "Then there are all these credit card bills in my name, as well as some joint accounts from my deceased wife."

"So does Alex know about these bills?" Pastor Martin pulled out a pair of glasses from his desk and put them on.

"Yes, she knows some of it. My first wife, Delilah, was something else. She believed in having all the finer things in life at whatever cost. Alex knows that, but she doesn't know how hard it is for me."

"I see."

"I don't like to talk about the details, but Alex knows the woman basically sucked me dry."

Dry was only the half of it. Delilah was like a barracuda when it came to getting what she wanted. I only wished I hadn't been such a weakling when she was alive and playing me.

"Okay," Pastor Martin said.

"Then with my tuition expenses, and money for the new baby . . ."

Pastor Martin pulled his glasses down on his nose. "Tell me about this new baby."

"Like I said before, we wanted a child right away."

"That much is obvious if you were seeing a fertility specialist, but you already have a daughter. And you never explained the reason for the rush."

"Well, to be honest, Pastor, ever since I lost Delilah and the child she was carrying, I've felt empty."

"Have you grieved the loss of your first family, Joshua?"

"I have, sir," I answered.

"It seems to me that you may be trying to replace that child that was lost by quickly having another one—a life for a life."

"I never looked at it that way before. I tried not to really look at it at all. Every time I did, it cut me to the core."

"That happens frequently with parents who lose children." Pastor Martin started plundering in his desk drawer. "How does Alex feel about it?"

"She used to think I was pressuring her, and we had a lot of problems because of it, but she's pregnant now so . . ."

"So the baby is not necessarily a problem?"

"No, the biggest problem is that I just don't know how to tell her that I feel like I'm drowning in debt when I promised to take care of her."

Pastor Martin looked directly into my eyes. "So you feel guilty?"

"I feel like I'm letting her down. Before we got married I told her she didn't even have to work. I wasn't even happy when she wanted to work part-time because I wanted her to be home with Lilah."

"And you wanted another child also?"

"Yes, I wanted another child also. Now, with everything that's going on at home and at work . . . I just don't know, Pastor," I said.

"What's going on at work?"

I remembered the missing money I'd discovered. I definitely didn't want to get into that right now, especially since I was probably worried about nothing. "Nothing important, just work-related stress."

"Sit down with your wife and talk to her. Sister Alex is a sweet woman. I'm sure she's not unapproachable."

"It's not just that, but we have a child in Kenya also waiting for us to adopt him."

Pastor Martin opened his mouth wide. "Another child?"

"Yes, we kind of promised the child, but that was before everything else went wrong."

"So there have been a lot of broken promises?" Pastor Martin shook his head.

I knew deep inside that this was probably the biggest issue with my wife. I promised her.

I promised her. She kept saying that over and over again. Didn't she know that sometimes things change? If she had been in the room she'd say that I should've kept my promise to her no matter what. Sure, my intentions were good, but it was other unavoidable circumstances that were messing up the promise. Not me. It wasn't my fault. Still, I felt like it was.

"Not intentionally, but yes, there has been a lot of stress on the financial end."

"Mmm, that's been a big problem these days with the recession and all."

"But what do I do, Pastor?"

"Well, Brother Joshua, may I suggest that you pray and consider your priorities. What is the most important thing first and foremost? Then go down the list as far as what needs to be done now and what may have to be postponed or cancelled altogether."

I thought about the obvious and knew Alex wasn't going to like it at all. "Right."

"I know you've made these plans in your mind, but what is God's will? What does God want you to do? A righteous man's steps are ordered by the Lord." Pastor Martin pulled his beard. "I don't think you need me to tell you that."

"No, you're right. I've got to pray for guidance concerning this matter. I've got to seek God's face because right now, sir, I'm a little lost."

"At least you're enough of a man to admit that you feel that way. Remember, son, you might feel lost, but His sheep hear His voice."

Chapter Thirty-five

Alex

By September I was in my seventh month of pregnancy. Our one-year wedding anniversary was fast ap-
proaching, and Joshua's dad seemed to be getting worse.
His mom had already hired a temporary replacement for
her husband, an interim pastor, a middle-aged minister
from one of their sister churches, Minister Ezekiel. Yet,
Mother Benning began sending little reminder notes
about her proposal to Joshua weekly. She would remind
him that he was her only son, that stepping up to pastor
their church was his responsibility, that she and his sickly
father were depending on him. Some of the notes were
pushed under the door of our apartment, some were left
at his office, some came by mail, and others came by e-
mail. They all said the same thing. "Your father is very ill.
What would Jesus do?"

The woman was absolutely relentless, and I could
tell that she was wearing Joshua's resistance down. He
looked weary. Sometimes he would stop by Kingdom
House Church to assist his mother with whatever she
needed, yet she still wasn't satisfied. She wanted more.
It was as if she wanted his soul.

I wanted to assure him that everything would be all
right, that his mother would forgive him, and that his
father would recover, but I wasn't sure I was the right

one to be giving guarantees. I knew a miracle was possible, but I didn't know if it was God's will.

In fact, whenever we visited his dad, he appeared to be getting weaker. Sometimes the chemo left him nauseated and incoherent.

One afternoon I went to the hospital by myself while Joshua was working. Pastor Benning seemed more alert than usual. He sat up high in the bed, with his back propped against numerous pillows, and his eyes were bright. Some of his color had returned to his pale skin, and his voice quivered less than it usually had.

"Joshua caught a good one when he married you, Sister Alex," Pastor Benning said.

"Thanks, Pastor Benning. Too bad your wife doesn't think so."

"My wife can be difficult sometimes. Don't worry about her. She'll come around eventually." He smiled, and I could easily see that his kind demeanor was in his son.

"I hope you're right."

"My wife is a very stubborn woman, but she's not stupid. Sooner or later, she'll realize that you're good for Josh."

"Please help Joshua to understand. He puts his mother on such a pedestal. She's only human, you know." *Got that right.* I had to really bite my tongue on that one.

"You know, you and Joshua have got to really understand each other."

"Yes, sir," I said.

"And you've got to sacrifice one for the other." He grunted in pain for a minute. "I know you all think you can put it over on us older folk, but the truth of the matter is that you can't. Sometimes you have to be willing to give up something for your true love."

"Oh, I do love Joshua. Don't worry," I said.

"Ah, I've got you this time," Pastor Benning chuckled. "He's not the true love I'm talking about."

What haven't I given up for the Lord? I wondered. That question kept running through my mind for the rest of the day. Is there a sacrifice I've been unwilling to make? I mean, I did my daily Bible reading. I decided to put the thought away until another time. I already had so much rattling through my brain.

On Sunday, I was feeling so badly that I couldn't even go to church. I stayed bent under the covers, sweating and trying to keep myself from throwing up everywhere. Joshua and Lilah went without me. Joshua was dressed in his three-piece suit, complete with Stacy Adams shoes.

Lilah wore her lilac and white striped satin dress with matching ribbons and black patent leather shoes. Joshua kissed me on the lips. Lilah hugged me. I hugged her back, hard, hoping she would respond to my maternal nature.

I tried to bond with her every opportunity I could, and we had made some progress, just not as much as I had hoped. Yes, I tried time and time again. Each day there was just a string of monotonous mommy duties and disappointments, with none of the mommy rewards.

"Good night, sweetheart," I'd say, holding her so tightly, smelling the fresh lemon scented detergent I used on her clothes and breathing in the sweet lavender-scented lotion I used on her skin. I wanted her to feel my love. I wanted her to feel a part of me.

Still she'd say, "Good night, Daddy. Good night, Sister Alex."

Sometimes, when reprimanded, she'd say "Mother Alex," but it just wasn't the same.

"Give it time," Joshua said as we settled into our own plush bed at night.

When Mother Benning came to pick up Lilah, she only aggravated the situation. "Come on, baby, come and kiss your big mommy," she'd say.

It would annoy me, but there was nothing I could do about it, except to pray. I was the only one in the family who felt like an outsider. I really hoped this baby I was carrying would change things. I thought that maybe then I'd truly be Mommy.

In any case, I didn't make it any easier when I almost lost Lilah at the mall. We were walking through the various stores, looking at both baby and household items. I held her hand tightly as we sped through each floor of the building. We even stopped to have chili cheese dogs and orange soda in the food court. Afterward, I had heartburn but kept on moving until I came upon a new baby store. It was nothing like I had seen in the mall before. They had very old-fashioned styles like lace dresses for girls and knickers for boys hanging in the window.

Since that suited my taste, I went in. That's when everything went wrong.

Somewhere between the racks of baby clothes, stacks of blankets, and the cash register, I lost sight of Lilah. Of course, I didn't realize it at the time. She had been twirling around the clothing carousels and having big fun at my expense the whole time. It was only at the cash register when I reached down into my purse for my wallet that I noticed she wasn't standing beside me. In fact, as I looked around and behind me, she was nowhere to be found. That's when panic set in. I jumped out of the line, yelling Lilah's name. There was no answer, but there were many solemn looks as people began to realize that my child was missing. I searched the small store with no success.

"Lord, please help me," I prayed. Then I left the store looking around, bumping into people, and apologizing along the way. I almost knocked over an older gentleman with a cane.

Frantically, I searched the entire area in front of the store until I was out of breath. I didn't know where she could've been, but the growing pit on the inside of my stomach didn't make things any better. Just as I was about to notify security and call the police, I spotted her in a crowd across the way. She was peeking in at a puppy in a pet shop window.

"Lilah," I cried out.

"Come and see." She grinned her biggest grin, which let me know that she didn't even realize she was lost.

I ran over and grabbed her up into my arms.

"Isn't he cute?" Lilah said, pointing to the cocker spaniel.

Personally, I never cared for pets, but he was cute. And I was relieved.

"Don't you ever scare me like that again, do you hear me, little girl?" I gently shook her, and then pulled her into my chest. Tears filled my eyes as I imagined the worst that could've happened. *Thank you, Lord, for your divine protection.*

Later on that evening after Lilah had gone to bed, I told Joshua what happened.

He gasped. "How could you have been so careless?"

"*Excuse me.* I *told* you it was an accident."

"Yes, but a dangerous one."

"You act like I told you that I left her on purpose. I just turned my head for one second while I made my purchase."

"I don't care. There was nothing you could have purchased in that store that could possibly be as important as my child's life."

"Of course not. No one said it was. I just said that's what I was there for. I was shopping, and it happened. She must've wandered away when I dropped her hand to take out my wallet."

Joshua sounded so stern. "Obviously."

"Why are you being so mean? I said I was sorry and that it was an accident."

"We can't afford accidents like that, not ones that could cost my child her life."

"Oh, so now she's *your* child. I thought she was *our* child," I said.

"Well, after today, can you blame me? It was a very irresponsible move, losing a four-year-old in the mall."

"What are you saying? I've taken care of Lilah every single day for the past how many months, without any issues, and the one day that I make a mistake, you won't let it go?"

"*Let it go?* I can't just let it go." Joshua talked with his hands. "That's *my* daughter we're talking about."

"There you go again with *your* daughter. She's *our* daughter. In the morning when I'm making her breakfast, she's *our* daughter. All day long when I'm doing what I do, she's *our* daughter. When I'm bathing her, dressing her, or tucking her in at night, she's always *our* daughter. So why in the world, Joshua, would she suddenly become *your* daughter?"

"I'm sorry. I didn't mean it like that," he said in a low voice, reaching out for me.

"Yeah, right." I pulled away from his reach.

"You know she's our daughter," Joshua said.

"Uh-huh." Now I was offended.

"Come on, now. You just scared me, that's all."

"Right." I sat with my arms folded tightly.

Joshua sat on the couch next to me. "Come on. I'm sorry; I know it wasn't your fault."

"Are you sure?" I was ready to go off on a brother, even though that was more of my sister's style than mine. "Because I can explain again and hold my own."

"No, I just love you and Lilah so much. I don't want anything to happen to either of you."

Joshua held me tightly against his chest. I didn't move, wondering what his tune would have been if Lilah hadn't been found.

Chapter Thirty-six

Alex

The Push It Fitness Center had always been an awesome gym, but ever since Taylor and Keith had purchased it, it was becoming even better. Besides state-of-the-art equipment, the center was now filled with African artistry. There was a glass showcase of shells, pottery, and figurines. Then there were the big prints on the walls, none of them original, but breathtaking just the same. Fresh paint covered most of the walls. The renovations were almost done.

I could tell that Taylor had pushed herself harder than ever, working out until her hair and face were dripping with sweat.

She looked over at me. "How are things going with Joshua now that you're having his baby?"

I smirked at her sarcasm. "Why, Taylor?"

"All right, I'm sorry. But you've got to admit your husband has been tripping for a while now." She shook her head.

"He's the same Joshua," I said, looking down.

Taylor smirked. "Yep. Uptight."

"He is not." I looked up and smiled. "But he is happy about the baby."

"I'm just playing. You've got a good one, I'll give you that."

Now was the time to ask her. "So do you, and by the way, how is Keith?"

"He's good." Taylor avoided eye contact at this point.

"If he's so good, when are you going to marry him?"

"I don't know." She threw one of her hands up. "Maybe never."

"Never? What's the point of being engaged if you're never going to get married?"

"I ain't so sure I wanna marry him anymore." Taylor put her hands over her face. "I'm thinking about giving him back his ring."

I pushed my head back. "Whoa. Giving back expensive jewelry. Now I know you're serious."

"I'm not playin'." Taylor didn't blink.

"I see."

She turned away from me. "I just ain't sure he's the one for me."

I shook my head. "Oh, you've got to come up with something better than that. I haven't met two people who are better suited for each other than you two."

Indeed this was true. Ever since she had met Keith, they had been a positive influence on each other. He helped her through the very excruciating physical and emotional pain she endured as a result of her accident. He also led her lovingly to the Lord. She, on the other hand, helped to renew his faith in miracles and challenged him to commit to a home church when he had become weary. Then, to top it all off, he invested in her dream to buy The Push It Fitness Center, and became her business partner. With Taylor as a physical trainer and Keith as a physical therapist, they had pushed each other to the brink and back again. There was no doubt in my mind that they belonged together.

"Well, maybe I'm just not with this whole marriage thing. Remember, that's *your* thing, not mine." Taylor turned to me and frowned up her face.

"Oh, please. Spare me the drama. A couple of months ago you were as excited about marrying Keith as he is about marrying you." I walked up close to her and got in her face. "Now what happened?"

"I don't know." She turned her back to me again.

"You don't know? I don't believe that. I hope this isn't about that little silly promise you made about having to walk down the aisle."

"It ain't silly. It's what I want."

"I know that. But if you've got a great man waiting for you at the altar, then what difference does it make how you get there?" I tilted my head to the side for emphasis. "Walk, run, hop, slide, or crawl, but get there and get your man."

"That's easy for you to say. You can use both your legs. I thought I would've been healed by now." When Taylor turned around I could see the sadness in her eyes.

"I'm sorry, Taylor."

Tears began to run down her cheeks. "Who would have thought that after one car wreck I'd lose everything."

"You haven't lost everything." I started counting her blessings on my fingers. "You still have your life, your family, your faith, and now you have Keith."

"I thought I would've been back to normal by now," Taylor yelled out. "After I started having feeling again in my legs, I just *knew* I was going to walk on my own."

"But look how far you've come—from paralysis to being able to get around on your own.

That's quite an accomplishment." I knew how important it was to be supportive.

Taylor dried her eyes with her sleeve. "It's nothing."

"It's a big something. Don't give up faith. The scripture says by His stripes we are healed."

"Yeah, yeah. Please don't go throwing scriptures at me, Mrs. Preacher's Wife."

"I've been giving you scriptures long before I ever met Joshua."

"Yeah, that's true. You were getting on my nerves then, and you're on my nerves now."

"Just marry the man, all right? I promise you it'll be okay."

"I told you already that I'll marry him when I can *walk* down the aisle *to* him."

"When are you going to give up this ridiculous idea of walking again before you get married? God is a healer and all, but you can't put time limits on God's work."

"You don't understand, I ain't never wanted nothing more than to walk down the aisle to Keith. He's the only one I ever dreamed about marrying at all," she sniffled.

"I know that but—"

Taylor's face looked like she was in deep pain. "No, you don't understand. It was never easy for me to give my heart away. I may look like you, but I'm not like you. Marriage ain't never meant that much to me."

"But you love Keith. I know you do," I pleaded.

Taylor squeezed her eyes shut. "But I don't want to be no cripple, having people feeling all sorry for me on my wedding day. That's just too much."

"Oh, Taylor."

"I want to be whole, not rolling in a wheelchair or on crutches, or a walker—just my own cute little toes in a cool pair of sling backs or something. Why can't everybody just understand that? I mean, God didn't create me with wheels, so why should I have them now?"

I looked at my very determined sister who wasn't ready to be pushed, pulled, or prodded down the aisle, not for anyone, not even for her fiancé. "I think you're just being stubborn and unreasonable."

That was always Taylor's dilemma. She was relentless even when she was wrong. It was that kind of bona fide hardheadedness that had contributed to her accident in the first place. She had no business out clubbing with that guy, and then letting him drive her home while he was drunk. The memory of her twisted-up body in the hospital was too much for me. I hoped that this time she would listen before she got herself into more trouble.

"My wedding means too much to me. It's a once-in-a-lifetime thing, 'cause I know if things with Keith don't work out, I'll never fall into this trap again." Taylor turned her back to me. "I won't even try."

"Come on, you can't be serious."

"I am, and I won't marry him unless I can walk down the aisle on my own two legs."

When Taylor first accepted Keith's proposal and told him under what conditions she'd marry him, I thought it was cute, but not anymore. "Keith is a great guy, and you're making him wait indefinitely."

"So?"

"So it's not fair." I walked over to face her. "It's almost like you're punishing him for loving you."

"Don't you think I know that? I owe it to him. Keith is more than just some dude. He's the best physical therapist around, and he's also my business partner, and next to you, he's my best friend. I was blessed to meet him right after the accident." Taylor looked me straight in the eyes. "I still remember not being able to feel anything below my waist. I thought I'd die."

"But God didn't let you die."

"But that junk was scary, even though everybody was praying."

I burst out into laughter. "That's because your heathen self didn't believe in prayer back then."

"Of course not. How could I have? Don't you remember Mama died with everyone praying. You don't know what it's like to be paralyzed, especially if you're like me, into fitness and stuff."

I didn't feel like hearing it again. "I know. It was a nightmare."

Taylor began to wipe the tears that were again running down her face. "I didn't want anything to do with Keith at first."

"I remember. Poor guy was so nice and sweet, and you were so . . . uh . . . difficult."

Taylor wiped her face with her sleeve. "I figured if my life was over, then there was no sense in making the pain worse. Shoot, I never knew he'd actually help me, help my pain, my mind . . ."

"And your heart," I added.

"Next thing I knew, we were good friends, even though he was one of those born-again types I didn't trust at all back then." Taylor picked up one of her leg braces. "He helped me to not feel so helpless, and then he stuck by me when I wasn't strong."

"Yep, he did." I nodded my head in agreement.

Taylor poked out her bottom lip. "Even when I had a stank attitude."

"Girl, your attitude was *worse* than stank," I laughed.

"You know I didn't care too much for men back then," Taylor smiled.

I jumped in. "Look, I know you still had issues with dad being gone and—"

"And Mom too. I mean, she had her problems for a while until she got right. Let's be real."

I had almost forgotten about that. It had been so long ago, I'd almost forgotten how disgusted I was with what my mother had become. I promised myself and Almighty God I'd never be like she was during that time in her life.

It wasn't that Mama didn't love us, but she'd always say, "A woman gets lonely sometimes." Of course, that was just an excuse for the goings-on that happened while my father was away. But man, I always thought she should've waited a little longer for male companionship. Don't get me wrong, Mama never bad-mouthed my father. Nor did she ever bring any man home, but we sure knew she was stepping out with them, whether they were deacons, ministers, or just regular members. Since Mama was the friendly sort, and I guess that's where I get this from, she definitely went out a lot. She must've dated every single, available man at the church or even passing through. That's probably the reason Sister Winifred still looks at me sideways sometimes. See, all the folk knew Mama was still married to Daddy, even though he left and she'd put that wedding ring away and vowed not to speak his name.

It wasn't until Mama became for real Holy Ghost-filled and sanctified that her prayers got through. It's funny that when she stopped stepping out and decided to wait on the Lord, that's when she didn't have to wait very long. Daddy came home to stay.

The sight of Taylor lifting herself from the couch jolted me back to the present.

"But guess what? Keith even helped me with my man-hating issues. Even though he's not a psychiatrist, he's the first guy I ever trusted. Gotta admit I never thought it would happen to me. Unlike you, I was never the romantic type." Taylor smiled. "But I guess love has a way of sneaking up on ya."

Taylor struggled to get to me, using her braces and her walker, and all the strength she had. No matter how strong she tried to be, I still felt so sorry for her.

"You can do it, come on," I said.

"I want to marry Keith—but free of all this mess I've got. I thought God would take it all away." Tears streamed from her eyes as she began to step forward.

"Alex, help me take off the braces. Let me just use the walker."

"But, Taylor, I—"

"Please, Alex . . ."

I helped her to get out of the braces as she propped her body against the wall. Then as soon as she saw me return to my original position, she took off using her own legs, transferring the bulk of her weight on the walker. Then without warning, her legs gave way and she came crashing down.

I watched my sister's strong body curled up in a heap on the floor, fighting back tears of vulnerability. I saw the defeat in her eyes as she struggled to get to her feet, and I knew that there was nothing anyone could do or say to help her. I knew that God would have to do a miracle, not of the legs, but of the soul, in order for Taylor to be whole again.

Chapter Thirty-seven

Alex

I longed for the days when I was working at Missionary Bible Institute. At least there were interesting people to talk to, and there was always Marisol to make me laugh. I missed having someone to talk to during the day. I even missed Seger, even though I didn't dare tell Joshua this. He had a funny way of starting his day at the job by stopping by everyone's desk with a joke for the day, and he'd always liven things up when things got too boring by starting controversial conversations. Marisol loved his corny jokes, but I loved his momentum. He always knew the right thing to say at the right time. He wasn't just an admissions director, he was a day-saver I thought to myself. But there was no need thinking about the job when I was no longer allowed to work. I was just stuck in the house with Lilah and the nicely decorated walls of our modern apartment. Sure, Joshua and Taylor would call to check in on me from time to time, but it wasn't the same. They were both busily working, and I had nothing. There was nothing like face-to-face interaction. Even though I wasn't the most social person in the world, I missed that.

So, against doctor's orders, I left that morning about an hour after Joshua went to work. I crept out of bed, took a fast shower, and pulled on a pair of maternity jeans and a big sweatshirt. Then I walked slowly downstairs to the parking garage and found myself in my carnation-pink Pontiac Sunfire. I drove down to the Push It Center. I was starting to love that place almost as much as Taylor did.

"Hi," I said as I approached my sister.

Taylor reached up from her wheelchair and hugged me. "What are you doing here?"

I twisted my lips. "Wow, I feel *really* appreciated."

"You know what I mean." She looked serious. "You're supposed to be at home and off your feet."

"I'm okay, and I'm not going to be here that long," I said, feeling like a child who had been reprimanded.

I wanted to help Taylor get the center off the ground before the baby came and before I started my graduate courses in the summer. It would be a combination of the new management grand opening and the launch of the young women's ministry workshops.

Since the Push It Fitness Center was a haven for young women, I knew it was a good idea to have the young women's workshops held there. The environment went right along with our commitment to women's health. It was also good for Taylor's business. Emotional fitness and physical fitness; I knew it was a match made in heaven.

Aunt Dorothy and Sister Trudy were already there volunteering, and everyone questioned my presence. I gave the same response as they each gave me the same suspicious look. Even Marisol called to confirm she would be able to lend a hand since she'd be there that evening for her tai chi class anyway. Keith painted and put up the banner. I put my hands on my hips and smiled, knowing we were almost ready to launch the women's ministry in its new location. Then I turned and saw him walk in.

"Seger. What are you doing here?"

Taylor rolled by and whispered, "Stalker."

"I was in the neighborhood. While I was driving by I happened to see your car."

"And you knew it was mine?" I smiled. "Of course, a pink car stands out in Brooklyn."

"Anyway, I just thought I'd stop in for a minute and say hello." Seger tried to give me a hug, but I grabbed his hand and squeezed it instead.

"Oh, well, it's nice to see you." I wondered what made this man so bold. Why was he still stopping by even for a minute when it was clear that his presence was causing unnecessary friction? Joshua was stuck at the bank for the next five hours, so I wasn't worried. But I wished Seger would stop taking chances.

"Is something wrong, Alex?"

"No, not at all. We're just very busy right now finishing up the final details for this project."

"That's great. That's your dream, right?"

"Right." I smiled because Seger was always so understanding and attentive to my needs. I remembered discussing my dream with him when we were in Kenya serving.

"We miss you down at work. In fact, aren't you supposed to be at home in bed now?"

"Actually, yes. I try to get out at least for a couple of hours per week. Nothing strenuous though. Just overseeing," I explained.

"I see."

"I miss you guys too," I giggled. "Marisol keeps me up on all the goings-on of the office."

Seger grinned. "You mean the gossip?"

"I try not to go there, but you know Marisol." I shook my head.

"Yes, I do," Seger nodded. "She's got a mouth on her—"

"Right, that's my girl," I said.

"Anyway it's pretty boring there without you." Seger's eyes seemed to dance with excitement.

I threw my head back and laughed hard. "Now, I don't believe that at all. Not with Marisol, Dr. Harding, Professor Daniels, old what's his name on the harmonica, and—"

"None of them can compare to you." Seger became serious. "You're a lot of fun, Alex."

"Well, thanks, but I won't be coming back to work. It'll be too much for me. Besides, Joshua doesn't want me to work now that I'll have the baby to take care of, so . . ."

"I understand." Seger began to stare into my eyes, making me uncomfortable.

"I'll be turning in my formal letter of resignation to Dr. Harding this week."

"Well, it's our loss." He leaned forward, and I could feel the heat of his breath on my face. "Missionary Bible School will have to make do without you."

"I'm sure you'll all do just fine," I said, taking a step backward.

"Anyway, do you need help with anything before I go?"

"Sure. You can take all these boxes of materials and put them into the storage room for me," I said.

"No problem." He began carrying boxes from the pile.

Before I could catch my breath, my husband walked in, and what would have been a productive and pleasant day immediately turned sour.

Chapter Thirty-eight

Alex

The argument started quietly down at the gym and continued at home. Joshua didn't make a scene because that wasn't his style. He merely pulled me to the side and whispered his opinions about Seger's intentions in my ear. Then we politely said good-bye to everyone and excused ourselves to our own private war.

Lilah had been spending the night with her grandmother so we were alone in the apartment.

"I don't know where to start. I decided I was going to surprise you by coming home for lunch. When I saw that you weren't home, I assumed you were down at the gym."

"You were right, but you should've called," I said.

"Oh? So I could warn you, right? Aren't you supposed to be at home taking care of yourself—resting?"

"Yes." I wasn't looking forward to this interrogation.

"Then why were you down at the gym working?"

"I wasn't really working, just supervising people who were working."

"Oh, I see." Joshua walked back and forth mumbling to himself.

"It's hard to stay away. I'm bored at home, okay?"

"Okay, that brings me to my next point. Why was Seger down at the gym?"

"I told you that he just happened to be in the area, saw my car, which is so easy to spot, and decided to stop in." I frowned up my face so much I could feel the wrinkles in my forehead forming. "He was just trying to help out."

Joshua paced back and forth on the hardwood floors. "I'll bet."

"What is that supposed to mean?"

"I told you before that I don't like the way he looks at you."

I was so tired of this same scenario. "Oh no. Not that mess again."

Joshua hit his fist on the back of the couch. "I know what it means when a man looks at a woman like he looks at you."

"What does it mean, Joshua? I'm surprised you even know. You haven't looked at me in months."

"So is *that* what this is about? I'm not giving you enough attention so you go looking elsewhere?"

"Nobody's looking for attention. I'm minding my own business. I didn't ask Seger to get a job where I work, and I didn't invite him down to the gym." I threw up my hands. "He just came out on his own."

"Right." Joshua's jaws tightened.

"Are you calling me a liar?"

Joshua threw his hands into the air as if he were giving up. "I don't know what to call you anymore."

"Oh, *don't* go there, Joshua Douglas Benning."

"I can't call you my wife because you're not acting like her, so—"

"I'm not acting like your wife? Why, Joshua? Because I'm not like Delilah? Because I can't be her."

"This is *not* about Delilah. This is about *you* and *Seger.*"

"Stop it."

"No, I can't stop it. Seger came down to the center because he wants you."

"As a friend."

Joshua clenched his teeth. "As more than a friend."

"Here we go again," I said.

"Yes, here we go again."

I threw my hands in the air to indicate surrender. "Joshua, what do you want from me?"

"I don't know, but I'm tired of this." Joshua walked away from me.

"Tired of *what?*" I followed him into the bedroom.

"Tired of being last."

"And what do you mean by that?"

Joshua's six foot two inch frame towered over me as I looked into his brown eyes.

"You risk everything for Taylor, everything for the women's ministry, and everything for Seger. There's nothing left for me."

"What do you mean there is nothing left for you? I'm just trying to—"

Joshua's eyes were wild and fiery. "I know. I know—to help. But help *us*. We're dying, Alex. We're dying."

"Joshua." I called out to him, but he didn't answer.

He had already turned his back on me and started toward the door. He reached into the hall closet, pulled his coat on, and left without a word.

I waited up for him until midnight when I started to get really tired, but he never made it home. Then I went to bed and tossed back and forth all night, aggravated and unable to pray.

He did call me the next morning and told me he was coming by to pick up a few things, that he'd be staying with Brother Jameson for a while until he could figure things out. Figure out what? That's what I didn't understand. He was supposed to be a man of God, an overcomer not a giver upper. Needless to say I was shocked and appalled. What about Lilah?

Would she continue to stay at her grandmother's house or would Joshua pick her up to let her stay with him? Either way, this kind of instability was not a good life for a five-year-old girl.

I tried calling to talk to him, but he wouldn't answer his phone. I left messages on his voice mail, but he wouldn't return my calls either. Finally, he called to tell me to say that he would be fasting and praying over our situation. *What situation?* Okay, Now I knew he was tripping. It has been two whole days already, and I haven't heard from him, and he won't let me speak to Lilah.

I prayed to the Lord to help me to understand my husband and this marriage covenant.

"You said in your Word that I'd be the head and not the tail. Please help me with what seems like a losing battle. I know this is spiritual warfare, and I bind up every hindrance, every demonic influence, every wicked power and principality that would come against my marriage on earth as it is bound in heaven. I loose blessings of peace, love, and joy in my marriage on earth as it is loosed in heaven. In Jesus' name. Amen."

Then I took out the double chocolate fudge ice cream and waited for an answer.

Chapter Thirty-nine

Alex

It was a warm but rainy day. I spent the entire morning crying, eating, and waiting for the phone to ring. It was mid-September, and I was going on eight months pregnant. I didn't want to get out of bed, shower, or do anything. All I wanted to do was inhale more ice cream and cookies, as if I hadn't had enough already. I was sure I had already gained an extra ten pounds just that week. I didn't dare get on a scale. In fact, if I wasn't so depressed, I'd bake a blueberry pie or some muffins.

I used to think it was the conception issue that made me sad, but I know now that it was everything. Yes, I wanted to give my husband babies, lots of them. But I was afraid then, and I was still afraid, even now, that I wouldn't be able to produce even one. What if a miscarriage suddenly took away what I had waited so long for? If I could fulfill that one little part of my destiny, I'd feel accomplished. I wanted to get rid of the depression and the fear. I wanted to get out of the bed and shout, but I couldn't. I was temporarily paralyzed in my mind.

I never knew Christians could even struggle with depression. I thought it was all about joy, joy, and more joy. Yet the depression was like a cancer of the soul, eating away at me a little each day. I hardly wanted to get out of bed. Folks always told me that when I got

born-again all my troubles would go away, and that I'd
be all right. Then I learned that wasn't necessarily so.
My troubles weren't going to roll away unless I rolled
up on some Word and got it deep in my spirit. So deep
that the Word of God would start talking to me about
my situation. That's what I needed, to be washed in the
Word again and again until my heart and mind became
like Jesus again. Then I knew the joy would come. How
did I get to that place of depression? I didn't know, but
what I did know was that I had to get out and get my
mind and heart right again.

I was busy thinking about what I was going to eat
for dinner when I heard a knock on the door. For some
reason I thought it was Joshua. I hoped he had mis-
placed his key. But it wasn't Joshua. It was Seger.

"Hello, Sister Alex."

"Hi." I was sure my disappointment was evident, but
I didn't care. I felt too bad for politeness.

Seger tried to squeeze past me, but I blocked him. "I
don't think it's a good idea for you to be here right now
so . . ." But didn't he get the picture by now? Was he
that bold or that stupid to show up at my house after
the last incident at the gym? Maybe he was deliberately
trying to cause conflict in my marriage.

"I'm sorry. I don't mean to cause you trouble, but I
just wanted to apologize for any trouble I've caused to
you or your husband."

"You could've called," I said.

"I've never been much of a phone person. I like to see
people face-to-face, even when my presence has caused
so much turmoil. I—"

"It's not your fault. You've been a really good friend,"
I said.

"I try to be."

I put my hand over my face because I was embarrassed. Joshua had made it very clear that he didn't like Seger and that he didn't want us to be friends. "Ever since we were in Kenya, you've been more than good to me. It's just that I've got some things to work out with my husband."

"Right, I understand that this is complicated—" Seger started.

I interrupted him, "And you being around all the time isn't really helping the situation right now."

"Fine. I'll give you the space you need. I just had to say that I'm really sorry for the way that things have turned out." He shook his head. "I never meant to come between you two."

"I appreciate that," I said, tapping my foot.

"But call me if anything changes or if you just need to talk."

I hoped he would get the hint without me having to be blatantly rude. That was more Taylor's style than mine. "I will if I need to."

"I'll always be here for you." Seger raised his hand to touch my face, but I turned my head away from him.

"I know you will. You're a good friend." I closed the door partially. "Thanks."

"Good night, Sister Alex."

"Good night," I said, closing the door.

I remembered what I heard at the women's conference about priorities. I remembered what my father-in-law said about sacrifice. Even then, I still wondered if I was doing the right thing by giving Seger the cold shoulder.

Chapter Forty

Joshua

Three weeks had gone by already and Alex and I still weren't seeing eye to eye. I'd only spoken to her twice, and every time I tried to talk some sense into her, she'd just shoot me down with that same old stuff. I decided to show her better than tell her. I was tired of these women trying to control me. First there was Delilah, then Mother, and now Alex. Since I couldn't continue to impose on Brother Jameson and his family, I rented a room at an extended stay hotel uptown. I hoped this separation wouldn't be for much longer because it was costing me every dime I had. Furthermore, I missed everything about my wife, everything except how she wouldn't listen to me. I sighed as I made up my own bed, straightened my own tie, and poured my own tea. I had to work things out with her soon because this single life, for me, was getting played.

I was tired of going to bed alone, waking up alone, and eating alone. On Sundays and Wednesdays, I'd attend Kingdom House of Prayer Church with my parents, which they were excited about, but I refused to move in with them. Every day I'd go to work and try to forget my marriage was such a mess while Lilah stayed at my parents' house. She whined about not seeing me every day and wanted to know when she could go home. I felt guilty about that too, but I didn't have any answers for her. I didn't have any answers for myself except that I needed God's intervention soon.

I couldn't get Seger off my mind, couldn't stop thinking about his hands on my woman that day at the hospital, and then showing up at my home, not to mention the gym. I knew it was supposed to be innocent, but still, that man did something to me. I didn't know what it was; maybe just the fact that he was close—too close—to my wife. Probably just that. It was like the brother had no respect.

I wasn't jealous. I mean, I didn't hate the brother. I just wanted him to stay away from my family, Kiano included. I didn't want him to touch anything that was mine. I certainly wasn't happy with him working with her at Missionary. With that Seger snake on the prowl, the missing money at the bank, and my father's health slipping away, I didn't know what to do. I was losing time fast. I prayed for God's immediate intervention.

As soon as I arrived at work that morning, I saw two policemen leaving the bank. I wondered what was going on as I pulled into the parking lot. Minutes later, I was in the building and staring face-to-face with Simon.

"What's going on around here?" I asked, walking past a few of my colleagues.

Simon didn't answer but signaled me to come into his office. Then he closed the door behind him. He was sweating profusely. "One hundred and eighty thousand dollars was reported missing this morning."

I froze in my footsteps. Every alarm on the inside of me went off, reminding me of the messed-up numbers, reminding me of the warning signs. "Missing?"

"Yes, I'm sorry, but the heat is coming down on me." Simon couldn't even look into my eyes.

"What happened?"

"I'm sorry, but I can't talk about this anymore." He turned his head away from me.

"You can't talk to me?"

"Listen, the heat is coming down on the bank. Unfortunately, all the evidence in this case is pointing to *you*, so I have to let you go."

"*What?* Pointing to me?" I couldn't believe what I was hearing.

"Soon, the feds will be all over this place." Simon shook his head.

I stood near him rubbing my temples. "But you know me."

"I'm sorry, man."

"You're *sorry?* That's *all* you can say?"

He shook his head. "Look, I don't know. I just don't know."

"You don't know? What are you saying? We've been working together for ten years.

You know I've dedicated myself to this bank. I would never steal from here." I turned to pound my fist on the desk. "In fact, I helped *build* this company."

"I don't know, Josh." He nervously ran his fingers through his thinning, gray hair. "Maybe that's why you felt entitled to the money."

I squinted my eyes as I began to process the nightmare that was taking place. "Are you crazy? Why would I risk my whole career and reputation?"

"You told me not that long ago that you've got a lot of debts and—"

"I told you that, hoping you'd give me the raise you'd been promising me."

"That doesn't change the situation."

"What do my debts have to do with this situation?" I resisted the urge to grab him by the collar. "I'm not a thief. You know me."

"I don't know anything anymore."

"What do you mean you don't know anything any-more?" I listened but I was hesitant to react. It took everything in me not to pin that guy up against the wall. After all, he was fooling around with my whole life, and then some.

"All I know is that almost two hundred thousand dollars is gone and that the only one who had access to that account information is you," he stuttered.

"And you." I swallowed hard and walked toward the door. At this point, I was so upset I was holding back tears.

"Yes, and me, but why would I steal from my own bank?"

I opened the door. "That's what I'm asking myself. I told you money was missing, and you told me not to worry about it, that you'd take care of it."

"That was just a little money you told me about, Josh. A mere couple thousand, and I did straighten that out. Just a glitch in the computer programming, that's all." Simon swallowed hard. "But *this*, this is big."

"It's big, but I didn't do it," I said.

"I'm sorry, Josh. I know you've been strapped for cash with the new baby coming and everything—"

"That's true, and I told you those things in confidence. Now you're gonna use it against me." I swung into the air with my fist. "Man, I was such a fool."

Simon loosened his tie and collar. "Joshua, this thing is bigger than both of us."

"I can see that." I looked him up and down with a blank stare.

"Everything will come out. Don't worry."

I put my hands over my head in disbelief. "Ha. You're telling *me* not to worry?"

"I've still got your back, but I'm going to need you to leave now. Please." He rushed over to the door and opened it.

I still couldn't believe what was happening to me. First, I had lost my wife, and now I had lost my job. And the way things were looking, I could possibly lose my freedom.

I went to my office and began to pack. *God, please help me.*

Imagine a minister caught in the middle of a big banking scandal. It just looked bad, really bad. To make matters worse, as it turned out, there were already reporters outside covering a special interest story on crime in the urban community. They had informed us the day before that they would be interviewing the owners of the boutique next door since it had recently been robbed. Unfortunately, when they saw the police snooping around the bank, the reporters started an investigation of their own. As I was walking through the door with boxes of my personal belongings, they turned their news cameras on me. One of the reporters actually recognized me from a news story she had done on my father's church last year. She put the camera right up in my face.

"Mr. Joshua Benning, son of the prominent Bishop Joshua Douglas Benning II, I see that you're leaving this bank with a box of your belongings. Does that mean that you've been implicated in this embezzlement case?" the young reporter grinned.

My heart sank. "No, I have not been charged with anything. I am completely innocent."

The reporter pushed the microphone in my face. "Really? Why, may I ask, are you the only one leaving then, sir?"

Some people who had been busily walking by stopped to listen, and a crowd began to form around us.

"I have no comment," I said as I pushed past her camera.

Then as if things weren't bad enough, a very sultry-looking, like she just fell out of the nightclub, Yvonne showed up out of nowhere and hugged me. "Joshua."

I didn't need that kind of help. What in the world made her do a dumb thing like that?

Those evil cameras caught her every move, her every curve, and they were sure to get a close-up shot of me and Yvonne cheek to cheek.

The reporter was in her glory. "Miss, are you aware of the embezzlement that's being investigated at this bank?"

Yvonne looked surprised by her question. "No, but I can say that Minister Joshua here is an upstanding citizen, always lending a hand to everyone at the church."

Yvonne made me sound guilty before I'd even been officially accused of anything. She was always interfering in other people's business, just like her busybody aunt, Sister Winifred.

Man, with her newly bleached hair, painted face, and spandex jumpsuit, I just knew I was doomed in the media. I was also doomed with my wife. What in the world would she say when she saw me on the six o'clock news with Yvonne Johnson?

The reporter continued. "Well, it appears that crime is running wild in this community.

First a string of robberies, and now embezzlement. We'll keep you posted on the outcome . . ."

I stopped listening as I walked to the parking lot.

My reputation was ruined. There was no way I'd be able to get any followers for my future church with that photo spread that would certainly follow me.

I tried to call Alex immediately. There was no answer. I was in such a jam. All I could do was bury my face in my hands and pray for divine intervention and mercy.

My phone rang, and I grabbed it, hoping it was Alex.
"Hello," I said.

"Joshua."

I recognized the voice right away.

Mother cleared her throat before she spoke again.
"Why in heaven's name have you decided to disgrace
your entire family by appearing on television with that
strumpet of a woman?"

That was the beginning of the end of life as I knew it.

Chapter Forty-one

Alex

Imagine my surprise when I turned on the news and caught a glimpse of the man I married, the father of Lilah and my unborn child, fired, possibly accused of embezzlement, and on the arm of that Jezebel of a woman. That was it for me. Joshua had left me several voice messages when I was in the shower, but by the time I called him back he didn't answer. His messages all said the same thing; that he was innocent, that Simon had let him go, and that he would probably be on the news because some nosy reporters just happened to be outside the bank while the police were there. Police? Probably on the news? I was in shock. The phone was ringing off the hook. My dad, Taylor, Aunt Dorothy, and Marisol were all calling back-to-back. I couldn't believe that one local news segment would attract this much attention. When would it all end? I didn't feel like talking to any of them. I didn't want to answer questions or hear their brilliant speculations. I just wanted silence, the kind that came with peace. Unfortunately, I didn't know when that kind of silence would come.

The next day, after seeing the latest headline of the local newspaper—and believe me, it was ugly—I didn't know if I was coming or going. I did know that I had to meet my dad in an hour. I had covered for Joshua long enough. It had already been three-and-a-half weeks since he'd left and no reconciliation was in sight. I had to let my dad know that Joshua had taken Lilah to his mother's house and had left me and my unborn child to fend for ourselves. Sure, he had left money for incidentals, but that wasn't enough to soothe my wounded soul. I was broken and crying out to God for answers. I tried to reach Joshua on his cell, but he wouldn't answer. I left him messages, but he wouldn't return my calls. Okay, so we were playing phone tag.

Eventually, I snapped out of it and decided not to keep sulking. That didn't mean that I didn't think about my husband, that I didn't miss his touch, his kiss, everything about him, even the things I thought I wouldn't miss. Sometimes I'd take a suit out of his closet and hold it close to me if it still had his scent on it. Then I would pray for him, asking God to strengthen him during this trial.

Between the media and my own mind, I had my fill of Joshua Benning. Still I waited for him to come by, but he did not. I waited for him to call, but he did not. I waited and watched the news, wondering if he would be officially accused, then arrested, indicted, and imprisoned. Then I realized I was letting my imagination run away with me. All I knew was that money had been stolen and that he had been fired.

Why wouldn't he come to see me? I was so angry with him I didn't know what I'd say if he did call now. I wanted to strangle him for allowing Yvonne to hop in front of the camera. Had he invited her to the bank? Had he called her down there for help? Or was she just passing by? I was so confused. It wasn't that I was jealous of Yvonne anymore. Call it confidence or insanity, but I didn't doubt that Joshua had nothing to do with her. I wasn't going to make a fool out of myself because I had definitely gone down that road before. Yet, at the same time, with Joshua being a public figure, I knew it didn't look good for him. In the church arena, reputation was everything.

I wondered why he hadn't turned to me for help. Didn't he know I was hurting for him?

It was so frustrating, playing these cat-and-mouse games. Why had he pushed me out of his life, and then virtually disappeared, at least from me? Then I began to rebel against my own heart. If Joshua wouldn't come to me, then I'd go on without him. I decided that I would make it on my own. I always had before.

And indeed I had. I had been single for over thirty years. I had roomed with my sister, paid my own rent and bills, and managed my own relationships. What made him think he owned me and could control every part of me?

Seger stopped by unannounced again. Hadn't I told him to stay away while I work things out? I see that he was not one to take no for an answer.

"Hi, Seger." I involuntarily let out a big breath.

"How are you, Sister Alex?"

"I'm sure you've seen the news so . . ."

"Yes, and I'm sorry." He shook his head. "It's very unfortunate."

"He didn't do it, of course, but it looks like he did, so that's bad enough, I guess."

"Yeah, it looks bad. How have you two been holding up under the pressure?"

I almost wondered if he already knew we had been separated. "Well, we've been separated for almost a month now."

"I see." Seger sat down on the couch. "I know you asked me to give you some space, but I only came by to ask about Kiano."

"I don't know. We were believing for a miracle, but now that we're separated and this scandal—"

"What has one thing got to do with the other? Kiano's village is being destroyed. Those children need parents—now."

That was the Seger I knew, the peaceful, world-changing missionary and activist, bringing the Word, aid, and revolution to the masses.

"I know, but it's really complicated, and I don't want to talk about it."

"I'm sorry. I didn't mean to pry."

"I just don't think it's appropriate to disclose all of this personal information to you."

"You're right. I might use it to my best interest," he laughed.

I smiled. "Yeah, something like that, I guess."

Suddenly Seger looked very serious. There was no smile in his eyes, only sadness. "I'm still willing to fund the adoption if you decide you want help."

"That's very generous," I said.

"It's the least I can do." Seger stood over me and pushed my chin up with his index finger. "I care about Kiano's well-being and yours."

"I know you do."

He looked into my eyes. "You're in my heart, Alex."

"Well, I'm getting a little tired, and I need to rest." I took a step back. I needed time to think. I couldn't just let my emotions dictate my actions. Even though I loved Kiano, even though I was afraid for his safety, I had to be calm. I had to pray.

"I'm sorry. I didn't mean to overstay my welcome." He turned his back to me and walked toward the door.

I shook my head. "No, it's nothing like that."

"Take care of yourself now." Seger quickly let himself out.

Now that he was gone, I began to give serious consideration to accepting his offer. I started to think that if by some extreme chance Joshua and I found our way back to each other, he would thank me for it later. I'd accept Seger's offer to help with Kiano's adoption costs. After all, what did Joshua's opinion matter when we were clearly separated, with little hope of reconciling? And besides, Joshua's whole ministry was on the line. Would he really have time to focus on being mad with me about Seger? Not when he and Yvonne were on the front cover of the local newspaper with the headline reading, "BISHOP'S SON FIRED DURING BANK INVESTIGATION."

On the social networks, people were asking, "Did Prominent Bishop Benning's Son Flee with More than the Offering Plate?" The gossip that spun from that one report was terrible, and my phone kept ringing. But the worst part was that I couldn't even talk to Joshua. I had left several messages for him, and he still hadn't returned my calls. That's when I really got mad and gave up on trying to please him. I was tired of trying to make things work while all the time he did his own thing. I was tired of feeling like an outsider in my own relationship. I was tired of being alone, doing everything alone. If I needed to call Seger for help, I would.

Chapter Forty-two

Joshua

I sat in that lonely hotel room, tired of hearing my name being mentioned in the media and online. I had been called in for questioning by bank authorities and by the police, but I hadn't even been formally charged. Regardless, I felt like I was trapped. I had picked up the phone to call Alex many times, but I had hung up each time. I didn't know what to say to her over the phone. What could I possibly say to her when I had failed in every area and our anniversary was next week. I was ashamed, and I was distraught. That kind of conversation needed to be done face-to-face. So I pulled on a pair of jeans, an old sweatshirt, and headed out the door. I hopped into my Lincoln Navigator, drove frantically through the overcrowded Manhattan streets and over the Brooklyn Bridge to see Alex.

When I reached our apartment building, I hurried to the parking garage downstairs. Just as I was about to pull into my parking space, I recognized Seger's car. I stopped in the middle of the lot and put my vehicle in park. Not again, and not in my space. Didn't this guy *ever* give up? No, why should he? I rubbed the temples of my head as an instant migraine came on. I started thinking that soon I'd be totally out of the picture once the police arrested me, and then he could have Alex all to himself. Within seconds, I realized that I was getting carried away and tried to push the negative thoughts from my mind. "No weapon formed against me shall prosper," I said. I leaned against the steering wheel, buried my head in my hands, and before I knew it, I was crying like a baby. What happened to my life? What happened to my vision? Everything was all wrong. When I heard another car coming, I wiped my face with my sleeve, put the car in drive, and drove away.

I went straight to Pastor Martin's office and begged him to see me. I didn't know where else to turn. I needed help. When I walked into his office, he motioned for me to sit down, and I did. The room smelled like lemon pepper wings, and I knew that was his favorite.

Pastor Martin sat down behind his desk. "Well, Joshua, I had hoped you would've come to me sooner."

"I couldn't, sir. I was ashamed and confused that everyone had seen that stupid news report." I dropped my head.

Pastor Martin leaned forward in his chair. "Right. You mean the one with you carrying your things out of the bank?"

"Yes, that awful one."

"Did you steal the money, Joshua?"

"No, sir." I shook my head vehemently.

Pastor Martin coughed hard as if he were choking, and I wondered if he had either a bad cold or asthma. "Then you don't have anything to be ashamed of. Don't worry about people talking. People *will* talk."

"I saw some of the numbers weren't looking right, but I let someone talk me out of what I saw. I trusted someone I shouldn't have."

"We're all human, and we all make mistakes. It sounds like yours was just a case of bad judgment." Pastor Martin covered his mouth with a handkerchief.

"*Very* bad judgment," I whimpered.

"What about Sister Yvonne? That situation looks pretty bad too."

"She just came to the bank at the wrong time and threw herself in front of the camera."

"I see. Well, you didn't steal anything, and you didn't have anything to do with Sister Yvonne, so . . ."

"But it looks like I did. 'Avoid the appearance of evil,' remember?"

"Oh, I remember the scripture, but you didn't do those things intentionally." Suddenly, Pastor Martin jumped out of his seat and came toward me.

"People don't know that," I said.

He stood beside me and put his big hand on my shoulder. "Why does it matter to you what people know or don't know, son?"

"Pastor, how can I ever build a church when the people don't trust me?"

The man of God sat on the edge of his desk in front of me. "I'd say let God handle the people. When that time comes, He will send those He wants to be in your congregation, and there is nothing anyone or anything can do to stop it."

"I feel like such a failure. I've left my wife, and now she has moved on with someone else."

"Whoa, wait a minute. Where did *that* come from?"

"Alex and I have been separated for a little over three weeks now."

"I wondered why I hadn't seen you all in church."

"I've been staying at a hotel, going back and forth to my parents' house to see Lilah and . . ."

"Okay, I knew things were bad from our last conversation but not that bad." Pastor Martin scratched his head as if he were deep in thought.

"We weren't getting along. Always arguing over money and the adoption, and this guy."

"What guy?"

"A friend of my wife's. He's a missionary she met when she went to Kenya last year. I think he's in love with my wife."

"That's a very bold statement. Could you be mistaken?"

"I don't think so, but she doesn't see it. Or maybe she does, and she's falling in love with him too. I don't know, Pastor."

"Do you really believe that your wife is in love with another man?"

"To tell you the truth, I don't know what to think. I just know I'm stressed out all the time, and this thing with Seger isn't helping."

"Have you tried talking to her about it?" Pastor Martin went back around to his desk and flipped through the pages of the Bible.

"Many times."

He stopped to think for a minute. "Maybe she just doesn't realize how much it's tearing you apart."

"No, she wouldn't, because she's too busy with her ministry and Seger, and what she wants," I said.

The pastor folded his hands in front of his face. "What do you want, Joshua?"

"I want my life back."

"And what exactly does that mean?"

"That means, I want my wife and child, my dreams of being a pastor. I want all of that back." I did. I wanted it all.

"If what you want is truly God's will, you shall have it all back. Get your life inperspective. Your wife didn't leave you. You left her. Wrong move." Pastor Martin jumped out of his chair again and went back to sitting in his spot on the front of his desk. He was just like that during service. Always moving. Never predictable.

"I know that now, but I just don't know how to fix it. With these legal problems and being out of work, the bills are piling up, and I've got to get an attorney, and—"

"Stop." Pastor Martin put up his hand. "Hear God's voice. You know the way home. In your spirit you know what to do. Stop fighting and listen. Just listen."

Immediately, I felt convicted. I had been so busy trying to handle things on my own that I had forgotten to trust God. "Thanks, Pastor," I said.

He immediately grabbed me by the shoulders and began to pray a short but powerful prayer.

"Now I want you to go home and pray for yourself. I'll continue to pray for you."

I went back to the hotel I was staying in, talked to Lilah on the phone at my parents' house, and then went into prayer. Since I was fasting, I didn't need food. I just drank water and got full from God's Word. I didn't speak to anyone, including the people from the church who claimed they wanted to help me. I buried myself in my Bible and listened to tapes of every sermon from Pastor Martin or my dad. I meditated on every piece of God's Word that I could get my hands on until I became everything I needed to be. I needed to be strong. I needed to be wise. I needed to be honest with everyone, including myself.

The next time I saw Pastor Martin he was more abrupt with me. It had been a week since I had seen him last, and he didn't leave his seat when I entered the room. He also didn't change the tone of his voice.

"Brother Joshua, we're not going to waste any more time during this session."

"What do you mean, Pastor?"

"The last time you were here, I told you to go and pray. Did you do that, son?"

"Yes, sir. I did."

"All right, then, what have you learned?"

"I learned that I've got to listen to God first, no matter what."

"And?"

He was pulling it out of me. "And I can't always be
in control of every situation, even when I want to be."

"What else, son?"

"I can't do it alone."

"What can't you do alone?"

"I can't solve these problems alone." I felt like I was
on the edge of a breakthrough.

"What about your wife?"

"I've got to stop being jealous." I dropped my head.
"I know I can't make my wife do anything or change. I
can only change me."

Pastor Martin pulled it out of me word by word. "Good.
What else?"

"I've gotta stop being angry about things that are out
of my control. Just because things aren't going my way
doesn't mean I can change it."

"And what about trusting your wife?"

"I've got to trust God and my wife too." I leaned forward in my chair and began rocking back and forth.

"What about your deceased wife versus your current
wife?"

I stood up and started pacing the room with my
hands clasped in front of my face. "Delilah is gone."

"And who is Alex?"

"Alex is not Delilah. She's not Delilah." Why didn't I
realize this before?

Pastor Martin watched me move around the room.
"And where is Delilah?"

"She's in the past. I can't ever bring her back or my
unborn child."

"And what else have you accepted about that Delilah experience?"

"I'll never know why she did what she did. I'll never know what made her tick." That was the rough part. I'd spent many nights on my knees over that one.

"And where is the past, Joshua?"

"The past is buried with Delilah." I tried to stop the tears, but the next thing I knew, they had a mind of their own. I wiped them away quickly with my hands. I couldn't have another man watch me crying like a little girl.

"And what about your future?"

"It isn't buried, and I can have a future with my wife, daughter, and child on the way."

Pastor Martin hardly moved. "So how do you feel, Joshua?"

"I feel alive again." The man was a genius.

"Good," Pastor Martin said. "Why?"

"Because my future is bright."

Finally, Pastor Martin stood up and shook my hand. "Why?"

"Because of Jesus my future is very bright." I knew at this moment that this was the truth. I had an epiphany right there in Pastor Martin's modest office.

The hard part, though, was receiving it.

Chapter Forty-three

Alex

It was October and Seger started helping me with the Giving Life plans since, at eight months pregnant, I could hardly move around. He called, dropped by, and ran miscellaneous errands on demand. If only I had received that much support from my husband.

Seger did everything I asked of him without complaint. He even purchased two plane tickets to Kenya so we could go and work on Kiano's adoption together, after I gave birth, of course. He didn't ask me. He just bought them and never said a word about repayment. At first, it seemed as if he were my hero, wanting all my dreams to come true. Then I remembered my real hero, Jesus.

And I remembered my vow to change; to put God's will first. That was enough to make me take a step back to reevaluate my life.

After having a conversation with my dad one day, he asked me why Seger was doing all of the things he did. And I honestly could not answer him. "Be careful," my father said. Was Seger just being a godly friend, or was there more to it than that? I honestly started to wonder why Seger was doing all of this for me; why he wanted to spend all of his free time with me. I wondered why Seger wasn't at least dating anyone yet. I thought about conversations I had with Marisol concerning his single status. Maybe Joshua was right. Maybe Seger had feelings for me that were deeper than friendship. The moment I accepted this possibility, I dropped everything I was doing, and I began to pray. Either way, I knew what had to be done.

Just as I picked up the phone to call Seger, the doorbell rang. I put the phone down and went to answer the door. I was surprised to see Keith standing there. He looked terrible, unshaven, with uncombed hair, and bloodshot eyes. I'd never seen the very handsome physical therapist look so bad.

"Hi, Keith," I said, looking around for Taylor. Keith never came over by himself.

"Hi," he said.

When I realized that he was alone, I stopped staring. "Come in, please. How are you?"

Keith came in and sat down on the couch. "Not so good."

"Why? What's wrong?" I sat next to him on the couch and slanted my body to face him.

"I'm thinking about accepting a position out in Chicago," he said.

I knew that meant trouble. "Oh, Chicago?"

He let out a deep breath. "I'm going to call off the engagement to your sister."

"Oh, no." I jumped up. "Not that."

Keith raised his voice a little. "I'm sorry, but I'm tired of waiting for her to change her mind and marry me."

I put my hand to my forehead and started walking around the room. "But, Keith, you know Taylor—"

"Yes, I do, and I'm tired of playing games. She promised she'd marry me, but now she won't." Keith put his hands up to his mouth. "I can't stay here and pretend I don't want her as my wife."

I stopped walking and stared at him. I could see the pain in his eyes. "I'm so sorry, Keith. I guess I didn't realize how badly it was affecting you."

He leaned toward me. "I can't stay here and *just* be her physical therapist or *just* her business partner. I can't *just* be her friend."

"I know. I know." I began to pace the floor again.

"I'm going to call and accept the offer in the morning," Keith said.

"Does Taylor know about the offer?"

He bit his lip nervously. Then he began cracking his knuckles. "Of course. I told her earlier, and she has until tonight to give me her answer."

"That's not much time," I said.

Keith stood up and threw his hands into the air. "No, but it's all or none. Either she agrees to marry me now, or I'm outta here."

"I understand." I followed him to the door and grabbed his hand. "I'll talk to her, but she's stubborn, you know."

"I know, but if anyone can get through to her, it would be her twin." Keith smiled a weak smile and withdrew his hand from mine.

I watched him walk through the door.

"Thanks for listening."

"You're welcome," I said, shutting the door.

As soon as he left, I called Taylor and told her I was coming over. I hung up the phone before she could protest. Then I drove as fast as I legally could, observing all traffic signs and lights, but knowing that this was an emergency of the soul.

"Mama didn't raise no fool," Taylor used to say whenever she saw a good-looking man.

She would never let one get by her without getting his attention, no matter what she had to do.

Unfortunately, it usually didn't take more than a slight jiggle of the hips and a hint of cleavage to get them interested in her. She would use them up, taking them for everything they had.

Afterward, she'd get bored and toss them aside. She never wanted to get caught up with any one man. She'd surrender her body, but never her heart, at least that's how it was until Keith came along.

Taylor was a new woman now, rededicated to Christ, softer, and kinder. I knew Mother would be pleased if she were alive. Lord knows that girl gave me grief for years while she was out there dropping it like it was hot. Nothing like a life-threatening car accident to cool a person off and set their mind straight.

When I arrived at Taylor's apartment building where I used to live before I was married, I knocked and then waited for an answer. When I didn't hear a response, I opened the door with my spare key. I hadn't seen her apartment in months, and it was a mess. So was she.

Clothes were thrown everywhere. Papers were on the floor. What looked like it might have been breakfast— two dried-up, not so sunny-side up eggs—sat on the coffee table forlornly staring back at me. Her hair was uncombed, and her ripped jeans and tee shirt looked like something for the slaughter. It was certainly not the glamorous image my sister liked to portray.

"Girl, you look tore up from the floor up," I said.

"Whatever." Taylor sucked her teeth and rolled away in her wheelchair.

"Get a hold of yourself or you're about to lose possibly the best thing that has ever happened to you, besides salvation, of course. And you know it."

Taylor rolled her neck. "Whatever, let him go."

"Oh, come on. Are you serious?"

"Yep, he don't need no cripple on his arm anyway. He's a good-looking brother. He can find somebody else."

"But he loves *you*. He wants you, walker, wheelchair, and all."

"How do you know that? How do you know he won't get tired of me being this way, not being able to walk or run? Can you promise me that?"

"No one can promise you anything."

Taylor sucked her teeth. "That's what I thought."

"But life is to be lived. You have to take chances to be able to succeed. You can't be afraid to live."

"Who says I'm afraid? I've never been afraid. I'm the bravest person I know."

"I agree with you. You have been—up to now. And now you've got this fear eating away at you, and you won't let it go."

"How can I let it go when it stares back at me every day in the mirror? My injury changed me." Taylor closed her eyes as if she were savoring a memory. "It changed my whole life."

"I know, and I know you've had to make some adjustments. We all have. But Keith really loves you, and you'd be a fool not to accept that," I said.

Tears ran down Taylor's face. "What if he stops loving me?"

"I have two totally functional legs, and I can walk, but my husband hasn't been home in weeks. There are no guarantees except in God's Word. Trust Him—not Keith and not walking.

Trust Him." I grabbed Taylor's wheelchair, pulled it to me, and leaned down to hug her. I felt her warm tears running down my neck and back.

I hoped that she would make the right decision.

As I drove home, I knew I had a few decisions of my
own to make also. The first thing I did when I arrived
at home was to check the mail. There was a pile of bills
for Josh and me, and another letter from the Kenyan
attorney that was supposed to handle Kiano's adoption. I held the letter in my hand, and then placed it
against my heart. It represented what I wanted from
my husband, what I expected from him. Sure, he had
promised me that we would adopt Kiano, but did I have
a right to hold that over his head and torture him with
it? Didn't I know that he was really doing the best he
could? Then I thought about Kiano himself, and what
would happen to him if I didn't go through with my
plans. *Trust in the Lord with all your heart and lean
not to your own understanding.*

I took a deep breath; and then I decided to trust God.
I called the airline to cancel my flight to Kenya. Seger
had booked the flight ridiculously early, despite the
fact that I couldn't travel and wouldn't be able to travel
any time soon. He claimed that he always booked all of
his flights far in advance, and had been doing so ever
since he started doing mission trips.

When I was done with the airline I called him.

"Hello." Seger answered on the first ring.

"Hi," I said.

Seger sounded anxious. "Do you need me to come
over to do something for you?"

"No, that's not why I called." I sat on the side of my
bed holding the phone in one hand and holding my
Bible in the other.

"Oh," he said.

"First of all, I'm sorry, but I'm not proceeding with
any of the adoption plans until my husband is back
home. And let me make that clear. I am believing that
he will come back home."

"But I thought you wanted to go ahead and get a jump start on saving Kiano."

Suddenly a boldness came over me. "I did, but I realized something."

"What's that?"

"God doesn't need a jump start. Everything is in His own timing, not mine."

"I see," Seger said slowly.

I didn't want to hurt his feelings, but there was no other way. I had been out of God's will long enough. "I'm also going to need to be alone while my husband and I are separated."

"Oh, no, I've offended you." I heard panic in his voice.

"No, you haven't. You've been an awesome friend. I just think that maybe our friendship may be standing in the way of the reconciliation between me and my husband.

I'm not blaming you for anything, but I'm just saying I can't see you anymore right now.

Not until I work some things out."

Seger began to nod slowly as if he were processing what he heard. "I see."

"I'm sorry."

"No, that's okay." Seger sounded like he was puzzled. A moment later, he continued, "But are you sure?"

I held the phone for a minute. "Thanks for everything, but yes, I'm sure."

"You know where I am if you need me." Seger's voice was low.

"Yes, I know where you are." I sighed. "Thank you, again, for your generosity."

"I'm not sure how good of a friend I am," he replied.

"What do you mean?"

Seger didn't speak right away. He let an uncomfortable beat of silence pass first. "I have a confession to make. Maybe I was just being selfish."

"How?"

Seger's voice seemed to caress his words as he spoke. "Sometimes, I'm a lonely man."

I was taken aback by his confession, and I certainly didn't want him to bare any more of his soul. "Seger, I'm sure there are plenty of people who would love your company. You don't have to be alone."

"Maybe I'm alone by choice because I'm selective."

"God knows all about your selections, and He'll work it out for you." I paused. "Just like He'll work this marriage thing out for me."

"You're right."

I paused. "I've got to go now."

"Good-bye, Sister Alex."

"Good-bye, Brother Seger." I shut the phone call down and shut him out of my heart.

That was the last phone conversation I had that day. After that, I went to my bedroom, kneeled down on my plush carpet, and repented about my attitude and my part in Joshua's and my separation. Clearly, I had been at fault as much as Joshua was. I realized I had let my feelings for Seger, no matter how innocent they might have been, to interfere in my marriage. My husband's needs should have come first, but I allowed pride and independence to rule me. I had refused to submit, and I had caused so much trouble as a result of it. Even though we still had issues to work through, I was willing to work through them in God's way and His time. Not mine. After the stress of the day caught up with me, I took a short nap.

When I woke up an hour later, the worst thing possible was happening. I started to feel my abdomen tightening like a fist. I walked slowly to the kitchen to get a glass of water and managed to drink some before I became too weak. Then I noticed a bloody discharge running down my legs.

Oh, Lord, no! Suddenly, I felt extreme pressure in my pelvic area and strong abdominal cramps hit me. I stumbled, and I knew something was terribly wrong.

First, I called Joshua, but I didn't get an answer, so I left a message on his voice mail.

Then I called 911 and my sister. I sat still on my bed and tried to stay calm, meditating on the Ninety-first Psalm. "He that dwelleth in the secret place of the most High shall abide under the shadow of the Almighty. I will say of the Lord, He is my refuge and my fortress: my God; in him will I trust."

About fifteen minutes later I was rushed into the emergency room where I was immediately hooked up to monitors. Clearly, I was in preterm labor, but I wasn't fully dilated and the baby's heart rate was dropping fast. I was told there was no time to spare.

"We're going to take the baby," I heard someone say.

So within minutes I was prepped for surgery. An epidural was placed in my spine. I was told to count backward. *Ten-nine-eight-seven* . . . I was drifting . . . *six-five-four-three* . . . I couldn't feel anything except that I was almost gone. I was practically numb. *Two-one.* Nothing.

I was out of my body and possibly out of my mind as well. The epidural took away the pain, but the stress was knocking me out.

The baby was being born too soon. Would our child survive being born at only eight months? Could our marriage survive if our child didn't? Would I want to live if he didn't? We already knew the risks, the danger involved. Then I saw Joshua come into the room, my knight in shining armor. He was wearing a face mask and surgical gown. How did he make it here so fast? I thought he was busy with his own life. No time to worry about that. I felt more and more pressure. I heard talking as I went in and out of consciousness; and then I heard my baby crying.

My baby, Joshua Jr., was born too soon. I couldn't hold him though. I was too sleepy. Through one eye I saw Joshua holding him. I smiled a weak smile before I lapsed into a deep sleep.

When I woke up in the recovery room, my father was standing over me. He looked tired and old with his head of gray hair and matching eyebrows.

"Daddy," I moaned.

Daddy smiled with his missing bottom teeth. "Don't talk. You're okay, and the baby is okay. That's all that matters."

"But I—"

"Josh is downstairs at the nursery. They're running some tests on the baby."

"I want to see him," I said.

"You'll have plenty time for that," Dad said.

"I want to see my son now."

He ignored me. "Thank you for giving me a healthy grandson."

"You're welcome, Daddy." A tear slipped from my eye and rolled on the pillowcase.

Minutes later a nurse rolled me down to my room from the delivery room.

When Joshua came through that door, the first thing he did was gently gather me into his arms. It was the way he had held me on our wedding day, the way I'd longed to be held for over the past months.

My body was sore, but the hug was way overdue so it soothed me. His rough, unshaven face scratched my skin. His shirt was wrinkled; he needed a haircut; and he smelled of engine oil. I wondered if he had been working under the hood of his SUV, which would've been a miracle since he didn't know anything about cars. He looked like he had been having a tough time without me.

"I'm so sorry, Alex," Joshua said, pulling up a chair to sit down by the bed.

"I am too." I touched his face and smiled. This certainly was not the neat, pine-scented Joshua that I knew. Regardless of how terrible he looked or smelled, he sure felt good in my arms.

Joshua fell to his knees and kissed my hands. "I love you. I never meant for anything like this to happen."

"I know that. It's not your fault," I said.

"Yes, it is. I should never have left your side. If I hadn't been such a fool, worrying about Seger, I would've been taking care of you. I'm sorry."

Although I still felt weak, all I wanted to know was if my baby was fine. "How is my baby?"

"He is small, but he is strong." Joshua swallowed hard. "God made him strong, and He'll not let us down."

"You're right." I wiped the tears from my eyes.

"Please don't cry. I'm sorry for all I put you through," Joshua said.

"It's okay."

Joshua wouldn't let me go. "No, I shouldn't have put you through this additional drama."

I must've had a confused look on my face because he explained. "First I left you alone because of my own foolish pride, and then I ended up messing up with the bank, losing my job, and then the media, and . . . I should've known Simon was stealing when I first saw the discrepancy with the numbers."

"You mean you knew?"

He nodded. "I saw small amounts of money missing. Not more than a couple of thousand in total, and it worried me for a while. But then I listened to Simon and chose to ignore it. Too busy with my own mess. Now I'm paying for it." Joshua dropped his head.

I felt sorry for him. "They'll find out the truth."

"Sure, after my arrest and a long, damaging trial," he smirked.

"Come on. They'll know you're innocent," I said. "Have they even questioned you?"

Joshua nodded. "Yes, they did on the first week."

"Well, I'm sure the FBI is doing their thing. No one in their right mind is going to suspect you of embezzlement," I stated, trying to reassure him.

Joshua let out a deep breath. "Maybe not. But that's not what they're saying on the social networks."

"Oh, no one cares about that nonsense. Did you tell the police about what you saw and about what you told Simon?"

Joshua loosened his grasp on me but still held my hands. "I told them everything."

I wrapped my fingers around his. "I'm sorry. What can I do to help?"

Joshua kissed me softly on my lips. "Just be yourself, your beautiful self. I missed you so much."

"Missed me? Why didn't you come and tell me?"

"I told you I was a fool." Joshua spoke low, as if he were ashamed. "Then I came by one day, and I saw Seger's car there, and I—"

"Seger and I were just friends. He was very supportive. Nothing more," I confirmed.

Joshua looked surprised. "Was?"

"I've decided to let that relationship go."

Joshua smiled. "For me?"

"Yes, for you and for our relationship." I smiled back.

"I should've never left," he said again.

I tried to sit up in bed, but I was too sore. "You're right. But I should've stopped hounding you about Kiano when I saw you doing the best you could. I should've stood behind your vision and trusted God."

"Okay," Joshua said, "where did all this come from?"

I looked up to the ceiling. "The same place all your revelations come from. Then I finally calmed down so I could hear a word from God—and it wasn't necessarily the one I wanted to hear."

Joshua looked directly into my eyes. "What do you mean?"

"I was too busy doing my own thing and asking God to bless it. That's something I heard a few months back at the women's conference, but I wasn't ready to receive it then. I've finally taken a step back and got back into His will. I'm no longer doing my thing or everything; just His thing."

Joshua asked, "So what exactly does that mean?"

"That means that I'm waiting for the doors to open concerning Kiano's adoption, and I'm trusting in God to supply all of our needs, and all of Kiano's needs too." I kissed Joshua full on the mouth.

He let out a breath of relief. "I'm so glad to hear that."

At that moment my dad ran into the room smiling. "You two will have plenty of time for that." He looked around for the remote. "Let's turn on this television."

Joshua raised his eyebrows. "Why? What's going on?"

"You'll see." Dad turned the television on and flipped the channels until he stopped at the news.

The breaking story was that Simon had been caught trying to leave the country, and he confessed to embezzling one hundred and eighty thousand dollars from the bank. Although Joshua was the one able to create new loans and adjust amounts in the accounts, Simon also had the authority to create and process certain adjustments. He had been transferring money from fictitious lines of credit to other accounts. Thanks to an anonymous tip, the feds had been checking him out for a while. They found that he had an undisclosed foreign bank account with deposits that matched the amounts of the missing monies. He was being charged with felony counts of bank fraud and embezzlement.

"Hallelujah!" Joshua jumped up from his seat.

"Oh, bless His name," I said with tears streaming down my face.

"Your sister is here, and she wants to see you," Dad said.

"Well, let her come in." I looked toward the door as my dad opened it.

Taylor and Keith came in holding hands.

"Oh, it's so good to see you two together," I said. I had hoped that everything would work out for them. With a strong-willed person like Taylor, I just never knew.

"I could say the same thing about you two," Taylor reached up to grab my hand from her wheelchair.

Keith hugged me very gently, careful not to hurt my sore areas. "Looking good, lady."

"I'm glad you're both here," I smiled.

"Well, I got here as soon as I could. I had to wait for slowpoke here to come by and get me." Taylor cut her eyes at Keith. "That's a beautiful baby out there."

"Thank you, girl." Now that my sister was there I felt like I was going to cry.

Taylor let out a deep breath. "Whew, you had me a little scared."

"I guess Josh Jr. was tired of waiting," I said.

"Got that right," Joshua smiled proudly.

"Well, we've finally set a date," Taylor announced. "I hope we can put together a cute little wedding in two weeks."

"Two weeks?" I started to grin, knowing we'd have to hustle to pull it all together.

"Yep," Keith affirmed.

"That should be more than enough time." I winked at Taylor. "I'm so happy for you."

"Congratulations, you two." Joshua pulled Keith into a quick hug, and then bent down to embrace Taylor.

"Thanks. I guess you two have finally rubbed off on me." Taylor never looked happier, even in her wheelchair.

Dad shook Keith's hand. "Welcome to the family, son."

"Thanks, Mr. Carter, sir," Keith beamed.

"That really is a beautiful grandson you two gave me out there," Dad grinned, revealing his perfectly even dentures this time.

"Yep, pretty big too for a preemie," Keith said.

Joshua and I looked into each other's eyes and smiled.

"Thanks," I said to my dad.

"We've been blessed." Joshua again took my hand in his.

Taylor yelled out. "Hey! Isn't tomorrow your anniversary?"

"Yes, it is. I guess Junior came early so he could celebrate it with us," Joshua smiled.

A few hours later, Mother Benning came in with Lilah on her heels. Lilah ran toward me and fell into my arms, pressing me into my pillow.

"Mommy, Mommy," she cried. Every part of my midsection ached, but I was so surprised I didn't dare stop her.

"I missed you so much, Mommy," Lilah said, never loosening her arms from my neck.

I looked at Joshua, and he smiled at me. "I missed you too, baby doll."

My heart fluttered with hearing that word—"Mommy." After all these months, she finally called me Mommy. I wiped a tear away before anyone saw it. From our wedding day all the way up to this moment, she'd called me Sister Alex, and then Mother Alex when she was reprimanded. After not seeing her for several weeks, when I least expected it, she blessed me with that one word. It was like music to my ears. Nothing could've been sweeter than hearing Lilah call me Mommy. I guessed I finally earned it.

Later, when I went to the nursery, I looked at my baby sleeping in his incubator, and I was happy.

Mama always talked to Taylor and me about faith. Sometimes she'd wrap her wide arms around us and hold us close and read the scriptures to us, word for word. But other times, she'd just sit one of us on each knee and talk to us about her life. She'd tell us how Jesus brought her a mighty long way, and that even though she didn't know where our father was at the time, she trusted God to change him and bring him home. Now that was big faith because in all the years of my growing up, I don't remember my daddy ever staying in one place too long. Yes, Mama had faith, and she spoke it over, and into, her girls' lives. I finally understood it and embraced it.

Some people have asked what joy is. I said it was a peace in your spirit, coming from the inside but spilling over on to the outside. Sometimes joy looked like it came in stages—a miracle here or deliverance there, but real joy was constant. It was faith in God's Word, His will, and His way. There was no doubt in my mind

what I knew about joy. I guessed it was God speaking it
to me Himself, but I knew what joy was supposed to be.
Just never quite got it 'til now. Just couldn't truly feel
it 'til now. Lack of understanding, I imagined. It was
like that at times—I just didn't know enough to bring
myself out. Then I realized I had to go back and fill up
on more—more of God, that is. He was the only one I
needed when it came to real joy.

Epilogue

Alex

Of course, Taylor and Keith became an old married couple, with the two of them working at the Push It Fitness Center and making it truly the best gym in the city. Me and the ladies of Giving Life Ministry met at the center twice a week. Taylor never gave up hope for her healing.

She just didn't put God on a timetable, deciding that she and Keith were good together whether or not she could walk on her own.

Joshua and Mother Benning finally came to a compromise. Joshua agreed he would be the interim assistant pastor at Kingdom House for at least a year. This would allow Bishop Benning to fully recuperate since his cancer was in remission. It would also allow his parents time to select a suitable person to serve as senior pastor.

Even though the embezzlement scandal was over and he was offered his old job back, Joshua declined to return to the bank.

After much prayer and meditation, we decided it was time to step out in faith and go into full-time ministry.

After a few months, with the salary he made as assistant pastor at Kingdom House, we were able to pay off all our debts and make a decent down payment on an old apartment building in lower Manhattan. We were also able to move into a three-bedroom apartment on the fourth floor, rent out two apartments on the third floor, and start to renovate the first and second floors for the church. Now there would really be room for Giving Life Ministry as soon as that part of the building was fixed up. I was excited about working on that.

With the additional income from the tenants, I was able to stay at home with Lilah and Joshua Jr., and I was finally "Mommy." The best part was that we were able to adopt Kiano about ten months later. We spent a few months in Kenya with Kiano, finalized everything, and brought him back with us. As it turned out, the orphanage received much-needed funding from a British missionary group and was never demolished. So the Mercy Group Home in Kenya continued to do God's will, which was to take care of His children.

Joshua, Lilah, Joshua Jr., Kiano, and I were finally a real family, dancing in God's goodness, living, forgiving, and counting it all joy.

Reading Group Discussion Questions

1. Why was Alex afraid of trying to have Joshua's baby?

2. Why was Joshua adamant about having a baby, specifically a son, so soon?

3. Do you think their trying to have a baby so soon was a healthy way to begin their marriage? Why or why not?

4. Do you think it was right for Alex to pressure her husband about Kiano's adoption?

5. How do you think Alex should have handled the adoption issue differently?

6. Why do you think Lilah refused to call Alex "Mommy"?

7. Why do you think Joshua was not suspicious of Simon when he first discovered the missing money?

8. Why couldn't Taylor just marry her true love, Keith, from the beginning?

9. Do you think that Seger was in love with Alex, or was he just being friendly?

10. Do you think Alex's relationship with Seger was emotional adultery? Why or why not?

11. Do you think Joshua was compromising by being the interim assistant pastor at Kingdom House of Prayer?

12. Do you think Mother Benning was right to push her son into pastoring at Kingdom House of Prayer?

Notes

ORDER FORM
URBAN BOOKS, LLC
78 E. Industry Ct
Deer Park, NY 11729

Name: (please print):_____

Address: _____

City/State: _____

Zip: _____

QTY	TITLES	PRICE

Shipping and handling-add $3.50 for 1st book, then $1.75 for each additional book.
Please send a check payable to:
   Urban Books, LLC
Please allow 4-6 weeks for delivery

ORDER FORM
URBAN BOOKS, LLC
78 E. Industry Ct
Deer Park, NY 11729

Name: (please print):_____

Address: _____

City/State: _____

Zip: _____

QTY	TITLES	PRICE
	3:57 A.M Timing Is Everything	$14.95
	A Man's Worth	$14.95
	A Woman's Worth	$14.95
	Abundant Rain	$14.95
	After The Feeling	$14.95
	Amaryllis	$14.95
	An Inconvenient Friend	$14.95
	Battle of Jericho	$14.95
	Be Careful What You Pray For	$14.95
	Beautiful Ugly	$14.95
	Been There Prayed That:	$14.95
	Before Redemption	$14.95

Shipping and handling-add $3.50 for 1st book, then $1.75 for each additional book.

Please send a check payable to:

Urban Books, LLC

Please allow 4-6 weeks for delivery

ORDER FORM
URBAN BOOKS, LLC
78 E. Industry Ct
Deer Park, NY 11729

Name: (please print): _____

Address: _____

City/State: _____

Zip: _____

QTY	TITLES	PRICE
	By the Grace of God	$14.95
	Confessions Of A preachers Wife	$14.95
	Dance Into Destiny	$14.95
	Deliver Me From My Enemies	$14.95
	Desperate Decisions	$14.95
	Divorcing the Devil	$14.95
	Faith	$14.95
	First Comes Love	$14.95
	Flaws and All	$14.95
	Forgiven	$14.95
	Former Rain	$14.95
	Forsaken	$14.95

Shipping and handling-add $3.50 for 1st book, then $1.75 for each additional book.

Please send a check payable to:

Urban Books, LLC

Please allow 4-6 weeks for delivery

ORDER FORM
URBAN BOOKS, LLC
78 E. Industry Ct
Deer Park, NY 11729

Name: (please print): _____

Address: _____

City/State: _____

Zip: _____

QTY	TITLES	PRICE
	From Sinner To Saint	$14.95
	From The Extreme	$14.95
	God Is In Love With You	$14.95
	God Speaks To Me	$14.95
	Grace And Mercy	$14.95
	Guilty Of Love	$14.95
	Happily Ever Now	$14.95
	Heaven Bound	$14.95
	His Grace His Mercy	$14.95
	His Woman His Wife His Widow	$14.95
	Illusions	$14.95
	In Green Pastures	$14.95

Shipping and handling-add $3.50 for 1st book, then $1.75 for each additional book.

Please send a check payable to:
Urban Books, LLC
Please allow 4-6 weeks for delivery

ORDER FORM
URBAN BOOKS, LLC
78 E. Industry Ct
Deer Park, NY 11729

Name: (please print):_____

Address: _____

City/State: _____

Zip: _____

QTY	TITLES	PRICE
	Into Each Life	$14.95
	Keep Your enemies Closer	$14.95
	Keeping Misery Company	$14.95
	Latter Rain	$14.95
	Living Consequences	$14.95
	Living Right On Wrong Street	$14.95
	Losing It	$14.95
	Love Honor Stray	$14.95
	Marriage Mayhem	$14.95
	Me, Myself and Him	$14.95
	Murder Through The Grapevine	$14.95
	My Father's House	$14.95

Shipping and handling-add $3.50 for 1st book, then $1.75 for each additional book.

Please send a check payable to:

Urban Books, LLC

Please allow 4-6 weeks for delivery

ORDER FORM
URBAN BOOKS, LLC
78 E. Industry Ct
Deer Park, NY 11729

Name: (please print):_____

Address: _____

City/State: _____

Zip: _____

QTY	TITLES	PRICE
	My Mother's Child	$14.95
	My Son's Ex Wife	$14.95
	My Son's Wife	$14.95
	My Soul Cries Out	$14.95
	Not Guilty Of Love	$14.95
	Prodigal	$14.95
	Rain Storm	$14.95
	Redemption Lake	$14.95
	Right Package, Wrong Baggage	$14.95
	Sacrifice The One	$14.95
	Secret Sisterhood	$14.95
	Secrets And Lies	$14.95

Shipping and handling-add $3.50 for 1st book, then $1.75 for each additional book.
Please send a check payable to:
Urban Books, LLC
Please allow 4-6 weeks for delivery

ORDER FORM
URBAN BOOKS, LLC
78 E. Industry Ct
Deer Park, NY 11729

Name: (please print): _____

Address: _____

City/State: _____

Zip: _____

QTY	TITLES	PRICE
	Selling My soul	$14.95
	She Who Finds A Husband	$14.95
	Sheena's Dream	$14.95
	Sinsatiable	$14.95
	Someone To Love Me	$14.95
	Something On The Inside	$14.95
	Song Of Solomon	$14.95
	Soon After	$14.95
	Soon And Very Soon	$14.95
	Soul Confession	$14.95
	Still Guilty	$14.95

Shipping and handling-add $3.50 for 1st book, then $1.75 for each additional book.

Please send a check payable to:
Urban Books, LLC
Please allow 4-6 weeks for delivery